Safe
Haven

A Historical Novel

DAVID R. GROSS

Outskirts Press, Inc.
http://www.outskirtspress.com

Paperback ISBN: 978-1-9772-5599-0
Hardback ISBN: 978-1-9772-5610-2

Interior Photo © 2022 Axiom Maps. All rights reserved - used with permission.
Cover Photo © 2022 www.gettyimages.com. All rights reserved - used with permission.

Outskirts Press and the "OP" logo are trademarks belonging to Outskirts Press, Inc.

PRINTED IN THE UNITED STATES OF AMERICA

CONTENTS

MAJOR CHARACTER LIST

Yusuf ben Ezia ibn Nasir, (Yusuf), physician, narrator

Abu Yusuf Hasdai ben Ishaq ibn Shaprut, (Hasdai), physician, diplomat

Abd-Ar-Rahman III, (the caliph), caliph of Cordoba and all of Andalusia

Dunash ben Labrat, (Dunash), friend of Hasdai, poet, Hebrew scholar

Menahem ben Saruq, (Menahem), friend of Hasdai, philologist, grammarian of Hebrew

Judah ben Shlomo, (Judah), servant of Hasdai

Abraham ben Moses, (Abraham), Hebrew trader and half-owner of the cargo ship *Fair Winds*)

Stephanopulus, captain and half-owner of the cargo ship *Fair Winds*

Hamza ibn Kafeel (Hamza), captain and owner of the ship *Shabh*

MINOR CHARACTER LIST

Vizier Ibn Bakana, finance vizier to the caliph of Cordoba

Grand Vizier Abu Ahmas, grand vizier to the caliph of Cordoba

Sancho I, (Fat Sancho), deposed king of Leon

Isaac ben Ezia ibn Shaprut, father of Hasdai

Al-Hakan, (crown prince), son of Abd-Ar-Rahman III

Rebecca ibn Hanoth, wife of Dunash

Sarah, housekeeper to Hasdai

King Joseph, king of the Khazars

Achmed, first mate to Hamza

Joshua ben Israel, young Hebrew of Panorma taught fighting skills by Judah

Abu Ahmadi, brother-in-law of Joshua ben Israel

Auda Al Thalabi, uncle of Abu Ahmadi, breeder of fine Sicilian horses

Aser ibn Adheri, prime minister of the caliph of Sicily

Elvira Ramiro, regent of Leon

Count Gonzalo Sanchez, leader of Leon's army

EUROPE AND THE MIDEAST (750-850 AD)

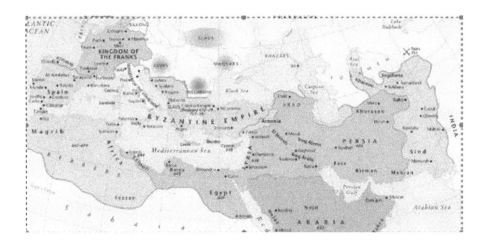

Printed with permission to publish by Axiom Maps Ltd.

Areas in light green were controlled by the Umayyad caliphates, darker green the Abbasid caliphates, light purple the Byzantine empire, darker purple the Kingdome of the Franks, yellow the Khazar empire.

The capital city of Khazar empire, Atil, is identified as Itil in this map, close to where the Volga river empties into the Caspian Sea.

CHAPTER ONE

S trident banging on our door shook the door and frame enough to vibrate the walls. It brought me out of my bed standing upright, barefoot, on the cold tiles of the floor. The banging was too loud and insistent to be made by a fist. I ran to the door, opened it just enough to see the pommel of a sword poised to continue the incessant pounding.

The soldier holding the sword wore the uniform of the Caliph's guard. Mail armor protected him from his neck to his waist. His polished helmet had been pushed back on his head from the violent pounding on the door.

"Go summon the physician," demanded the soldier.

Two drops of blood fell from the tip of the sword. Two other soldiers supported a fourth man whose expensive robe was soaked with blood.

I felt something and glanced over my shoulder to see my master, Hasdai ibn Shaprut, standing behind me in his night clothes. He pushed me aside and opened the door wide. "Pick him up, don't drag him. Follow me," he ordered the soldiers.

He led the way to our treatment room, the first door on the right after the entry. "Put him on the couch with his wound up. What happened?"

The soldier still holding the sword carryied the injured man's legs. As they lowered the man to the couch he spoke. "He was attacked by a now dead would-be assassin. We were leaving a party in his honor not far from here. The assassin leaped from the shadows and stabbed him."

My master quickly cut away the clothing from the face-down patient. "Was it a knife or a sword?"

"A knife."

"Long, short, wide, narrow?"

"Medium length, a stiletto. Why is that important?"

"I need to know how deep the wound might be."

The patient's bare back was exposed. Bright red froth burbled from a wound below his right shoulder, spreading across the skin of his back and down his right side.

"Yusuf, go quickly, wake the house. I will need many clean cloths, hot and cold water, and containers of the salted water. First, bring me the box of clean compresses and the flask of distilled white wine from the cupboard. Thank you. Now go."

I glanced over my shoulder as the patient moaned and tried to rise from the couch.

Hasdai put his hand on the small of the injured man's back to prevent him from rising. "You men hold him down. He must not move, or the bleeding will worsen. Good. I have something in the cupboard that will make him sleep. One of you, press this cloth on the wound and hold it. You two, raise him up so I can give him the medicine."

I returned from awaking the household to find my master slowly pouring a brownish liquid into the corner of the patient's mouth. It was the concoction made by mixing distilled white wine with the dark sticky substance harvested from the poppy pods grown in his medicinal plant garden.

All three soldiers' faces were frowned with worry, not certain how their failure to protect the man on the couch would impact them. All of us were crowded around the couch.

Good. Now place Vizier ibn Bakana back face down," ordered Hasdai.

"You know this man, Physician?" asked the leader of the soldiers.

"Of course. Does not all of Cordoba know this man and his good works? I am surprised he has enemies who would attack him like this."

"All powerful men have enemies, Physician," responded the leader, "especially if they are good men who obey the teachings of the Quran.".

"I suppose you are correct."

The finance vizier moaned softly. Hasdai ibn Shaprut carefully washed his hands and arms with soap and warm water, then nodded at me to pour distilled wine over his hands.

"Unroll my boiled instruments, Yusuf, and bring the jars of suture to the small table. Move it closer so I can reach it. Thank you."

The suture jars held two kinds of suture, both soaking in the distilled wine. One contained fine silk thread. The other one was made from thin twisted strips of carefully washed cat intestine. It had taken me many weeks of practice to learn to cut the strips of intestine thin enough to meet Hasdai's standards.

"I would be obliged if you men would stand outside the door while I work on the vizier. Make certain only my servants can enter with the objects Yusuf directed them to bring. Your job is to make certain nobody bothers me."

"Will the vizier live, Physician?" asked the leader.

"I will do the best I can for him," said Hasdai, "but if he lives or not is the will of God. If you know the prayers for the ill or injured, you should recite them now."

Hasdai motioned to me to come closer. "Wash your hands and pour the distilled wine over them," he instructed. "I will need you to hand me the instruments I call for and sometimes to hold one of them for me."

"Yes, Effendi.

"Before you do that, bring the mirror on the stand over and adjust it so the light from the big lamp reflects directly on the wound. Yes, that's good. Now clean your hands."

"You see, Yusuf, the patient is fortunate the wound is on the right side, if it had been on the left, it probably would have penetrated to his heart. It is between the fourth and fifth rib and has injured the lung, that's why the blood is bright red and frothy."

"He is the finance vizier?" I was astounded. "What if he dies, will we be blamed?"

"If so, it is God's will, Yusuf. But I think, with God's help, we will save this man. We'll see. Hand me the scalpel."

I watched as Hasdai enlarged the wound. Then he placed between the ribs the device he had designed that spreads tissues and holds them apart. Once the spreader was positioned to his satisfaction, he slowly spread the tissues apart, only stopping when the ribs made a faint cracking sound. He carefully probed the wound with a special clamp that held a soft, clean cloth pledget. He discarded the pledget when it was no longer able to absorb more blood and took up a clean one.

"Ah, good, the wound has only injured a small part of the lung. Observe, Yusuf, I have located the source of the blood. Hand me the curved clamp. Thank you. Now hold the compress in place while I clamp the area. Yes, good, the bleeding has stopped. Now I will have a length of catgut please. Thank you. I will tie this around the lung tissue behind the clamp. Thus. Now I will hold on to the adjacent tissue with this small clamp while I release the large curved one. If I have tied the ligature tight enough there will be no bleeding. Yes, you see, no bleeding. The jars of salted water were boiled and cooled before they were stored?"

"Yes, of course. There are four jars in the cupboard."

"Good, get two of them and pour the salted water into the wound to clean out the wound. I will suck out most of it with the suction bulb but will leave some in the wound. It will be absorbed and, hopefully, replace some of the blood he has lost."

I watched as Hasdai pulled the ribs back together with silk sutures placed with a large, curved needle. He then closed the muscle layers with the cat gut using a smaller needle. Finally, he closed the skin with individual silk sutures. I wondered how long it would be before Hasdai trusted me to place sutures. I had been practicing tying knots in the manner he instructed by suturing closed openings made in a thin piece of leather.

"Now we will bandage the wound with the wound poultice and leave Vizier ibn Bakana in the hands of God."

Hasdai ordered the servants to bring in a bed with clean sheets and blankets. He pointed to the corner of the room where he wanted the bed placed. The three bodyguards and I carried the bandaged, and now moaning more loudly, finance vizier to the bed, putting him on his uninjured side, and propping him in place with pillows.

"Have the servants clean and put away everything, Yusuf. You stay and watch our patient. When he is fully awake, give him small sips of water and send someone to fetch me. I am going back to sleep."

For the next few days, I helped Sarah, Hasdai's housekeeper and nurse, bathe and dress Vizier Bakana. We changed his bandage and poultice twice daily. I knew to report any redness or swelling near the wound immediately to Hasdai, but it wasn't necessary.

By the fourth morning the Vizier was much improved. He graduated from rich chicken broth to substantial stews full of fresh vegetables and easily chewable meats.

"Yusuf, you assisted your master when he treated my wound, didn't you?" he asked.

"Yes."

"How serious was it?"

"Extremely serious, Vizier. The knife lacerated a portion of your lung, and you were bleeding profusely. My Master opened the wound so he could find the damage. He was able to clamp off the injured portion of the lung and tied a ligature to stop the bleeding. He then cleaned the wound and sutured it closed. I don't think any another physician in Cordoba could have saved you."

The vizier shook his head. "Then I am extremely fortunate, and thankful, that the soldiers brought me to this house."

That same afternoon I ran to answer an authoritative knock on our door. I opened it to find a large delegation of functionaries and soldiers. The man leading the delegation was dressed in a brilliantly white robe decorated with gold threads. Judging by his clothing, and the way the other men deferred to him, he was a very important personage.

"This is the house of the physician who saved our finance vizier's life?" the man inquired.

"Yes, Effendi, please enter. I will run to fetch my master, ibn Shaprut."

"No need, Yusuf," said the voice at my back. "Welcome, Grand Vizier, I am Hasdai ibn Shaprut. Please follow and I will take you to our patient. He is improving rapidly."

The grand vizier indicated to his entourage to stay where they were and followed Hasdai.

Vizier ibn Bakana sat in his bed, propped up by pillows. Sarah, holding the bowl that had held his lunch, bowed to the grand vizier, and backed out of the room. When the grand vizier entered the room ibn Bakana's face flushed, he sat up straight, adjusted his robe and smoothed his blanket. Then he moved his legs to stand, but Hasdai put a hand on his chest.

"Not yet, Vizier, you are not quite ready to get up, but will be soon. I'm certain the grand vizier understands."

"Of course, stay on your couch, Bakana. I must say, given what I am told about the wound you received, that you are looking quite fit. The caliph sent me to inquire after you. It appears that your physician, according to the reports I received, follows many unorthodox methods in his treatment of patients. However, he has brought you back to life and reasonable health. How do you feel?"

"Better every day, Vizier. Hasdai ibn Shaprut assures me I will be able to get to my feet soon and return to my duties shortly thereafter."

"Well, our caliph is anxious for your return to the Alcazaba. We have been doing everything possible to identify the persons responsible for hiring the man that attacked you, but nobody seems to recognize or know anything about him. It is possible we will not discover the perpetrator of this obnoxious affront, but we will continue our investigations and hope to discover who was responsible."

Hasdai spoke up. "My plan is to get our patient on his feet tomorrow. If he can walk a few steps by tomorrow afternoon, he could, perhaps, return to the Alcazaba the following day, providing there are people there who will follow my instructions for his care."

"We have many physicians at the Alcazaba. Do you not trust them to care for ibn Bakana properly?"

"I only know of the work and methods of two of them, and their philosophy and methods are quite different than mine. I would trust them—if they were ordered to follow my instructions."

"Very well. If I can convince the caliph to allow it, will you be willing to visit the Alcazaba to oversee your patient's full recovery?"

"I would be honored to do so, but I must also be able to attend to my other patients and to my studies."

"Studies?"

"Yes. I constantly scour medical texts written in Arabic, Latin, and Hebrew. Many of those are to be found in the most complete library in the western world, thanks to our enlightened caliph. When I learn about a text not in the caliph's library, I can usually find a copy from my contacts throughout the Hebrew diaspora. I am always on the hunt for new, to me, ideas for the diagnosis and treatment of all the medical problems I might encounter."

"And these studies have resulted in your unorthodox methods?"

"Some, yes. But some resulted from my own experiments and experience."

"I will speak with the caliph. You will send me a message when your patient can return, and I will arrange for his comfortable transfer."

The grand vizier turned to Vizier Bakana.

"Well, my old friend and colleague it is good to see you looking and feeling well considering your injury. Get back to full health as soon as possible."

"Vizier Abu Ahmas, thank you for your concern. I learned from the apprentice to ibn Shaprut that the wound was very nearly fatal, but the extraordinary skill and dedication of the physician clearly saved my life."

I was only fifteen years old when these events happened. I wondered if Hasdai would take me with him when he went to the Alcazar to treat his patient, curious and excited to learn about the wonders that huge, imposing, and mysterious structure might conceal.

CHAPTER TWO

This is the year 4695 of the Hebrew calendar, 935 according to the reckoning of the Christians. I was born in Cordoba fifteen years ago, and it has always been my home. My mother, may she rest in peace, was a first cousin to Hasdai ibn Shaprut's mother. My father, Ezai, ignored the scholarly wishes of his family and embarked on a career of buying and selling. He became a merchant and enjoyed moderate success. He was lost at sea while travelling to the Holy Land with goods he hoped would bring good profit. My mother, when she received the news, fell into a deep depression and, not long afterward, succumbed to measles complicated by pneumonia. She had no will to live. Hasdai, already well known for his medical skills although only twenty-five years old, was not called to our house until it was too late for him to work his magic. I was ten years old when orphaned, but lucky that Hasdai considered me family. He took me to his house and there I have remained.

Hasdai has seen to my education, employing tutors as required. He made certain I learned everything necessary to be bar mitzvahed after which he made me his only apprentice. He taught me to read Arabic and speak it with confidence. I am present when my master examines, diagnoses, and treats patients. Before the next patient is seen he tells me his observations, gives the reasoning for the tests he conducted, and the results of his examination. I take notes then transcribe the notes at the end of each day and file them for easy access. He continues my education by helping me translate Latin medical texts into Hebrew or Arabic. In this way I have been learning to read, write, and speak Latin.

Hasdai's father, Isaac ben Ezira ibn Shaprut is a rich and pious man. He was originally a member of the large Hebrew community of Jaen and even founded a synagogue in that city. He patronizes Torah scholars and publishes their writings. Isaac moved to Cordoba after Abd-Ar-Rhaman III consolidated all of Andalusia by defeating the rebellion of the notorious ibn Hagsun as well as securing victories over several Christian states that abutted his territories. Abd-Ar-Rhaman also conquered a host of dissident tribes and political enemies, restoring a powerful caliphate headquartered in Cordoba. Six years ago, he declared himself Caliph of Cordoba and all of Andalusia.

The new caliph espoused a policy of religious tolerance, particularly of the Abrahamic religions. He settled tribal feuds and discontent with a combination of shrewd diplomacy, granting of favors and rewards, and swift, brutal force when necessary. His strong central authority created a strong economy to encourage enterprise benefiting all classes. As a scholar himself, he emphasized the importance of scholarly activity. He promoted learning and established a library containing several hundred thousand books. Library use was free to all his subjects, although there were strict rules enforced to assure the books were respected and well cared for.

My benefactor, Abu Yusuf Hasdai ben Ishaq ibn Shaprut, was born in Jaen. He was twenty years old when his family moved to Cordoba, the largest and most progressive city in the whole of Europe. Not even Rome can match our over six hundred mosques, nine hundred public baths, and more than two-hundred thousand homes. Many of the homes have water running into them and are connected to an underground sewer system. The streets are cleaned regularly and lit at night with lamps. While living with Hasdai I learned, from his mother my aunt, that when his family was still living in Jaen, he was tutored by the best teachers available in Hebrew, Torah and Talmud. She also told me he was an excellent student who absorbed and remembered almost everything he was taught. However, he was not especially enamored with his Hebrew education. He did develop a strong interest in languages and was a keen student of them. His father encouraged learning in any form and paid for the best available tutors in Arabic, mostly imams, who encouraged him in both the spoken and written language. They did their best to convert him to Islam, to no avail. After he was fluent in the formal grammar and classical styles of Arabic, including Arabic poetry, he embarked on his study of Latin. For this his father employed one of the Christian Mozarab clergy, and it wasn't long until he mastered both church Latin and the common Latin used in daily commerce, science, and history.

When I was about twelve years old, I developed a significant interest in the history of my homeland. Hasdai was happy to encourage me to learn as much as possible about anything that interested me. He encouraged me to take out books of history from the caliph's library that was open to all residents of Cordoba. I learned that more than two thousand years before the beginning of the Christian calendar, the Romans invaded the lands they named Hispania. They found Visigoths of Celtic origin, who had come to these lands centuries earlier and stayed. The Visigoths intermarried with the indigenous people and spoke a mixture of related Celtic languages. Over time, they evolved a mixture of Latin and Celtic that many of the inhabitants of Andalusia still use today to converse. There was, Hasdai told me, no written form of this language, but, of course, he could converse in that language as well.

In one our many long conversations I learned that during his early study of languages, Hasdai encountered medical texts written in Arabic. He became completely absorbed in the study of medicine. In the caliph's library, he discovered a trove of medical texts, most of them only read by an occasional scholar or physician. Many of these texts were written in Arabic, but some were in Latin, and a few in Hebrew. He learned that many of the Arabic texts were translations from the original Greek. He found several descriptions of discoveries made by the most revered physicians of history. Many of these scholarly physicians were from the near east, particularly Egypt, which seemed to have been the birthplace of much medical knowledge. The texts that were Arabic translations of Greek writings also incorporated the principles of Greek medical knowledge. His initial studies prompted him to study with a succession of Arab physicians. From those men he adopted what he considered to be their most effective treatments and methods. He was meticulously observant and analytical. It didn't take him long to ascertain what was real and what was smoke and mirrors.

Shortly after the finance vizier returned to his duties Hasdai's family hosted a large party for his twenty-sixth birthday. As a relative, more likely because I was his apprentice, I was invited. At the sumptuous table, groaning with delicacies and jugs of white and red wine, both of excellent vintage, Hasdai's father addressed him in a voice loud enough to be heard over the tumult of conversations.

"Hasdai," he said, "your mother tells me there are several young women of our faith, who would be receptive of a ketubah with you. Your mother is anxious for you to meet these girls in hopes of grandchildren."

Hasdai, who was sullenly pushing food around on his plate looked as if he would rather be anyplace but at this table. He looked up, frowned, and fixed his gaze on his father.

"I am very busy with my medical investigations and just this morning I was instructed to appear next week before the Caliph to be interviewed for something he may want me to do. I have no time to waste interacting with women of marriageable intent. I also have no interest."

"Hasdai, my son, do you not want a life partner, someone to share your life, be a reliable companion, give you children, care for you when you are old?" asked his mother.

His father leaned forward and grasped Hasdai's left shoulder. "Children are the one true blessing, my son. I speak from experience."

"Yes, yes, I understand. I see and understand the blessing of your relationship, but I am not ready. I have no time nor interest to devote to that sort of enterprise now."

His mother didn't give up easily. "It will not require a major effort or expenditure of time, my son. A few minutes—maybe once a week—to meet with each girl. I will pre-select only those I deem most suitable."

"And what do you think I will find to talk about with these girls, Mama? Will they be interested in language, grammar, medicine, Torah, Talmud, medicinal plants, cures, what?"

"Don't be mean spirited, my son. The girls I choose will be intelligent, educated, interested in what you are doing. They will be able to read Hebrew and to converse with you. They will be interested in music, poetry, and other subjects you might find interesting to learn. You will have common interests."

"Will they be attractive?"

She frowned. "Don't be like that, Hasdai. Do you think I would select a girl for you that you would be ashamed to escort to synagogue?"

"I attend synagogue with minimal interest these days, Mama."

"Don't blaspheme, Hasdai," scolded his father.

"Can we please end this discussion?"

Both parents shook their heads and dropped the subject. I smiled into my hand at Hasdai's discomfort. It was exceedingly rare for him to not control any situation, any conversation. It was this commanding presence that gave his patients their confidence in him and in his skills.

Two days later my wishes were answered, and I was allowed to be present when Hasdai had his interview with the caliph, Abd-Ar-Rhahman III. We did not go to the old Alcazar located within the city limits. That walled fortress, built on the ruins of the fortress of a Visigoth king who built on the ruins of a Roman fort, now housed the multitudes of minor functionaries who conducted the everyday business of the government.

We walked to the new Alcazar, on the outskirts of the city, recently completed under the caliph's direction. While we walked Hasdai told me some facts about the new Alcazar, a huge walled and protected compound that housed the caliph's palace as well as a large collection of small, medium, and large villas. The larger villas housed the extended family of the caliph. Several large, and a few very large, buildings housed the official offices of the emirs, members of the royal family with specific responsibilities, and viziers, high ranking political advisors and executives responsible for overseeing the daily functioning of the government. In addition to all the buildings, the compound contained many gardens, baths, and a royal cemetery. There were two main gates into the Alcazar, the Iron Gate on the north side and the and the most used Gate of the Embankment on the south facing the River Guadalquivir.

We approached the Gate of the Embankment. Hasdai spoke to a guard who peered at us through a small window in one of the massive oak double doors. Hasdai gave his name and mine. The guard consulted a list. A few moments later one of the doors, the one without the window, swung partially open. We walked through, and the door was forced shut behind us. We walked through a passage about eight cubits long. The distance of the passage was the thickness of the wall at its base. We entered a large plaza.

I stopped in amazement. "I had no idea the Alcazar was this huge. How much ground does it cover?"

Hasdai leaned toward me, speaking softly. "I am told it is about eight parasangs long and six wide."

I shook my head. I had never been in a place so large that it would take eight hours to walk from end to end.

"I don't know the answer to that question Yusuf, you should do some research. When you find the answer, please tell me. This plaza is where the public gathers for executions, military parades, and festivals such as the caliph's birthday," said Hasdai who proceeded in his usual way to impart information he considered I should know.

He turned and pointed to the top of the gate we just came through. "You see that covered balcony? That is where the caliph comes to observe the events held here. Do you see the door to the left of the gate?"

"Yes."

"Behind that door are stairs that lead down, deep below the wall. The unfortunates to be executed are kept there. After the deed is done, their heads are hung from those hooks over the doors to the gate."

I shuddered. "I will do my best to avoid that fate."

He pointed to a large, ornate building. "That is the Grand Mosque. As you see it is outside the wall. The caliph wanted the people to have easy access to it. But you see there is a covered bridge that connects that large building in front of us to the mosque. I am told the caliph uses that bridge to go to the mosque for prayer. We will enter that building shortly. It contains a huge room known as The Perfect Hall where the throne of the caliph is."

He pointed with his chin to another large building. "That building is the House of the Viziers. It houses all the offices of the various viziers. I have visited the offices of ibn Bakana several times since he returned to his duties. He is very interesting and intelligent. I am learning a great deal about the finances of the caliphate and how they are managed."

"Did you notice as we approached the gate the waterwheel on the banks of the Guadalquivir?" he asked.

"Yes, of course. It is called the Abulafia, is it not?"

"Correct. Do you know when it was built and its purpose?"

"I was told it is over a hundred years old and supplies water, via a system of aqueducts, for the Alcazar and all of its gardens."

"Very good, Yusuf. I am pleased you show curiosity and take the time to learn things by your own initiative. Now, do you know the reason why the north gate is known as the Iron Gate?"

"Because the iron door knockers were taken when we conquered Narbonne after the Arabs invaded this land."

"And do you know how many other gates and how many gardens are contained within these walls?"

"Let me count. There is the Gate of the Garden, the Village Gate, the Gate of the Mosque, and another southern gate above which is a pavilion with views of the river. There are also the Gate of Justice, the Gate of the River, perhaps that is the one with the pavilion, the Gate of Seville, the road outside it leads to Seville, the Gate of the Lion, and the Gate of the Bathhouse. Some I've missed, no doubt, but all the gates are secured and well-guarded. There are many, many gardens including the cemetery of our rulers and their families, all watered from the river. There are too many for me to remember all the names."

"That is enough of my quizzing you for now. Straighten your robes, stay two paces behind me and mimic anything I do, is that clear?"

"Yes."

"Let's find out why the caliph summoned me."

I followed Hasdai to the door of the Perfect Hall. It opened as we approached.

"I am Hasdai—"

The guard, resplendent in glittering chain mail and a polished steel helmet topped with a purple plume, cut him off. "Yes, Hasdai ibn Shaprut. I recognize you from the description given me. Enter and wait in the vestibule. I will summon ibn Bakana to escort you into the presence." He nodded at another guard who slid through a door on the opposite wall, closing it softly behind him.

The walls of the vestibule were decorated with tiles of intricate, geometric design, some spelled out specific Arabic quotes

"Are those quotes from the Quran?" I whispered in Hasdai's ear.

He nodded and put a forefinger to his lips.

In a minute or two a door opened. Vizier ibn Bakana motioned us forward. He leaned into Hasdai, whispering. "There is a delegation from Rome presenting their credentials and gifts to our caliph. They speak very rapidly, and the interpreter seems unfamiliar with much of what they are saying. Grand Vizier Ahmas told me to ask if your Latin is good enough to translate what is being said."

"That shouldn't be a problem if they are speaking educated Latin."

The finance vizier motioned us forward with a wave of his hand. "Follow me. Yusuf, stay behind us."

The hall was the largest I had ever seen inside a building. Hasdai's entire house would have fit inside. The room was ablaze with light from glass-covered windows high up on the ten-cubit high walls, several skylights, and hundreds of glowing lamps. The walls and ceiling glittered with even more ornate and colorful tiles than those in the anteroom. A particularly large skylight illuminated a platform at the end of the hall. buried in cushions. Nestled amongst them was an imposing figure of a man, leaning forward, concentrating on what was being said. Standing on the floor, about half a cubit below the caliph, stood the grand vizier. He glanced at the three of us and waved us forward, impatiently. He held up his hand to stop the obvious struggles of an interpreter. A man resplendent in red robes and a red skull cap, stood next to the interpreter and in front of three men dressed as monks.

Ibn Bakana had told us that when we first came before the caliph we should kneel and bow our heads to the floor.

Hasdai came even with the grand vizier and bowed. He did not kneel. I sucked in a fearful breath and mimicked my master.

"This is the physician Hasdai ibn Shaprut, Excellency," said the grand vizier. "He is fluent in several languages, a learned man. I thought he might be useful."

"You and the young man with you are Hebrews," the caliph said.

It wasn't a question. His voice was deep. It resonated throughout the room because of the acoustics of the hall.

Raising his eyebrows, Hasdai glanced at the grand vizier.

"You may speak directly to the caliph, Physician."

"Yes, Your Excellency, my apprentice and I are both Hebrews."

"I assumed so since you did not get on your knees."

"Our sages teach that we only prostrate ourselves to God, not to mortals."

I inhaled sharply, making a sound that was repeated by many in the room, I held my breath.

The caliph smiled. "And your people have paid an enormous price for this over many years."

"I cannot deny the truth of that, Your Excellency."

"All right, Physician. Now, tell this delegation to start over. I am not even certain who they represent."

"Of course, Your Excellency."

Hasdai turned to the man in the red robes, spoke rapidly in Latin, and waited for the reply.

"This delegation is from the pope, Your Excellency, not the emperor. The pope is the head of their religion, very wealthy and powerful. He is responsible for all religious practices and doctrine. The emperor is the head of the Roman Empire and responsible for governing the people and protecting them with his armies. The emperor of the Christians cannot rule without the approval and support of the pope. The relationship between the church and the state is very complicated. I will be happy to tell you what I understand about that, but it is probably a subject for another time. The leader of this delegation is Cardinal Francis." He bowed slightly to the cardinal. "He is one of a select group of men who form the pope's council, analogous to your viziers. He is here to give you greetings from the pope and to present the gifts that have been spread out to show you. The cardinal speaks a very educated and precise Latin which is probably why your interpreter was having difficulties. The cardinal's Latin is quite a different form than that spoken in the streets."

"I notice you speak an educated form of Arabic, Physician, also unlike the Arabic spoken in the streets."

"Thank you, Your Excellency. I consider that a compliment and testimony to your own level of education and learning for you to say so."

The caliph glanced at Abu Ahmas and smiled. The grand vizier returned the smile.

The caliph turned to Hasdai. "So, what does this delegation from the pope want from me?"

Hasdai faced the cardinal to repeat the caliph's question. He listened with great concentration as the man spoke.

"The cardinal says the pope would like to establish an embassy here in your capital and the cardinal has been honored to be the pope's ambassador if you are agreeable. They have the necessary funds to purchase an appropriate building for this purpose."

"What do they hope to accomplish with this embassy?"

I was concentrating on all that was happening and noticed that sweat was accumulating on the cardinal's forehead, drops were running down the sides of his face.

Hasdai asked the question and waited for the response. "The cardinal says they will act to represent any of their people who need to interact with your government and to establish and maintain relationships with the appropriate viziers. Most of their work will relate to commerce, but hopefully they will be able to mediate misunderstandings that might occur between the Roman state and yours. He also says that the size and completeness of your library is a legend amongst the most learned of his people, and he hopes members of the pope's clergy, selected because of their academic accomplishments, will be allowed to travel here and take advantage of the accumulated wisdom and knowledge available there."

The caliph put his left elbow on his left leg and rested his chin on his hand. He closed his eyes in thought. After what seemed an eternity of silence, he spoke.

"Well, that is a worthwhile cause, don't you agree, Physician? Should we share our knowledge with these infidels?"

The cardinal fished a square of linen from his left sleeve and moped the sweat from his forehead and face.

"The sharing of knowledge is a holy thing according to my understanding of what the Quran teaches, Your Excellency. It is most certain that it's taught in our Torah."

"Tell this cardinal to proceed, Physician. I give my blessing. They and their colleagues are welcome to use our library, as are all free men in our caliphate, if they treat our books with respect and honor. After they leave, you stay. I want to speak to you at length."

After the delegation from the pope had backed out of the throne room the caliph extricated himself from the cushions and stood. Accounting for the height of the platform, he was at least four cubits tall with broad, muscular shoulders and a waist that was just beginning to thicken. His beard and hair showed flecks of gray. He beckoned for Hasdai to approach. When Hasdai reached the edge of the platform the caliph stretched out his arm and put his hand on Hasdai's shoulder.

"Ibn Shaprut, I have received accounts of your activities and your successes as a physician. Accounting for understandable jealousy from some of your colleagues regarding your medical achievements, you enjoy a remarkably excellent reputation as a scholar and judge of character among your people. I have witnessed your facility with Latin and Arabic. I assume you are equally, or perhaps even more, educated in Hebrew. What other languages do you command?"

"I have a smattering knowledge of written Greek, Your Excellency, but not to speak it. I can converse in the so-called street Latin, a mixture of several Celtic languages and Latin that is used by many of your indigenous subjects, but that language does not have a written component or literature that I am aware of. The history and legends of that culture seem to be transmitted orally, mostly in song, some in poetry. Their poetry falls far short of the sophistication and intricacy of the efforts of our Arabic poets."

"Good. I have arranged a small villa for you within the Alcazar grounds. It is larger than your current home. I will send people to gather all your belongings and servants. They will be instructed to take special care of your medicines, instruments, and books. I have instructed people most familiar with these things to rent your house at a fair price and you will have an income from that rental. Your villa within the Alcazar is rent-free. "

"What about—"

The caliph held up his hand. "You will be able to continue to care for your patients. You will supply all your patients with official passes that will be prepared for your signature. They will be escorted from the Gate of the Embankment to your villa. The villa you will use has a garden, significantly larger than the one at your house. I have also ordered experienced gardeners to transplant all your medicinal plants. They will help you secure any others you need or desire. Have I missed anything you require?"

Hasdai bowed his head. "Not that I can think of Your Excellency. I assume if I can remember something it will be provided. What am I to do in exchange?"

"You will be my official translator and join the physicians that attend me and my extended family, including my harem. Will that be onerous for you?"

"Not at all, Your Excellency."

"Good. As you may know, we are constantly in danger of encroachment from Christian kingdoms north and east of us. Any correspondence or treaties with those people must be conducted in Latin, none seem willing to learn the nuances of Arabic or its forms. I need a scholar of both languages to make certain anything agreed to is clearly stated in both languages. I don't think this will be too difficult for you."

"I am reasonably certain I can perform those duties, Your Excellency."

"I also want you to continue to learn from our vizier of finance. Specifically, how import and export taxes are applied, managed, and collected. Ibn Bakana tells me that in addition to your other accomplishments you have a head for mathematics and accounting. I may have work for you to do in that regard."

Hasdai stood silent.

"Ah, you are modest as well. It suits you."

Ibn Bakana, Hasdai and I kept the caliph in front of us as we stepped backwards the long distance of the throne room. The caliph turned to the grand vizier and started a discussion of some other matter of state.

"I will take you to your new home," said Ibn Bakana.

We followed him walking rapidly until he stopped in front of a gate in a tall, plastered wall. "This is your gate, here are the keys to it and your house. I will leave it for you to explore. Your household will arrive this afternoon. I am pleased that you accepted the caliph's proposition."

Hasdai unlocked the gate, and we entered a paved courtyard filled with shade trees, flowering bushes, and raised planters resplendent with flowers. Water fell from a stone wall into a small pond with fish swimming in the clear water, in and around water plants. The door to the house stood open.

I followed Hasdai into the house where we entered a square vestibule with a door on each side and two doors in front of us.

Hasdai opened the door on our left and we entered a good-sized room. "This will serve well as an exam room." He crossed it to open another door finding a room of equal size. "This can be a surgery."

A door from our future surgery led to a small room with many shelves and a sink with two faucets. I turned on the left faucet and put my hand in the flow of water. "It' warm, no wait, it's getting hot. "This is fantastic Master."

"Let's see where the other door from the surgery leads," he said, smiling.

We found ourselves back in the vestibule. Another hallway led to a well-equipped kitchen, a room I could picture as a large office, and a small room off the kitchen that could be a bedroom for Sarah and her husband who helped Sarah with household chores and tended the garden. Another door from the kitchen hall opened to a room with a tub, a sink, and a commode. I pulled the lever handing from the ceiling over the commode and water filled the bowel underneath then drained away. The tub and sink both had hot and cold-water faucets.

Up a flight of stairs were three rooms and another bath.

"I think you have managed a significant increase in your standard of living Master," I said.

Hasdai's smile included his eyes. "I believe you are correct in that assumption, Yusuf. Let us hope there is no bad side to this arrangement. Let's find the door to the back garden where I assume our medicinal plants will also find a new home."

The back garden was at least twice as big as the one at Hasdai's former home, supplied with a drip irrigation system and carefully sited fruit and shade trees.

"Yes Yusuf, this will do nicely."

CHAPTER THREE

T wo days later we were moved in and settled. I went to answer loud knocking at our gate and found Dunash and Menahem, Hasdai's closest friends, and my tutors.

"Come in, come in, Hasdai has been expecting you," I said.

There ensued a pantomime as each indicted for the other to go first.

I laughed at their exaggerated antics.

"Do we amuse you, Yusuf, said Menahem? "Have you been working on defining the Hebrew words I gave you at our last session?"

I knew that Dunash was five years younger than both Hasdai and Menahem. He gained his scholarly reputation as a poet, a grammarian, and a ruthless polemicist. His writings attacked, and systematically refuted, the work of grammarians with whom he disagreed. He was especially aggressive about the correct definition of Hebrew words. Dunash was born in Baghdad but travelled to Sura, in Babylonia, where he studied with the renowned Rabbi Sa'adia ben Joseph. In Sura he began composing poetry in Hebrew using Arabic meters, the first to do so. Sa'adia considered that innovation brilliant and spread that opinion, with samples of Dunash's poetry, to his correspondents throughout the Diaspora.

Menahem was born the same year as Hasdai, but in Tortosa, on the Ebro River. Tortosa originated as a hamlet named Dertosa by the Iberians. It grew larger under the governorship of the Roman general Scipio Africanus, then it was transformed into a large municipality by Julius Caesar. When Menahem was born it was a frontier city of the caliphate of Cordoba. A backwater at best, its citizens were considered second class to natives of Cordoba. Menahem had a prickly personality, abrupt with no patience for anyone whose intellect he considered less than his own. He was a recognized expert in comparative linguistics and a philologist with a special interest in Hebrew and Arabic.

When Hasdai's father learned of the academic achievements of Dunash and Menahem, he sponsored their moves to Cordoba, took them into his house, and supported the continuation of their studies. The interests of the three overlapped. They frequently went to the library to study and spent many hours in friendly argument about the meaning of various Hebrew and Arabic words based on how they were used in what they considered to be the most erudite texts. The three were good friends, each recognizing and valuing the learning of the others. Hasdai encouraged Dunash to write poetry in both Arabic and Hebrew and Menahem to initiate work on a dictionary of Hebrew words. At that time Jewish biblical dictionaries were written in Arabic and then translated into Hebrew. All three believed there was considerable loss in the translation. The three considered all the existing dictionaries inadequate.

Two weeks after we moved into the Alcazar Hasdai received a message to go to the offices of Abu Ahmas. He took me along. We arrived after the midday meal and were taken into the grand vizier's private office immediately. Abu Ahmas got up from his desk, walked around it, and embraced Hasdai. Until that moment I was worried this meeting might not be something good.

"Ibn Shaprut, you have made great progress in a very short time. My reports from ibn Bakana indicate that you are quite ready."

"Ready, Excellency?"

"The caliph has been searching for the right person to put in charge of the collection of import and export duties. I assume you know from the time you've spent with the finance vizier the size and importance of this income. The caliphate depends heavily on those funds."

"Yes, Vizier. I know those funds comprise a significant percentage of the total income our caliph has at his disposal each year."

"That is true. The overseeing of the customs agents at all our ports requires a man of intelligence, honesty, and administrative ability. I suggested to the caliph that you are that person, and he agreed."

"I am honored, Excellency," Hasdai bowed his head.

"Tell me what you think this job will entail."

"The caliphate's customs agents have extended experience as traders and merchants prior to their appointment. They access the value of the goods being imported or exported and tax them at seven percent of the presumed value. Most of the merchants consider that a fair tax, compared to what they must pay in other places, but spirited negotiations over the true value of the goods are commonplace."

"And how are the custom agents renumerated?"

"They are allowed to keep half a percent of what they collect as their payment. This provides a comfortable living for them, especially those located at the large ports such as Sevilla and Malaga. The customs agents sell their percentage of the goods collected, when it is not paid in coin, usually at wholesale prices to merchants. Some have their own family run markets or shops but six and a half percent of the value of the taxed goods finds its way to the caliph's treasury."

"All that is true, and the reason we are able to select fair and honest men of experience for these positions. However, I'm certain you understand there is ample opportunity for cheating and graft in the system. An important aspect of your position will be to keep close track of these officers and make certain they are fulfilling their responsibilities with honesty and honor. I must explain that this position would ordinarily warrant an appointment as a vizier, but the caliph has pointed out to me, and I agree, that to give a Hebrew that title would, inevitably, cause consternation and jealousy amongst our Muslim brothers. That could lead to serious consequences for yourself, your fellow Hebrews, and for the caliphate. Do you understand?

I knew that Hasdai understood, as did I, despite my age. Yet another, not subtle, reminder that our faith made us second class, even in the eyes of the enlightened and tolerant.

"I understand completely, Vizier. Titles mean little to me. However, those working under my direction must understand that my authority comes directly from the caliph."

"Certainly. That fact will be made abundantly clear to everyone concerned"

"You will be given a suite of offices in the Old Alcazar and a staff. You will be responsible not only for the work of the customs agents, but for safely transporting the funds due the caliphate to Cordoba. The military will supply guards for the transport. To accomplish your duties, you will retain one and a half percent, one percent for the wages of the people you need for your staff to operate the system, the other half percent for your personal use."

"That will make me a very wealthy man in a short amount of time, Grand Vizier. Are you certain? Last year the duties recorded in the office of the finance vizier were valued at slightly over one hundred thousand gold dinars. A half percent of that is five hundred gold dinars a year, a fortune. I can't imagine how to use that much."

Abu Ahmas smiled. "The use of gold is like smoke trapped in a jar. It expands to fill the volume of the container. You will, I have no doubt, find good use for the gold you acquire."

Hasdai got to work immediately. He acquainted himself with his new offices and staff, then summoned each of the customs agents, one at a time, to Cordoba so he could interview them and take their measure for himself. As each was summoned, he dispatched Menahem, to travel to the same port city to make inquiries about how the customs agent was perceived by the merchants. Menahem went first to the synagogues and spoke to the rabbis, who knew of his scholarly work by reputation. They introduced him to the Hebrew merchants. Those merchants comprised a significant percentage of the traders that interacted with the customs agent. The rabbis also referred Menahem to their Muslim and Christian colleagues. He was thus able to ascertain the honesty and fairness of the custom agents and report his findings to Hasdai. It was my job to sit in on the interviews with the agents and, in writing, document them and Menahem's notes on his findings.

Only two agents were relieved of their positions because of these investigations, but Hasdai was making enemies.

During this same period Hasdai was studying and interpreting two copies of a medical book of pharmacology, *De Materia Medica*. One of the copies was written in Latin, the other was a translation of an earlier Latin version into Arabic. He told me he found both versions frustrating.

"They were transcribed by a person or persons with little, if any, knowledge of medicine. The drawings of the medicinal plants frequently don't match the names I know, and many drawings are incorrectly rendered. Often formulas for various cures are incomplete, particularly for a cure-all known as Therica. We've talked about Therica previously, Yusuf. What do you remember about it?"

The compound is of Greek origin. It was known and used in the late first century, BC. The original formulation was used as an antidote for the bites of snakes and the stings of poisonous insects and spiders. It was, according to legend, first discovered by King Mythridates Eupator and perfected by Andromaque of Crete, physician to Emperor Nero. Andromaque's formulation allegedly consisted of sixty-one different components and was commonly used throughout the Roman Empire as a cure for almost any medical condition. At some time during the third century, the formula was altered or lost. Therica is no longer considered effective."

Hasdai smiled and punched me gently on my left shoulder. "Good Yusuf, you do not disappoint."

When I was twenty years old, and still learning to be a physician, Constantine VII, Emperor of Byzantium, was fighting with the Fatimid Caliphs of Egypt. He was made aware of the enmity between Abd-ar-Rhaman III and the Fatimid Caliphs, so he sent an emissary to Cordoba with the intension of negotiating a treaty of friendship and cooperation.

Hasdai was brought in to translate. At the caliph's direction, and with the help of both Menahem and Dunash, he crafted a treaty as a formal response. The caliph was very pleased with the tone and artistry of the response and sent a delegation to Constantinople bearing the document with appropriate gifts for the emperor. The delegation was delayed by bad weather and didn't arrive in Constantinople until a year later.

Constantine VII responded swiftly with suggested changes and suggestions. The head of the delegation he sent to Cordoba was Stephanos, Constantine's Head of Protocol. He was empowered to negotiate additional changes agreed to by both parties and to sign the formalized treaty which pledged friendship but limited collaboration. Amongst the many gifts sent by Constantine in response to the caliph's gifts was a copy of *De Materia Medica* written by Petanios Dioscorides. It was the original Greek version of the translations Hasdai struggled with. The treatise was illustrated with magnificent and accurate drawings and the Greek names with which Hasdai was familiar. The Caliph also gave Hasdai Orosius' book of Greek history, full of information about important Greek Kings and reliable information about Greek culture and science.

Hasdai immediately recognized potential importance of the *Materia Medica* but told me his knowledge of Greek was not sufficient to allow him to translate the text on his own.

He asked for, and received, an audience with the caliph. "Your Excellency, this book," he held it up, "could contain medical knowledge that would be immensely important to your caliphate. But I will need someone with an extremely good command of both Greek and Latin to work with me on a translation. Would you allow me to compose a letter in your name, to ask the Byzantine emperor to send someone for me to work with on this?"

"That will cost me nothing Hasdai, you have my permission. However, I want you to work to formulate a treaty making the Arabic and Latin versions as identical as possible. You will work with the grand vizier on the details."

"Of course, Your Excellency. I will start on that immediately."

The caliph rolled his eyes and chuckled. "Calm yourself, ibn Shaprut. We don't want the infidels to think we are overly anxious to commit to this relationship."

Several months later a monk named Nicholas arrived. Hasdai brought Nicholas as a guest into his home and supplied food and lodging far superior to anything the monk was accustomed to. They worked together diligently for at least two hours each day for months. Although Nicholas was able to translate the Greek words into Latin, he was not familiar with the various medicinal plants or formulations or for what medical conditions they would be appropriate. Hasdai was able to fill those gaps.

Hasdai found a talented artist from the Hebrew community who was able to recreate the drawings of medicinal plants. He made accurate drawings of all the plants in Hasdai's medicinal plant garden and copied many more from the drawings in Diosorides' work. The Latin text resulting from the collaboration contained descriptions and drawings of over six hundred medicinal plants, oils, and minerals. A great number of these were missing from the previous Arabic and Latin translations. Hasdai had no prior knowledge of a significant number of the medicinal plants, nor what they were used for. He subsequently sent requests with copies of the drawings to Jewish physicians throughout the Diaspora asking for them to look for and, if possible, send him specimens and seeds.

I did all I could to assist Hasdai with this work, and he trusted me to treat some of his patients when he was occupied with it. We awoke early each morning and spent at least an hour reviewing the most recent translations and drawings, all to contribute to my education.

Amongst the many important new discoveries in the work was the original formula for Therica, all sixty-one components, and their measures. Hasdai and I immediately set to work gathering all the ingredients and formulating the cure. It wasn't long before we were able to use it, and the results were almost too good to be believed. We learned it was helpful for a wide variety of illnesses but especially useful to control a fever, to relieve moderate pain, and to resolve a host of women's complaints. His reputation as a physician and mine were enhanced greatly. I became well-known throughout Cordoba as the dispenser of the cure since one of my jobs was to formulate batches of it and give it to any physician who requested it. Hasdai considered the substance quite safe to use, so he did not have to see most patients to prescribe it. He confided to me that although some of the ingredients were, no doubt, effective for some problems, the overall effectiveness of the formula as a cure-all was probably due to the belief on the part of the patient that it would affect the cure.

CHAPTER FOUR

T wo years before Hasdai received the copy of *De Materia Medica*, Menahem, Hasdai, Menahem, and I were crowded in the office filled with three desks, desk and visitor chairs, and shelves of books on three walls. I looked up from the patient record I was working on to see an ominous frown on Menahem's face, he was not happy. For some time, he had been travelling to many of the port towns and cities of the Caliphate.

"Hasdai, I am distracted from my studies by all of this travelling. I want to start my own yeshiva and educate students in my work."

"Yes, I know this is a burden, brother, but you are doing important work. There are still some customs agents not collecting or sending what they should to the caliph, based on your investigations. Most of the agents you visited made the necessary improvements, but some haven't. You will need funds to start your own yeshiva. Am I not paying you well enough? How many more ports do you have to visit?"

"Yes, yes, you are very generous with my wages, of that I can't complain. I recently made my way to Algeciras, on the Bay of Tariq. While there I visited several smaller port towns where smuggling seems to be concentrated. The customs agents in those places seem helpless to stop it. In the larger ports, where ships must load and unload under many watchful eyes, smuggling is less of a problem. Most of the Hebrew, as well as the gentile, merchants have some sort of understanding with their agents. There is little doubt in my mind that coins change hands. This is particularly true with the assessment of value when the traders do not have receipts for the goods they purchase. Even then it is not difficult to obtain a receipt for less than the actual price paid for the merchandise. There are many ways to cheat."

"What do you suggest?" asked Hasdai.

"Suggest? These problems are not my responsibility."

I gasped as Menahem threw his cloak onto the large table that served as Hasdai's desk. The cloak knocked over a rare vase. Fortunately, it did not shatter. I put it back in its place.

"I may be able to offer some suggestions that might, or might not, be effective. I will provide you with a list of suggestions. However, I do not have any ideas about how to enforce morality amongst our own people, let alone the gentiles."

Hasdai removed his turban and placed it on the desk. He scratched his head vigorously. "These problems occupy too much of my time. Remind me which port cities you have visited."

"As I said, Algeciras. I have also visited Alum E'car a very old port on the Mediterranean Sea, and Torremolinos, on the western shore of the Bay of Malaga."

"And where have you yet to visit?"

"Metril at the mouth of the Guadalfea River, Moguer at the mouth of the Tinted River, near Huelva, Shaluga on the left bank of the mouth of the Guadalquivir. The larger, navigable rivers also have ports with access to the sea such as Sevilla. All those have yet to be visited."

Hasdai groaned. "It is a monumental task, Menahem, but I cannot do this work without your help. Here is what I propose. You visit all the ports on your list and interview the customs agents. More importantly, identify members of the Hebrew community who are known to be honest and moral. I will recruit those men as my eyes and ears. They will also help us identify men in other places who can fulfill that role. In return, in addition to your monthly stipend, I will purchase a suitable house here in Cordoba where you can set up your yeshiva. I will also promise you an annual stipend to support you and your students. Does that sound fair?"

"You have the resources to do all that?"

Hasdai looked solemn, then smiled. "In fact, I do, and I will. If you need a written contract, draw one up and I will sign it."

Menahem frowned. "You think I value our friendship so little I need a contract?"

"No." Hasdai laughed. "Brother, I just need your help with this task."

"I will do as you ask."

Menahem stood up and the back of his legs pushed the chair he had been using to the wall. "Something else you should be aware of. The former agent removed from the Malaga post has been causing trouble for the Hebrew community there. Rabbi Shmuel wrote me that the man has recruited a group of thugs who attack Hebrews on the street. They are trying to organize a rampage through the Hebrew section of the city."

"Ah, Menahem, will our people ever find a place where we can live without the fear being attacked because of our faith? I know our people want to live separated from the gentiles. They feel they need to live together, close to their synagogue and to their extended families. The desire to be part of a community is natural, but by isolating ourselves we invoke the passions of those who are looking for, and need, scapegoats. Do you think the Hebrew community of Malaga can band together to protect themselves? You know our culture. The rabbis will argue against such an action for all the old, tired reasons."

Menahem shook his head. "We will not be able to stand up for ourselves unless we have a nation of our own. Have you heard the rumors of the Khazar empire?"

"Yes, of course, but they are just that, rumors. Perhaps someday we can find someone who has been there to verify what we've heard."

"Yes, I suppose you are correct. Well, I will speak with the grand vizier. Perhaps I can convince him to bring that man here to Cordoba so I can reason with him."

"Reason with him?"

"I will convince him that I have the power, not only to take away his position, but to instigate charges against him for his wrongdoing, the reasons that precipitated his removal. I will charge him in the caliph's court where, as you know, sharia law can be very harsh."

"You have the power to do that?"

"Not me personally, but I am pretty certain Abu Ahmas or ibn Bakana will be happy to act for me."

Menahem turned to face me. "Yusuf, did you realize how ruthless Hasdai can be?"

I nodded my head. "It is always in the cause of justice," I smiled.

During the next few months Hasdai was able to build a network of men he considered honest and trustworthy. They monitored activity in the ports and reported to him on a regular basis. He promulgated strict rules, with severe penalties, for giving or taking bribes. He instituted an appeals process, with mediation, to establish the true value of goods. The taxes collected increased significantly.

The troublemaker in Malaga was brought to Cordoba. Hasdai took him into his office motioning for me to join them.

"Please have a seat, Effendi." Hasdai indicated the chair in front of his desk, then sat down in his chair. I leaned against the bookshelves on the far wall.

"I have strong evidence that you have been charging for more than the merchandise passing through your port is worth, You have also been taking more than your share of the duties collected,"

The man started to protest but Hasdai held up a hand. "Stop, don't say anything, you will only make your situation worse. I have the evidence. If you chose to fight, I will charge you in the caliph's court. I assume you know the severity of the punishments handed out by that body. My advice to you is to return to your home, find other employment and stop making trouble for the Hebrew community. Do we understand each other?"

The man sat quietly in the chair. I moved to the opposite wall to study his face. There was no sound in the office except our breathing. Finally, the man stood.

"May I leave?"

"Yes, of course, but please modify your behavior and cause no more problems. You will not get a second chance."

Two weeks later I was again present in the office to overhear the following conversation: "Brother, I am drowning in tasks. I am unable to devote the time necessary to compose and write down the official documents and correspondence required of me. Yusuf is keeping up with my patient records and taking on more and more of my patients, but I am asking you to serve as my confidential secretary. I will communicate with you what needs to be said and leave it to you to craft the eloquent phrases and exact meanings expected from me. Would you be comfortable doing this? I will, of course, pay a handsome salary for you to act for me in this way."

"To whom will the correspondence be directed, Hasdai?"

"Mostly to officials in the government of Cordoba, but also officers in other Muslim countries. All the documents will, of course, need to be in the most impeccably correct Arabic. Grammar and spelling must be perfect, with the necessary flowery expressions our rulers seem to covet. I must provide constant diligence and attention to the business of duty collections. The caliph has recently added to my other duties by appointing me nagid for all the Hebrew communities in the caliphate. My primary responsibility will be to oversee the collection of property taxes from them, but I will also be the final authority to settle disputes the rabbis of those communities are unable to resolve. This will entail a significant amount of Hebrew correspondence, most of which I will also leave for you to deal with in my name. We will, of course, discuss the issues to make certain our ideas are the same. As you may be aware, I am becoming increasingly well known throughout the Diaspora and contacts with the leaders of the various communities need to be established and cultivated. I am receiving more and more correspondence from rabbis living in Christian states, and from Muslim states outside of Cordoba. Sometimes the rabbis use Hebrew forms from the Torah and Talmud and the meaning related to everyday problems is difficult to understand. However, we still need to help those people solve their problems. I know you and Yusuf share my concern about the continued persecution of our Hebrew brothers and sisters. If only there was a safe place for them to relocate. At this moment Cordoba is a refuge, a haven, but we all know how quickly that can change."

Here it is again, the need for a safe haven. I wonder if the Khazar empire actually exists and if so, where is it?

Dunash nodded in agreement the Hasdai continued. "The grand vizier and the caliph also rely on me to correspond with the various Christian states and kingdoms. All that correspondence must have the same meaning in both Arabic and Latin. That task consumes a great deal of my time."

"Is that it?" Dunash laughed. "What has taken you so long to ask for my help with all these tasks?"

Hasdai smiled. "You, Menahem, Yusuf and I know I am gaining power and now have the means to be of significant help to some of our persecuted

Hebrews. I had to be reasonably certain you would be receptive to taking on some of the more mundane chores I am responsible for."

"And are you providing that help?"

Hasdai and Dunash stared into others eyes for several moments. The room was silent and I could hear my own breathing. "Yes, I am," Hasdai said.

Dunash went over to Hasdai's writing desk, sat down in his chair, pulled several sheets of the special paper made according to the exacting specifications for official correspondence of the caliphate, and selected a calligraphy galam, a pen made from dried reed, from a container filled with them. He took the top off a small pot of ink and looked up at Hasdai.

"To whom do you wish to write first and what message do you want to convey?"

Although Hasdai continued to resist all efforts of his family to see him happily married, his two friends were not so reticent. Independently, they asked Hasdai's mother to introduce them to appropriate girls of marriageable age and desire. Both were good looking men of learning and substance. They were friends with, and worked with, her increasingly powerful son. There was no dearth of families willing and anxious to take advantage of the opportunity. Perhaps shortsightedly, the wife of Isaac ibn Shaprut, selected the same six young women to spend time with each of his two friends, separately, of course.

Rebecca was the bat Kohen, the daughter of Rabbi Moses ben Hanoth, who had taught all three of the friends. She was the treasured child of his old age, born when he was over fifty years old. Rabbi Hanoth was a renowned scholar and Rebecca a beautiful, spoiled, nubile young woman. The rabbi acceded to her demands and allowed her to study Torah and Talmud with his students, amongst whom she excelled. For her own amusement, Rebecca allowed both of her two new swains to believe she was infatuated. Before either could realize what had happened, they found themselves in competition, each doing his best to win the heart of Rebecca, and the approval of the rabbi.

Hasdai was oblivious to their dilemma but when we were alone in his office keeping up with his patient notes he stopped and looked up at me. "Are you also starting to think about married life, Yusuf? You are now eighteen years old."

"No, I have too many things to accomplish. I want to become a physician equal to your skills and I have one other burning desire."

"Yes, what is that burning desire?'"

"I want to travel to the Khazar empire and learn if it can be the place our people can go to and be safe."

"Well Yusuf, perhaps I can give you that opportunity. Let's achieve the first goal first."

Hasdai's time was often interrupted by the need to treat illness and injury amongst the caliph's large extended family. That family consisted of brothers and sisters of the caliph as well as uncles, and aunts, all with their own children. All the emirs had three or four wives and numerous concubines. Both wives and concubines had children. Hasdai's ability, if not to cure the complaints of this multitude, at least to relieve pain and suffering, had not gone unnoticed.

To tend to the caliph's family Hasdai, sometimes with me along, went to their homes. If necessary, they came to his house, usually for surgical procedures. Hasdai and I were in his exam room having just seen our last outside patient. "Now the caliph has given me yet another task, Yusuf."

"What now?"

"He wants me to start a yeshiva to train the court physicians in my methods."

"Most of them will not be happy about that."

"He anticipated that. He has given them the choice of learning how I treat the various illnesses and injuries, and following those precepts, or being banned from the Alcazar."

I shook my head smiling, wondering how much of this new task would fall on my shoulders. "How will you find the time for this?"

"I will have to give lectures, but most of the time they will have to follow me in groups of no more than four as I see patients. I will ask questions. If they answer wrongly, I will ask the others to correct their answers. I will only intervene if no one has the correct solution. I will try to lead them to it. It will be tiresome, but perhaps if they learn and embrace my methods, I will not be so essential to the care of the household in the future. Most of them are intelligent, some are even inventive with their treatments. A few have extended knowledge of medicinal plants and two of them are extremely skilled at setting fractures and dislocations. Hopefully, this will improve medical care. I will count on you to teach them the ingredients, formulas, and techniques used to concoct the various medicines I use. Will you do that for me, Yusuf?"

"Of course."

Hasdai became the head of Cordoba's Academy of Medicine and most of the court physicians benefitted from learning his methods. With the passage of time, I was gaining more and more medical knowledge and skill, particularly as a pharmacologist.

It wasn't long until the army physicians were sent to the academy to learn Hasdai's methods. Medicinal gardens were cultivated throughout the caliphate. The extract was harvested from the capsule of *Papaver somniferum*. After the poppy flower fell, horizontal slits were made in the capsule, the substance that had oozed from it was allowed to harden, then scraped off with a knife and dissolved in distilled white wine. This cure became widely available for the treatment of many conditions for which it was marginally, if at all, indicated. It was effective for controlling a cough and for diarrhea. It was also an important component of Therica.

A year after the translation of *the Materia Medica* was completed, I was then twenty-three years old. Hasdai and I were part of a large army involved in war with Ramiro II, the king of Leon. After retaking several frontier towns with their fortresses, we had laid siege to Ramiro's fortress at Zamora. Because Hasdai was by then the sole personal physician of the caliph, we accompanied the forces besieging Zamora. Ramiro was recognized by our caliph as a brilliant military leader who extended his territories south to Salamanca taking several frontier strongholds from the caliphate. He defeated Cordoba's forces, at the battle of Simancas but while the caliphate forces were fighting under the generalship of the crown prince. Now Abd-Ar Rhaman led his army to continue the war with Ramiro.

Another attack on the fortress where Ramiro had decided to stand, and fight was underway. The whoosh of the catapults accompanied the shouts of sergeants, the clashing of swords against shields, and the screams and cries of the wounded. I had not realized that battles would be so loud or smell so bad. Our pavilion, which served as a hospital and medical supply, as well as our home, was pitched just a few minutes away from that of the caliph.

"Follow me, Yusuf," ordered Hasdai.

I followed Hasdai as he trotted toward the large pavilion of the caliph at the center of the camp. I carried his heavy medical chest tight against my chest.

I struggled to catch my breath. "What has happened?" I asked as I caught up.

"The crown prince, Al-Hakan II, has been seriously wounded trying to storm the fortress. We must attend to him."

We were immediately passed through the guards into the caliph's pavilion.

The caliph paced back and forth at the foot of a couch on which the crown prince laid, his armor stripped away, his underclothing soaked with blood.

"This idiot son of mine sought to regain his honor by being the first up a ladder. Do your best for him, Physician."

"Of course, Your Excellency."

Hasdai pushed his way through the several men surrounding the couch. "Please, Your Excellency, have the pavilion cleared of all except yourself. Yusuf, put the chest with my instruments and medicines within my reach."

I opened the chest. Hasdai grabbed a scalpel and swiftly started cutting away the prince's underclothing to expose his wounds. There was a crossbow bolt protruding from his right shoulder, an arrow, with the shaft broken off, embedded in his left thigh, and slashing sword wounds on his left shoulder and abdomen.

"Swab the abdominal wounds and bandage them tight with compresses, Yusuf. The arrow in his thigh might have penetrated enough to hit the femoral artery. It is the most dangerous of his wounds. I will deal with it first."

Hasdai took a bottle of the distilled poppy extract from the chest and poured some into the corner of the prince's mouth. The patient coughed some of it back but swallowed all a second dose.

"Your Excellency, I require several bowls of clean water that has been brought to a boil, and soap. I need to wash my hands and arms thoroughly."

The caliph shouted orders. Within a short time, water must have been boiling for some other purpose, several servants entered with bowls of water. The caliph cleared a large table of maps and papers with a backward sweep of his right arm. The servants set down the bowls and retreated hastily.

Hasdai began by soaping up his hands and forearms. He took a brush and scrubbed each finger on both hands, the palms, and backs, then his arms up to his elbows. He rinsed both hands and arms by dipping both hands into the second bowl that had by then cooled, allowing the clean water to run off his elbows. He repeated the rinsing three times. I held out a towel that had been boiled then dried in the sun. He used it to dry first his hands then his forearms.

"I will need two servants in the room now, Your Excellency. They must do whatever I or my assistant tells them without hesitating."

The caliph roared again.

I winced at the volume of his roar. Hasdai didn't. Two servants silently glided into the pavilion.

Hasdai held out his hands. "Yusuf."

I poured distilled white wine over his extended hands and arms. He waved them in the air to shake off droplets then took a clean scalpel from the chest and carefully dissected around the broken shaft of the arrow.

I washed my hands and arms after handing another container of the distillate to one of the servants, a solidly built man, dressed in a short tunic with no sleeves. His well-defined musculature, of both arms and legs, suggested he hadn't always been a servant. He was taller than me and his expression suggested calm confidence. I noticed he had carefully observed how I poured the distillate over Hasdai's hands and arms. When I held my arms out, he mimicked what I had done. I glanced at the compresses covering the patient's abdominal wounds. There had been some bleeding, but it appeared to have clotted and stopped. No blood was coming from around the bolt in his shoulder. I took up a forceps, grabbed some soft cotton cloth sponges from a container of them and began to clear the blood from the wound Hasdai was making. He also held a forceps with a sponge in his left hand, holding the tissue back away from the blade of the scalpel.

The caliph had been looking over my shoulder, watching closely. I saw him blanch and start to sway. I looked over my shoulder at the second servant. "Get a chair for the caliph, now."

"I need light to see properly," Hasdai said, loud enough to be heard by everyone in the room. The same servant who had poured the distillate reacted immediately, grabbed a large lamp, and brought it over to the couch.

"Stand to the right of me, over my right shoulder," Hasdai directed. "Try to hold it as still as possible. When you tire and need to change hands tell me first. Do you understand?"

"Yes, Rabbi, I do," the servant said quietly in Hebrew.

Hasdai glanced at the man and smiled.

Hasdai kept his voice low. I heard him but the caliph apparently did not. "You are Hebrew?"

The man nodded.

"Slave or free?"

"Slave."

"If God wills it, I will see what I can do."

I saw the man's eyes glisten with tears.

Hasdai continued his careful dissection and the prince moaned.

The caliph spoke again, his tone harsh. "Be a man, suffer in silence,"

Hasdai straightened up and stretched his back. "The artery is intact. Let's hope the arrow wasn't dipped in feces to contaminate the wound."

He carefully extracted the arrowhead, sniffed at it, then dropped it into one of the empty water bowls. He glanced at the caliph.

"I smell feces on the arrowhead. That means I will not be able to close the wound. I will pack it with a poultice after flushing it thoroughly with boiled, salted water. The wound will have to be kept open to heal slowly from the inside. It will take a long time and will leave a large scar."

"If God wills it." The caliph scowled, then his expression softened. "Perhaps it will remind him to not attempt foolish acts."

Hasdai next extracted the crossbow bolt. It must have been fired from a long distance, as it had only penetrated through the skin to embed itself in the collarbone. It was swiftly dissected free and Hasdai sutured the wound closed.

The sword wounds were next. The sword wound to the shoulder had cut to the bone near the joint, but the joint was not open. Hasdai dissected to freshen the edges of the wound, cleaned it of all foreign bodies, flushed it with salted water, then sutured it closed.

Hasdai bent close to inspect the abdominal wound. "This is good. The wound is only superficial; it didn't penetrate the abdominal cavity. I will be able to clean it and suture it closed."

Hasdai finally straightened, stretched his back, and rotated his shoulders. "How long were we occupied?"

The servant holding the lamp bowed his head and stepped forward. "Three turns of the hourglass, Rabbi." During the entire procedure he had held the lamp in just the right place to illuminate the surgical field, without changing hands.

Hasdai turned to face the slave, bringing his mouth close to the man's ear. "What is your name?"

"I was Judah ben Shlomo in another life."

"How did you come to be here?"

"I was conscripted into the army of Umar ibn Hafsun from my home in Jaen. I was captured and brought to Cordoba as a slave," he murmured softly.

"What are you whispering about with my slave, ibn Shaprut?" demanded the caliph.

"I was curious about his history, Your Excellency. I could use a man of his strength and intelligence. Will you allow me to purchase him?"

"No." The caliph replied gruffly. "But if my son lives, I will gift him to you."

"We will offer special prayers for your son," replied Hasdai.

"I will have him moved to your tent and you will take extra special care of him."

"Of course, Your Excellency. I would have suggested that in any case."

A few days later Abd-ar Rhaman ordered a portion of the moat surrounding the fortress of Zamora be filled with corpses from the fighting to provide easier access to the fortifications. Following heavy bombardment from his trebuchets, the fort was stormed and taken.

Several of the army physicians had trained in Hasdai's medical academy and he trusted them. Each day he inspected all the hospital tents, making certain the physicians had all the necessary supplies and medications needed to care for their patients.

The crown prince's wounds made good progress. After Zamora was again part of the caliphate we returned to Cordoba. Hasdai and I went daily to the quarters of the crown prince and tended his wounds. It took a little over six weeks for the thigh wound to close completely and, as Hasdai predicted, it left a huge, ugly scar.

Judah ben Shlomo joined our household. He told me he was thirty years old. His military training had given him a powerful physique and he moved with the grace of an elite athlete. Hasdai immediately freed him since he believed slavery was an evil institution. He told Judah he could return to Jaen if he wished to do so, but Judah said he wanted to stay and serve Hasdai anyway he could.

If I ever have the opportunity to travel to the Khazars I want this man as my companion.

CHAPTER FIVE

· ·

After our return from Zamora, Hasdai, Dunash, Menahem and I
met each week for an hour or so after breaking the overnight fast.
As the titular head of all the Hebrew communities of Cordoba,
the nagid, Hasdai's responsibilities were expanding beyond his control.
He asked me, Dunash and Menahem to seek the names of responsible
Hebrew leaders so he could appoint them as surrogates in all the Hebrew
communities of Andalusia. They were empowered to act in his name and
to keep up regular correspondence with him about their actions. At the
same time, he reached out to Hebrew communities outside the borders
of Andalusia. Most of these he found by interrogating traders coming to
Cordoba from essentially all the known world. His intent was to learn as
much as possible about how Hebrew communities were faring throughout
the Diaspora. When he learned of a community, within or outside of the
caliphate, being persecuted or oppressed, he invoked the considerable
power of his office and the support of the caliph to intervene and do all
possible to correct the situation.

At the same time, he gave, from his own considerable resources,
financial support to the rabbinical yeshivas. He also paid for the editing
and publishing of scholarly books reflecting his own opinions, opinions
that varied from his, and a wide variety of other books that might be of
interest to scholars. He also paid to import books from the libraries and

cultural centers located in all the dominions of Islam, adding to the caliph's growing library.

One of my regular tasks was to receive all correspondence sent to Hasdai, determine its importance and how soon it needed to be answered. After establishing communication with Hebrew communities in Southern Italy, he received a letter listing the names of rabbis and Torah scholars who had survived persecution by the late Byzantine emperor Ramanus I Lekapenos. Although that despot was dead the decree which forced the Hebrews to convert or face exile, was still being enforced. The same letter informed Hasdai about three Rabbis; Isaiah, Menachem, and Elijah who, with all their disciples, had committed suicide rather than convert. The authors of this letter made it clear they were not asking for Hasdai's aid, but only wanted to inform him of their situation. Fearing, with good reason, that the letter might be intercepted or copied, Hasdai gave my translation of this letter to the grand vizier who transmitted it to the caliph. The caliph agreed to support Hasdai's efforts to end the persecution of the Hebrew communities.

We were all present for our regular once weekly morning gathering. Hasdai told us about the caliph's support. "I am certain we are all grateful to have a caliph who is so tolerant, but the Hebrew communities are desperate for a place in this world that conforms to our teachings and is governed by members of our faith."

"We still don't know if the Khazar empire is Hebrew, nor where, exactly it is, or how difficult to get to," I said.

"We hear you Yusuf, and we are aware of your desire to go there. Be patient, we must learn more about this place before sending you."

Abd-Ar Rhaman acted on Hasdai's request and sent a delegation headed by his ambassador to the Byzantine Emperor. Hasdai supplied the ambassador with a letter to be delivered to the emperor. The letter was carefully composed, in exquisitely correct Hebrew, by Menahem. Hasdai anticipated the emperor had monks who were fluent in Hebrew and could translate the contents of the letter. The translators who did so were unable to refrain from commenting on the eloquence and exactness of the Hebrew. They pointed out the merit of the quotations made by the author from their own Old Testament, translated from the Greek. The quotations emphasized the importance of treating all peoples with kindness and compassion. The same letter to the emperor also promised to act in favor of the Christians living in Andalusia. The Muslim caliphate was, of course, already being lenient to all the Abrahamic religions and traditions, since the Hebrews, Christians and Muslims all derived from Abraham.

The emperor found merit in the arguments presented. He decided to address the issue but directed that the interventions he proposed should be done in Hasdai's name, since he did not think it appropriate for him to defend the Hebrews. He sent two letters, in Hasdai's name, but clearly from the emperor's desk. The first was to his daughter, Empress Helen. In this letter he referred to the Hebrews as "the rest of the survivors of the community among us." He asked that she should not oblige the Hebrews to act against their will and, further, that she should name one of her subordinates to deal specifically with matters relating to the Hebrew communities. The second letter was sent to Constantine VII Porphysogenetus, the emperor of the Macedonian dynasty of the Byzantine Empire, asking for the same concessions.

Correspondence with leaders of the Hebrew communities ruled by the two despots indicated conditions had improved, slightly, but prejudice and malice towards the Hebrews was deeply impeded in their cultures, the fires fanned by the church clergy.

Byzantium was not unique in persecuting the Hebrews. It was another bright, sunny morning, early in spring shortly after Hasdai had finished dealing with the situation of persecution in Byzantium. Dunash, Menahem and I were in the office when I opened a letter addressed to Hasdai. It was yet another plea for help. Hasdai returned from a meeting with the finance vizier.

"Any new correspondence for me," he asked?

"I just received this today," I said, holding up the letter.

"What is it? Summarize it for us."

"Apparently the city of Toulouse, in the Germanic kingdom to the north has an ongoing annual tradition. On the eve of Passover, a Hebrew male is forced to present himself at the cathedral door. His charge is to provide thirty pounds of wax to make candles for the church. The thirty pounds of wax represents the thirty silver coins Judas received for the betrayal of Jesus. The bishop stands at the door, takes the wax, then slaps the man's face. On at least one occasion the bishop hit the man so hard he was knocked off his feet, hit his head on a cobblestone, and died as a result."

Everyone in the room was outraged. Hasdai sat behind his desk rubbing his forehead. I stood and paced the office feeling hopeless.

Dunash finally spoke. "I want to leave immediately for Toulouse and knock some people in the head with a club."

Menahem stood. "I will join you."

Then reality took hold and we all slumped into chairs, defeated and despondent.

"I ask all of you to help me compose a letter to the caliph's ambassador to Leon and ask him to present the letter to King Otto I. We will send a copy of this same letter to the city administrators of Toulouse. Maybe we can do something to end this shameful tradition."

Unfortunately, this effort had no effect and the tradition endured. However, Hasdai's ability to protect Hebrews encouraged many, particularly from North Africa, to emigrate to Andalusia to escape persecution and avoid the endless warring between the Shia descendants of Fatima and the Sunnis.

Dunash and Menahem sat across from each other, their desks butted up together. They seemed not to notice I was in Hasdai's office with them. I made myself busy transcribing patient records. Hasdai was out of the house, treating one of the caliph's favorite concubines for some woman's disorder. I would learn what it was when he returned. I looked up as Menahem suddenly broke the silence.

"Dunash, Rebecca told me you visit her at least twice a week. Is that true?"

"She tells me you do the same Menahem."

"I care for her very much and want to marry her."

"As do I."

It was obvious to me that both were struggling to not show anger. Their red faces betrayed them.

"Is she playing a game with us to you think?" asked Dunash. "If so, why would she want to turn us against each other?"

"I have been wondering the same thing. What do you suggest we do?" asked Menahem.

"One of us should withdraw."

"Are you volunteering?"

Menahem chuckled. "And leave her to you? You wish."

"Do you think Rebecca will eventually choose between us?" asked Dunash.

Menahem shrugged. "Or maybe she has a rich merchant in mind and is waiting for him to join the competition."

They both sat, silent, pensive, each with his chin resting on his right hand. I noticed that their fingers were stained with ink, as were mine. After what seemed to be a long time both sighed and went back to what they had been working on.

I found the silence ominous and disturbing. How could a young girl have caused two good friends to feud and cause pain to each other? I wondered if their friendship would be broken.

Hasdai stalked into the office, put his medical bag back in its empty place on one of the shelves lining the office. Most of the shelving sagged, some more than others, from the weight of books. He plunked into chair behind his large table and tossed his turban in the general direction of an empty corner of the desk. It slid to the floor.

I started to get up from my small desk.

"Leave it, Yusuf. I will pick it up myself, eventually. Why is this office so quiet? No lively discussion of some obtuse Talmudic question? Menahem and Dunash, both of you have your noses buried in your writing and serious frowns on your faces. What's going on?"
"They are both in love with the same woman," I announced.

"Nobody asked you, Yusuf," Menahem shouted.

Dunash also raised his voice. "Yes, Yusuf, mind your own business."

Hasdai coughed. "Don't take it out on Yusuf. Why was I not aware of this wonderous person?"

There was a long silence. I watched all three wondering who would speak first. It wasn't going to be me.

Hasdai lost patience. "Well, one of you satisfy my curiosity. How did this come to be?"
"We both asked your mother to select some girls of marriageable age to introduce us to. Ever efficient, she chose the same group for both of us," volunteered Dunash.

"And?"

"One of them was Rebecca, the daughter of Rabbi Moses ben Hanoth."

"Rebecca? She is an infant. You are speaking of our Rabbi Hanoth, our teacher, not some other Rabbi Hanoth?"

"She is a beautiful young woman, now already eighteen years old," answered Menahem.

"No, not possible. I remember clearly when she was born. The rabbi was so proud."

Menahem sighed aloud. "Yes, well she grew up while you weren't paying attention. I think your mother had in mind that we would tell you how beautiful, well-educated, and intelligent she has become and maybe get you interested in her. We all know your family is anxious to see you married."

"I know what they want, but I have no time for a wife and children. Go on, tell me more."

"There is no more," answered Dunash. "We both visit her regularly, but she shows no preference for either of us."

"Well, I can understand. You are both well-educated, successful, good looking, devout and available. She, perhaps, is unable to choose between you. How should this be resolved? I know, I will make long lists of pros and cons for each of you. I know you both, perhaps better than you know yourselves. Then, I will go meet this wonder of nature and present her with the lists. Don't worry, I will be both fair and honest. That should help her make up her mind."

Menahem spoke first. "Hasdai, we both appreciate all you do for us, but please God, do not interfere in this. The situation is bad enough as it is."

"I agree with Menahem," added Dunash. "Please stay out of this."

Hasdai laughed. "I am just teasing. I will not stick my nose in. However, I would like to see the object of so much adoration."

I smirked. "If you tell your mother that, I am certain her feet will not touch the ground as she runs to the house of the rabbi."

Hasdai turned to me. "Did anyone ask for your opinion, Yusuf?"

Judah entered the room carrying a tray with a coffee urn and cups in one large hand. I cleared a corner of my desk so he could put the tray down.

"Should I serve, Effendi?"

"Yes, please, Judah, and take a cup yourself."

We sipped at the dark, sweet syrup.

"The new girl is making herself comfortable in your house next door," said Judah.

"New girl?" The three of us were incredulous.

Menahem's cup slipped out of his hand, but he caught it before it hit the floor, but what remained of his coffee spilled over his hand. "What new girl?"

"Yes, the caliph has insisted I accept another concubine as a gift. She is from the far north, a Slav, very pretty, blonde. I was not allowed to refuse."

"And this was a reward for what?" asked Menahem.

"We are all aging," answered Hasdai. "One of the caliph's favorites is a beautiful woman, already mature when he was a youth. She taught him all the skills necessary to be a good lover and he still cherishes her. That is who I am back from treating. She has sudden periods of feeling feverish and her menstrual periods are now irregular, sometimes skipping months. I explained to the caliph that this time of life comes to all women if they live long enough. She, of course, knew exactly what was happening to her. I gave her some medications to ease her symptoms and told her to eat foods containing flax seed meal or oil. It contains a substance that seems quite useful for this condition."

"Let's return to the more interesting subject. Just how many young women are you housing next door now?" asked Dunash.

"Four."

I couldn't restrain myself. "Do you visit all of them at the same time?"

"Do not be crude, Yusuf. Of course not. They share meals and socialize but each has her own bedroom and adjacent sitting room."

"No wonder you have no interest in marriage," observed Menahem.

"If any one of you allow this information to reach the ears of my mother you will be cast out. Is that clear enough?" He was no longer smiling.

All three of us held up both hands in surrender.

"Are you the only one allowed to tease," I laughed?

About six months after we learned of Hasdai's harem Hasdai returned from a meeting with the finance vizier. I handed him a letter from his surrogate in Seville, one of the most respected and scholarly rabbis of that city. The rabbi complained about recent events and expressed worries concerning the safety of his community. I had read the letter to Menahem and Dunash.

Hasdai read the letter quickly then looked up and spoke. "All rulers have enemies. A powerful caliph has powerful enemies. Our caliph's old enemy, Ibn Hafsun, was recently killed by an assassin."

"Did the caliph have a hand in this," I asked?

Hasdai ignored the question. "Did you read this letter to them, Yusuf?'

I nodded.

"Then you all know that one of Hafsun's sons, Assad, has a following in Seville. He has decided to make a surreptitious move to undermine the caliph. He imported a radical, fundamentalist imam from Tunisia and encouraged the man to foment discontent and hatred against the Hebrew community.

"Yusuf, I want you to come with me when I visit Grand Vizier Abu Ahmas to ask his advice. I suspect he will suggest I go to Seville and if so, I will want you and Judah to accompany me.

Abu Ahmas welcomed us, directing us to sit with him.

"You are always welcome, Shaprut, but I am curious about the reason for this visit."

"I am concerned about events in Seville."

Abu Ahmas held up his hand. "The caliph is very aware of what is happening in Seville, and the person responsible for it. Assad thinks he will be able to take control of Seville when the rioting gets out of hand and from that position of power instigate a revolt against the caliphate. The caliph wants you to travel to Seville, rally your people, and convince this imam to return to Tunisia. If you do not feel safe performing this duty, I will assign a company of experienced soldiers to accompany and protect you."

"My servant is a former soldier. He is big and powerful and I'm certain he will be able to protect me. My colleague Yusuf," the grand vizier nodded his acknowledgement of me, "is extremely efficient. He will make all the necessary arrangements for our trip to Seville next week. I will write the rabbi and inform him that we are coming."

Hasdai continued. "I have an idea about how to resolve this, Vizier. Would it be possible for you to arrange a debate between myself and the imam? I believe I can identify the quotations from the Quran he is using to incite his followers. I am certain I can refute those ideas by quoting other sections of the Quran and the writings and interpretations of respected Islamic scholars."

The grand vizier looked concerned. "You feel confident you will win such a debate? What if you do not?"

"I am quite confident, with the help of my good friends to prepare me, I will be able to. I want to do it."

The grand vizier thought for a long moment. "I will insist that Assad host a gathering where you and the imam can debate the issues. It is, after all, a very Arabic traditional entertainment. It will go even better if you can bolster your arguments by quoting some Arabic poetry."

"I will prepare myself to do so."

"Good, I will make certain you have the opportunity."

We returned to Hasdai's house where Hasdai enlisted Dunash and Menahem to help him prepare. Menahem agreed to scour the Quran for quotes the imam might use to incite his followers and justify his antagonism of the Hebrews. Dunash said he would identify relevant writings of scholars and poets, particularly Arabic writings that promoted tolerance.

"Good," said Hasdai. "Give me what you find as soon as you have it and I will organize, catalogue, and memorize. I will leave for Seville in only ten days, so we have a great deal of work to do in a short time."

I made all the travel arrangements and made certain we had everything we needed for the journey. I was also included in the study sessions to prepare Hasdai for the debate, and even allowed to voice my opinion on the material to be used.

The four of us worked long hours finding and discussing every possible interpretation of each quotation we believed relevant to the arguments Hasdai would be making. I worked with Menahem and Dunash to anticipate what the imam would argue. Hasdai rehearsed how he planned to answer each anticipated statement from his opponent. Then the three of us provided criticism and suggestions for improvement. I was still in awe of how their minds collated and organized the writings they collected, identified various possible interpretations, and selected those interpretations that most strongly presented their preferred arguments.

The morning we departed Dunash grabbed Hasdai's arm. "Do you feel ready, Hasdai? Menahem and I could come with you and rehearse your arguments as we travel."

"No, I need you both here to take care of the everyday responsibilities and correspondence. I trust you both to act as I would act. Thanks to both of you, I am well prepared. It would not have been possible without your diligence and help. Yusuf can quiz me while we travel."

Judah, Hasdai and I mounted the strong horses I had purchased after Judah evaluated those offered.

"These horses will make easy work of the twenty-seven parasangs to Seville," said Judah.

Two of Hasdai's other servants drove a wagon pulled by two mules, loaded with our supplies, equipment, and gifts for Assad, the imam, and various important functionaries of the Hebrew community of Seville.

The horses and mules easily covered ten to twelve parasangs a day. The road between the two major cities was well maintained, bore a lot of traffic, was guarded by units of the caliph's army stationed at regular intervals, and paroled both night and day. It was quite safe. The grand vizier had agreed to send messengers ahead to make arrangements at comfortable inns for the two nights of our journey. He had also convinced Assad that it was in his best interest to host the chief customs officer of the caliphate and to treat him with the respect the caliph demanded for his officers.

Assad provided everything expected for an honored guest. Upon our arrival at his mansion, we were shown to a large private bedroom for Hasdai with a small adjoining room for Judah and me. Our two servants were housed with the servants of the house. After making ourselves comfortable, we were escorted to the baths located in the basement of the mansion and enjoyed the steam, expert massages, and relaxing water of a large pool. The meal that first evening was extravagant. Hasdai and Assad held a relaxed and informal conversation about Arabic poetry. Assad was quite knowledgeable about that subject, and Hasdai encouraged him to pontificate. After a while Assad addressed the real issue at hand.

"Well, Efendi Shaprut, you have an enviable reputation as a scholar and a man of learning. We are looking forward to your debate with our imam tomorrow evening. I hope you are ready for it. Our imam is a man of extraordinary learning and is a fiery debater."

"I believe I am adequately prepared, Effendi. I am anticipating a lively and educational debate. Thank you for making the necessary arrangements. Do you anticipate a large gathering to witness it?"

"Oh yes. I have invited many of the most influential citizens of Seville and there is great anticipation. I hope you will also invite some members of your Hebrew community to join us."

"Thank you, Effendi. How many will you have room for?"

"I am certain we can accommodate at least a dozen."

"Good. I will ask Rabbi Solomon to invite some of his scholars when I visit him in the morning."

"Excellent. Did you taste the goat? It is prepared in a very special way, marinated for a full day and night in a secret concoction invented by my chef, then wrapped in banana leaves and cooked in a pit of coals covered by earth."

Hasdai pointed at a large serving dish. "Is it that dish?"

"Yes."

"It is extraordinarily good. I kept taking more. I assumed it was halal."

"Of course. Everything served in my house is halal. Our food traditions are, I understand, very similar to yours."

Hasdai nodded in agreement. "Yes, almost identical. Perhaps that helps explain why Muslims and Hebrews coexist so peacefully under the watchful eye of our caliph."

Assad grinned. "Perhaps."

The following day Hasdai met with Rabbi Solomon and some members of the Hebrew community who had suffered abuse. I carefully recorded the details of all the incidents they related. Some had been personally attacked and injured, others had suffered extended verbal abuse, and some had their property damaged or destroyed. Hasdai distributed coins for reimbursement and made it clear that the payment was from the caliph, who knew of their problems and had sent him, Hasdai, to correct the situation.

That night Assad hosted another banquet, this one much more lavish than the one the previous evening. At the head table the imam was seated to the right of our host; Hasdai was on his left. As everyone at the head table finished eating, Assad leaned to the imam and whispered. The imam rose to his feet, gathered his robes around himself and, in a loud, penetrating voice, quoted a passage from the Quran, then turned to face Hasdai. Hasdai rose to his feet and spoke, just loud enough for the people seated at the far end of the large banquet hall to hear. We had tested the acoustics of the room earlier and he knew just how loud he needed to speak so that the audience had to lean towards him but could still understand what he was saying. He spoke slowly, carefully, and distinctly. He quoted other passages from the Quran and cited the written works of Moslem scholars explaining how the passage quoted by the imam could be interpreted to have the opposite meaning.

The debate continued for close to an hour. The iman became increasingly strident, shouting his interpretation of the passages he quoted. All were from the Quran. On two occasions, Hasdai corrected mistakes the imam made in quoting. Other times he quoted respected Arabic theologians who had written different interpretations of the meaning of the passages quoted. Each time his response was calm, measured, and scholarly. I was seated at the furthermost spot in the room, holding my face impassive, but a huge grin was smothered inside me. I had never suspected that Hasdai could be such a brilliant debater. The debate ended abruptly when the imam stalked out of the room, head down, muttering to himself about being trapped.

Hasdai addressed our host. "Effendi, I'm afraid I offended the iman. I have gifts for him from the caliph. I will leave them with you and perhaps you will make certain he receives them? I will send him a letter of apology. I was probably overly aggressive. He acquitted himself to the full extent of his abilities, but I may have had the advantage of a superior education."

Assad's countenance was impassive, but his voice couldn't hide his disappointment. "I will make certain he receives your gifts, Effendi Shaprut. If you will excuse me, it has been a long day and I am tired."

"Of course, Effendi Assad. I will take leave of you and take this opportunity to thank you for your hospitality. You have been a most gracious host. We will return to Cordoba early tomorrow morning."

"It has been my great pleasure to host you, Physician. Please extend my greetings and best wishes to Abu Ahmas and the caliph."

"It will be my pleasure to do so."

We returned to Hasdai's room where he dictated a letter to the iman. In it he explained that the caliph had authorized the expenditure of one hundred gold dinars, included with the letter, to finance the imam's return to Tunisia. This was in addition to the gifts from the caliph that Effendi Assad was holding for him. Hasdai pointed out that the large audience attending the debate had been witness to the weakness of his arguments and would, without doubt, incite considerable comment and conversation throughout Seville. This would, in all probability, make his continued residence in Seville uncomfortable, especially among the several Muslim scholars who had been present at the debate. The letter was a masterful example of the carrot and the club.

After I finished writing, Hasdai quickly scanned the document, signed it, affixed his seal, and called for Judah.

"Will you please deliver the letter with the coin pouch? See that the imam receives both into his own hands. Thank you. We'll wait to see if this has the desired effect. Be particularly careful and watchful. I would not be surprised if Assad is watching our movements. He may interfere with your errand. I suspect he will be planning something for our return to Cordoba. It is unlikely he will try anything on the road, it is too well patrolled, but during our overnight stays something might be in the works."

Judah nodded. "Do not be concerned, Effendi. I will be well armed, and I have not forgotten how to defend myself. Unless he sends a host to confront me, I will be fine."

"Good, hurry on your errand and hurry back. Here, take my sealing ring and show it if you have any problems with the authorities. You can explain you are doing an official errand for the chief customs officer."

Judah returned within the hour. The right sleeve of his tunic was torn, there was still drying blood on the tunic and his trousers, and he had a wound on his left forearm.

"What happened? Let me see that wound," said Hasdai.

"It is minor. Don't worry, Effendi. Shortly after I left the imam, I was accosted by two sinister looking men. They demanded to know the nature of my business with the imam. I told them I was just a delivery person. They demanded to know what I had delivered. I told them it was a letter. They wanted to know what was in the letter. I told them it was sealed, and I didn't know what was in it. They screamed something rather insulting about my ancestry and then attacked. They made the mistake of coming at me side by side. I easily side-stepped the man on my left and used his forward momentum to divert him into the path of his partner. I held a good grip on his right arm, ducked under it, twisted, and shoved it up high enough to dislocate his shoulder. He dropped the knife he tried to stab me with. The other man regained his balance and swung his knife at me, but I deflected with my left forearm and stabbed him in the chest with my own knife."

"Street guards were soon on the scene. I showed them your ring and explained I didn't know the reason for the attack. I assumed the motive was to rob me. I was just a poor servant on an errand for my master. While they were questioning me the man with the chest wound breathed his last. They told me to be on my way and they would find out why I had been attacked when they questioned the survivor. I don't think either of the attackers expected to encounter someone who could defend himself. I also don't think the man with the dislocated shoulder will give up the person who hired them, even if he knows who it was. It was, no doubt, arranged by an intermediary."

At that moment I determined that I would do well to make an extra effort to befriend Judah. If I was ever sent to seek the Khazars I needed a companion I could count on for protection.

"I think you understand the situation very well, Judah," said Hasdai. Yusuf, please bring your medicine bag and treat this wound. We don't want to risk infection. Thank you, Judah. I am very happy God brought you to my house."

The next morning, we were on the road early. The weather was pleasant, sunny but not too warm. In the late afternoon we reached the same inn where we had stayed the second night going to Seville. The landlord was prepared to receive us. Our rooms were clean and ready. His wife prepared a special meal for us. We retired early intending to get an early start in the morning.

Judah approached Hasdai in the hallway leading to our rooms, his forehead wrinkled with worry. "Effendi, I am worried about another attack from the Seville rebels. Assad might be the lead instigator but there are probably other malcontents who might try to gain his favor by assassinating you. If you don't mind, I will stay in your room and stand guard."

"You need to sleep too, Judah. You can't stay awake for the whole trip."

"I am accustomed to going without sleep from my days as a soldier. If I do doze, I will awaken at the slightest sound. I will not allow any harm to come to you."

"Thank you, Judah. I feel quite safe with your protection."

During the earliest hours of the morning, I heard a loud grunt from the room next to mine. I rushed to my door and tried to open it. The light from the hall lamp showed one man on the floor, blocking my door from opening completely. Judah had hold of the wrist of another man who was still holding a knife. A third man was slowly getting to his feet while shaking his head. I grabbed the heavy book I had been writing in prior to getting into bed. I squeezed into the hallway and hit the man shaking his head as hard as I could with the book. He fell prone, his face smashing into the floor.

"Thank you, Yusuf," Judah twisted under the arm he was holding, wrenching the arm upward. I heard a loud pop and knew the attacker's shoulder had dislocated. His knife clattered on the floor. It was clearly an often-practiced move. It must have been exactly what Judah had done to the man the previous night.

The landlord pounded up the stairs, panting, holding a cudgel in his right hand. "What is happening?" he demanded.

Hasdai's calm voice came from his bed, where he was sitting up. "Those three assassins broke into the room. As you can see my guard took care of them. I am surprised your house is so easily broken into, landlord."

"A thousand apologies, Effendi. If I had known you were in danger, I would have posted guards."

The landlord took the lamp from its bracket on the hall wall and held it aloft to peer at each of the men on the floor. He prodded the one I had hit with the book with his free left hand. The man groaned.

"I have not seen any of these men before, Effendi, at least not that I can remember. I think we should bind them. I will send for the caliph's guards to come and collect them. Perhaps they will say who sent them."

The landlord looked at Judah. "You subdued all three of them with just your hands?"

Judah shrugged. He nudged the groaning man with his right foot. "Yusuf hit this one with that heavy book."

"But he was still trying to recover from whatever it was you did to him before I arrived!" I said, but I was pleased I had contributed to Hasdai's defense.

We returned to Cordoba. Hasdai was called to the grand vizier's office three days later. He reported his interview at our gathering the following day.

"The grand vizier said he was relieved that Judah was able to subdue those three who intended to do me harm. He told me that one of the three had confessed, after a prolonged, and no doubt painful, interrogation, that he and his companions were hired by one of Assad's stewards. The steward was arrested, and the grand vizier was certain it will only be a matter of time until he implicates Assad. He has already admitted that he hired the two that attacked Judah in Seville. The troublesome imam has returned from whence he came. All seems to be under control and Assad has fled. So far, we don't know where. The vizier also said he wished he could have been present for the debate. He told me he heard that I demolished the imam's arguments. I told him I was very well prepared by my friends and that my opponent seriously underestimated our combined scholarship."

CHAPTER SIX

During the next six months my life changed markedly. I was then almost twenty-five years old and Hasdai declared that I was ready to take over his medical practice in the city. I knew his patients and they were good about accepting me as their physician. They knew I would consult with him when I was not certain about a diagnosis or treatment.

Hasdai consulted with me to select the most talented student from his medical academy to take my place as his assistant. I spent a month training him to do all the tasks I had taken care of for the past several years.

Hasdai rented me his house in the city, at a reasonable, nay, small rate, and I conducted my practice from that familiar place. I visited my mentor at his house inside the Alcazar on a regular basis and he always had a task or two for me to accomplish to make his load lighter.

I had heard stories about the king of Leon, Sancho I, but it was a surprise when I became involved in his life. Although he came to be called Fat Sancho, he was not a fat child. As a youth he was quite athletic and even excelled in the use of the sword and shield. After reaching maturity and assuming the management of his kingdom, he exercised less and ate more, gaining weight at a rapid rate. He became so fat he was unable to mount a horse. Not to be deterred, he ordered a platform and steps to be built, but he was unable to climb the stairs without a person on either side.

Once on the platform, he was able to sit on the horse, but had difficulty maintaining his balance. Even the strongest of horses were unable to carry him more than a short distance and that only at a hesitant walk.

Eventually he became so obese he needed to lean on someone just to waddle in a rough semblance of walking. The nobles of Leon, always looking for a reason to gain additional power at someone else's expense, began a campaign of ridicule directed at Sancho I. They murmured, albeit in the shadows, that the king had lost his ability to reason by virtue of being so obese. The prime instigator, Ferran Gonzalez, had, at least once before, attempted to place a cousin of Sancho I on the throne, but that effort had fallen short of fruition.

With time Gonzalez and his cronies managed to convince enough generals that ridding the kingdom of the overly fat king was the only way to keep Leon safe from its enemies. Within a month soldiers invaded the palace and seized control of the administrative offices. Sancho's loyal adherents managed to hide him in a wagon and flee Pamplona. They arrived safely in Navarra where Sancho had powerful allies. Queen Toda of Navarra was his grandmother, and the king of Navarra was his uncle. They provided refuge for him and his handful of loyal followers.

Ferran Gonzalez and his co-conspirators chose Ordono IV, a cousin of Sancho I, to be their new king. The justification for the choice was that Ordono IV was the only other living male of the royal family. The new king was not much easier to stomach than the obese Sancho I. He was hunchbacked, bad tempered, and not overly bright, but Gonzalez and his junta believed they would be able to control him. Ordono proved to be not only truculent, but vindictive, exacting severe discipline on anyone who displeased him. It proved easy to displease him because he gloried in perversions that any moral person would consider despicable. His nickname was Ordono, The Evil One.

Once she learned of the coronation of Ordono, Queen Toda resolved to restore her grandson to his rightful throne. Mentally sharp and ambitious, she knew that to restore Sancho's title she would need a militarily powerful ally and, just as important, a doctor capable of curing Sancho's obesity. Cordoba was the only available option, but she knew the cost of asking for the help from Abd-Ar-Rhaman would be high. Even though the caliph was her grandnephew, by reason of marriage, Navarra had been involved in an on-again, off-again war with Cordoba for more than thirty years. A year before Sancho was driven out, Cordoba's army had devastated several of Navarra's agriculturally productive valleys and set fire to some of the cities in those valleys.

Queen Toda summoned General Ignacio Valdez. Valdez was highly intelligent, well-educated, a decorated soldier, and had the additional reputation of being a very capable diplomat. He was also the son of her youngest sister. She sent him to Cordoba as an ambassador, bringing a proposal to form an alliance.

The general travelled with a substantial entourage to Cordoba. He presented his credentials and the written proposal from Navarra. The grand vizier, after a suitable delay, arranged an audience for the ambassador with the caliph. Hasdai was asked to attend the audience, but he told the grand vizier he was inundated with obligations and asked that I attend in his place. Surprising me, the grand vizier agreed.

We were gathered in the throne room filled with spectators. General Valdez made his formal presentation to the caliph. It was mid-morning, the sun illuminating the platform where the caliph, resplendent in deep blue robes and turban sat unmoving, a serious expression on his face. I was extremely nervous, but, I hope, managed to hide it.

"Your Excellency, I am here representing my country of Navarra, and especially our Queen Toda, your relative, to ask for the help described in the proposal you hold in your hand." The general was in an immaculately tailored dress uniform, resplendent with a myriad of medals. His spoken Arabic was much more eloquent than I had anticipated, I had assumed I was present as an interpreter.

The caliph seemed interested. "Yes, thank you, General Valdez. I presume from all those medals that during some occasion, possibly more than one, we have been on opposite sides of a battlefield."

"That may well be, Your Excellency, but perhaps we should ignore the possibility and focus our attention on the matter at hand."

"As you wish. My counselors and I have carefully examined your proposal. I understand Queen Toda's motivation to reclaim the throne of Leon for her grandson. I also understand that unless Sancho can regain his physical well-being, and demonstrate he can lead his country, the likelihood of his regaining power is slim. I have discussed the situation with my physician, Hasdai ibn Shaprut and his colleague Yusuf ben Ezia." He pointed with a fist at me. I was flabbergasted since the caliph had never spoken to me. I was amazed he knew who I was. "They have agreed to accompany you back to Navarra to conduct a thorough medical examination of Sancho to determine if the patient can lose the required weight. If so, the physicians will ascertain what will be necessary to accomplish the goal of getting him into good enough physical condition to accomplish the desired outcome of an invasion of Leon."

"I find that request not only completely acceptable but wise," replied the general. "And the request for your military aid to recapture Leon?"

The caliph stared at the general for a long time while he considered his answer.

"That is a separate issue dependent upon Sancho's ability to regain the physical strength necessary to reconquer and lead his country. Ibn Shaprut is also one of my most trusted diplomats. I will give him the authority to negotiate all aspects of an agreement between our two countries at the appropriate time."

"That seems agreeable to me, Your Majesty. I welcome both Effendi ibn Shaprut and Effendi ben Ezia to accompany me back to Navarra."

The general was left to cool his heels for over a week while preparations were finalized for Hasdai's state visit. The distance from Cordoba to Pamplona is not more than one hundred and fifty parasangs, about eight to ten days of travel, depending upon how fast Hasdai wanted to get there. Officials were sent ahead to arrange for suitable housing at inns, or where none were available, suitable campsites were identified and marked.

We finally departed Cordoba, with the retinue of General Valdez swelled by a unit of the caliph's bodyguard, Judah, me, Hasdai, a half-dozen servants, and three wagons of tents, food, and supplies. We rode at a leisurely pace, with stops mid-morning, noon, and mid-afternoon for rest and refreshment. We never spent more than a total of six hours in our saddles. It took us twelve days to reach Pamplona. General Valdez managed to hide his frustration and displeasure extremely well. Hasdai was cruelly amused.

The day after we arrived in Pamplona, we had an audience with the king, his mother, and Sancho I. Following the required formalities, Hasdai and I, accompanied by Sancho and two servants who supported his weight by holding him up by the armpits, conducted a complete examination of the morbidly obese former monarch in a private room. I had never encountered a person in that condition before. We took our time, conferring in whispers about our various measurements and observations of each organ system. We were both surprised the man was still alive, considering the amount of sugar I tasted after dipping a finger in his urine. the function of his heart, liver, lungs, liver, and kidneys were significantly affected.

The following morning, we met with the three monarchs again.

"My colleague and I agree that it will not be possible to treat King Sancho here in Pamplona. We cannot spend the necessary time here, and we also require special medications and absolute control over his diet and daily exercise. That will only be possible in Cordoba," explained Hasdai.

"Very well," answered the queen. She fixed Sancho with a cold stare. "I assume you want your kingdom back and will do everything required of you by the physicians."

"Yes, Grandmother. I will do everything they require of me."

"Will your caliph be helping us with his army?" asked the queen.

"Ah, yes," replied Hasdai, "the caliph assured me he was willing to do so, in principle, but many details remain to be negotiated. In any case, the first order of business will have to be restoring King Sancho's physical well-being. He must be physically capable of accompanying our combined forces into Leon."

The queen frowned. "That seems reasonable, I suppose."

Hasdai took the initiative. "You must also understand the personality and nature of our caliph and the constraints under which he operates. He is a man of considerable pride. Once King Sancho is physically able to regain his throne, my suggestion is for you and your son to travel to Cordoba for an in-person audience with the caliph. It will be necessary to follow the protocol of his court, that is to approach him humbly and beg for his help. Without that, he will lose face with his subjects by helping you."

All three noble faces showed expressions alternating between disappointment and anger. This was, obviously, not welcome news.

Hasdai's face betrayed nothing as he pressed on. "The caliph also informed me that there are a number of your frontier fortresses that have proven problematic for him over the many years of conflict between our two countries. The list is rather long I'm afraid. The caliph suggests that they be conceded to Cordoba as a sign of good faith for our future collaboration."

The three were silent for a long time. The queen alternately grasped and loosened her hands. Sancho was unable to sit still. The king fidgeted with a button on his coat. Not one of the three looked at Hasdai directly but glanced, furtively at me to see if I would give anything away. Hasdai sat quietly, his arms folded, quite comfortable with the silence.

Finally, the king of Navarra spoke. "I assume some of these fortresses are well inside our borders and those of Leon.?"

"Indeed," answered Hasdai.

"I guessed so." Now the king was clearly upset. "Leave us the list of the fortresses your caliph has in mind. We will consider each and give you a decision tomorrow."

"That's agreeable."

Hasdai turned and spoke directly to Sancho. "Meanwhile, my colleague, Yusuf ben Ezia, has written out a diet for you to follow for the next three days. It involves drinking a great deal of water and eating only the vegetables and amounts listed. You will eat only three meals a day, nothing between meals, other than the prescribed amounts of water. This is extremely important since we need to make certain your kidneys are flushed as you burn up excess fat for energy. It will also demonstrate the extent of your commitment, Your Highness. We need that information to be able to estimate the amount of time necessary to return you to top physical condition."

Fat Sancho looked very distraught, depressed. He slumped in his chair.

"Well?' said the queen, "Will you do as you are told?"

He nodded dejectedly, said nothing.

Back in Cordoba Hasdai put me in charge of formulating a nutritious diet for Sancho and making certain he took the various medications we decided to use. Judah was put in charge of his exercise regimen. The deposed king was dedicated and focused on what he had to do to regain his kingdom. The first week after we returned, Hasdai gave me a list of medications to prepare and took me into his medicinal plant garden.

He showed me a *Gymnema sylvestre* plant, a climbing vine with soft hairs on the upper surface of its elongated-oval-shaped leaves. "A tea made from the leaves of this plant will curb his appetite, especially for anything sweet. Whenever he complains about being hungry, and I'm certain he will, give him unsweetened green tea, that will curb the hunger pangs somewhat."

He pointed to a small tree. "This is *Commiphora wightii*. We slit the bark, like this, and collect the sap in a cup tied to the bottom of the slit." He tied a cup in place. "The gummy resin is supposed to cause weight loss and can be added to soups or stews, once your patient has progressed to that level."

He pointed to another plant with bunches of bright green obovate to oblong leaves. "Do you recognize this?"

"I am embarrassed to admit that I do not."

Hasdai frowned. "Well, you should be embarrassed, Yusuf. During the evening meals of Rosh-Hashana we eat the ground up seeds from that plant mixed with water, turmeric, and lemon juice as a relish. Rabbi Yitzchak called the relish *milbeh*. It is described in the Talmud as *rubia*. The sprouted seeds and leaves are often used in salads. A salad with these could make a filling meal for our patient and will not convert to fat."

My face flushed, upset I hadn't remembered what was in the *milbeh*, but I now recalled what I knew about *Commiphora wightii*. I did my best to keep my voice calm and strong.

"I remember now. The plant is reported to be useful in treating kidney problems, body aches, improve digestion, cleanse the intestines, and supposedly will cure skin diseases, asthma, bronchitis, sore throat and lower a fever. It may also aid in building muscle mass. Are you convinced it will do all that?"

"What do you think?" he said.

"I find it hard to believe it is able to be of use in all those various illnesses. I do recognize that," I pointed at another plant. "It's the same family as the daisy but is *Inula racemosa*. The roots are ground up, boiled and the liquid is used as a tonic."

"Good, but it will also decrease appetite. You should also give him doses of Therica. You remember that the formula contains extracts of *Glucomannan, Griffonia simplicifolia* and *Caralluma adscendens*. All of those extracts act as tonics and aid in weight loss. In any case I want you to take charge of getting him in shape. I have many other obligations. Will you assume that responsibility along with your other commitments?".

"Of course, I will. But he will be taking so many medications and fluids, what foods will supply the energy he will need to follow Judah's exercise regimen?" I asked.

"He can eat citrus fruits, clear broths and limited amounts of broiled meat. His ample body fat will provide plenty of energy. Don't forget to force him to drink copious amounts of water though. If we don't keep his kidneys flushed, he will produce excess ammonia. Smell his breath daily for the smell of ammonia. If it is present, he must drink even more water."

We left the intoxicating odors of Hasdai's medicinal garden and entered his house through the kitchen door. We were overwhelmed by the aromas from the meal being prepared for us that evening. We would be enjoying an abundance of rich flavorful dishes while poor Sancho would have to be content sipping a clear broth and masticating a small, broiled, venison steak.

Judah was very limited in what he could require of our patient. For the first two weeks he had to aid him to walk. The first day he managed only ten steps and was winded. By the end of the first week, he was up to fifty steps, still with Judah partially supporting him. He progressed to a hundred steps with Judah's assistance, then fifty without Judah's help. The third week Judah had him lifting small sacks of rocks and every other day the weight he lifted, and the distance he walked, was slightly increased. At the end of the month Judah had him jogging, rolls of fat oscillating in every direction. He jogged until he was gasping for breath. Judah allowed him to walk and when he was breathing normally, they resumed jogging.

The regimen of strict diet, medications, tonics, and exercise produced the desired effect. After three months Sancho lost at least a third of his body mass. Muscle was gradually replacing fat. Judah then started him, along with the ever-increasing distance and speed of running, on calisthenics and sparing with sword and lance.

One early evening Hasdai and I stood, each of us with our arms crossed over our chests, watching Sancho spar with Judah in the front courtyard.

"I have convinced Sancho that he should walk to Pamplona when he returns. It will demonstrate that he is fit and capable to rule. He has agreed. He has made remarkable progress, don't you think?" I asked.

"Yes, Yusuf, he has. You and Judah have accomplished a great deal with him. I will report to the caliph. I think we are nearing the time for Queen Toda and her son to swallow their pride and beg for our caliph's help. It is necessary that our caliph appears magnanimous as well as shrewd. I have been corresponding with the king of Navarra. He has signed a treaty to cede ten frontier fortresses to Cordoba and join with us to invade both Leon and Castile. We will gain lands in Navarra, Leon, and Castile, providing the invasion is successful. Our generals and their soldiers will be rewarded with new estates. I am happy that you convinced Sancho that he march, on foot, all the way from Cordoba to Pamplona. It will prove his determination as well as his fitness to be king once more."

Sancho marched all the way back to claim his kingdom, with the aid of the caliph's army. The caliphate gained territory and income from its new holdings.

CHAPTER SEVEN
· ·

With the passage of only six months Hasdai's official duties acting for the benefit of the caliphate took up more and more of his time. However, when I had a medical issue and needed his advice, he always found time to consult with me.

"I have a problem patient Hasdai. Over the past few weeks, he has lost considerable weight, and grows weaker daily. His heart and lungs sound normal, his pulse is relatively strong, but his heart rate is increased. There is no sign of sugar in his urine, and his urine is clear. His mucous membranes and sclera appear normal. He shows no sign of jaundice. I am unable to palpate any enlargement of the liver although his abdomen seems sensitive to my prodding. There is no discernable blood in his feces. I am at a loss for what to do next."

He listened carefully to my description of the symptoms of my patient, the results of my physical examination, and of the various tests I had conducted.

"It sounds as though you have tried everything I would have. It could be a tumor of the pancreas, although I would think he would have more digestive problems. Perhaps a tumor of the stomach or intestines that hasn't yet started to bleed. I can't think of anything more you can do, except watch him carefully and look for signs of bleeding. If it is a tumor, it might also spread to the lungs or liver, and you should be able to discover that. You know that sometimes there is just nothing we can do."

"I have something unrelated to ask of you, Yusuf," he said.

"Of course, you need only ask."

"You might want to know what it is before agreeing," he said, with a smile.

"I cannot imagine anything you might ask me to do, that was within my power to accomplish, that I would not agree to."

"That's nice to know. Here, I want you to read this."

He handed me a letter written in Hebrew. I scanned through it once then again more slowly.

"The grammar and spelling are confusing, but I think the message is clear. Rabbi Moses ben Israel reports acts of outrage against members of his congregation in Palermo. It seems his congregation is experiencing acts of outrage against their properties as well as their persons. He asks for your help. What do you want me to do?"

"To be able to help I must know by whom and why these acts are being perpetrated. To accomplish this by correspondence might take so long the community will be obliterated."

"So, you want me to travel to Sicily and find out?'

"Yes, you and Judah. I have found a ship and captain who will take you there. The captain will sail from Malaga in seven or eight days, depending on winds and tides. If Judah is willing, I want the two of you to go to Sicily, find out everything you can, correct the situation if possible and then return. If you and Judah are unable to rectify the situation, return as quickly as possible and I will seek a remedy here.

"You know Judah will do anything you ask of him, as will I. I am very pleased that you have enough confidence in me to entrust me with this mission."

He smiled broadly, "Yusuf, you are my pride and joy. You were a willing and able student and you have not only always done what I asked of you, you are an accomplished and respected physician."

A week later we found our captain and his ship and introduced ourselves.

"How much time to arrive in Panormus?" I asked the captain.

"It is not far from Malaga to Panormus. If the winds are steady and favorable, we should arrive in forty-five to fifty hours." I looked at Judah. He shrugged. "There isn't any other way to get there."

The ship we took was large with comfortable lodgings for passengers as well as cargo. The weather was clear and the winds steady and favorable.

In less than two and a half days we left the ship in search of the Hebrew section of Panormus and the rabbi whose letter had brought us to the island.

We found the synagogue by asking a man who was removing his tallit for directions. He waved an arm at the building behind us. Embarrassed, we entered the building to find a short, wizened man, with a long white beard, shrouded in an old, frayed tallit. He was bent over the table holding a Torah. He and the table were standing on the bimah, a raised platform. He was completely absorbed in the Torah passage he was studying, his lips moving.

"Rabbi Israel?" I asked.

He looked up, surprised, his head swiveled, searching the room for who had called out. "Yes?"

"I am Yusuf ben Ezia, and this is Judah ben Shlomo. We were sent by Hasdai ibn Shaprut in response to the letter you sent him."

The old man's eyes opened wide, the white sclera forming a frame for his deep blue irises.

"So soon? I never really expected him to send someone. I just hoped for a letter of encouragement and perhaps some advice about what to do.

Please help me roll up the Torah and replace it in the ark. I was puzzling over the passage we read this morning."

Once the Torah was safely dressed and back in place, with the appropriate blessings rapidly muttered by the rabbi, he seated himself on one of the front benches, patted it and motioned for us to sit down next to him.

As I sat next to him our legs touched. He did not recoil so I stayed close, keeping, contact. Judah leaned against the nearby wall; his arms folded across his chest. The room was dark, the only light filtered in from two small windows high on the wall that Judah was leaning against, and the open door behind us. There were oil lamps on the walls and a chandelier holding candles hung over the bimah, but none were lit. The room smelled of old books and rarely bathed bodies. I turned my head and found the women's balcony over the entrance, with steep stairs leading up to it.

"We have come to see firsthand the problems you are experiencing," I explained. "How many Hebrews are in your community here?"

"We are now down to only sixty families."

"Are there more who are not observant, do not attend services?"

"Yes, of course, but only a handful, and they still must live within the borders of our section. Since we have become targets of discrimination and hate at least three families have returned to the synagogue seeking the comfort of community. Perhaps Adoni, our Lord, tests us to bring us together?"

"I am not the one to answer that, Rabbi. How long has there been a Hebrew community here on this island?"

"The most often told story is that we were brought to this island as slaves shortly after the destruction of the Second Temple in our year 3830 or 3831, the Roman year 70. For certain by the year 3900 there were well established Hebrew communities in Syracuse and here in Panormus.

Our numbers expanded significantly when the Arabs took over the island in 4708."

"Have you always been isolated, I mean forced to live, in a Hebrew ghetto?" Judah asked.

"Of course, but we are allowed to own land and buildings and most prefer to live in our own community with our extended families and friends. Under Arab rule we live relatively freely but do have to pay the *kharaj* and the *jizya*."

"Sorry Rabbi, what are the *kharaj* and the *jizya?*"

"They are special taxes which go directly to the Muslim leaders of Panormus to be used as they see fit."

"What has changed to result to cause the problems you are having? Who is persecuting the community?" I asked.

"The Hebrew community is administered by a dozen of our most respected citizens, called the *proti*. By law they can act against those slow in paying taxes. They even have the authority to impound property to force payment. The proti also authorizes weddings, divorces, ritual slaughter, and the election of synagogue officers with the approval of the rabbi. They act on our behalf with the government authorities. Ten years ago, the caliph of the island installed his brother as the mayor. Within a short time, this brother recruited a group of thugs to enforce his edicts. He raised taxes on all Hebrews and additional taxes on Hebrew merchants. Non-Hebrew merchants are exempt from those additional taxes. If the taxes are not paid immediately the thugs arrive to take merchandise in payment, usually more than the tax. If the merchant objects, he is beaten."

"Has not your proti complained to the mayor?" I asked.

"Of course! We complained in writing. A delegation was sent to make a plea in person. The mayor ignored them, so another delegation was sent to the caliph in Syracuse. Nothing has changed. Lately the thugs invade the community, attacking people on the street and threatening to burn down our synagogue."

"Nobody has fought back?" Asked Judah.

"No, the proti advise the people to endure. They fear that any resistance will lead to more severe reprisals and the situation will become even more difficult. Our hope was that ibn Shaprut could convince the caliph of Cordoba to put pressure on the caliph of Sicily and induce him to remove his brother from office, or at least to make him stop his thugs from persecuting us."

"We will, naturally, take your concerns to Effendi Hasdai, but our caliph is not usually anxious to interfere in the affairs of other Arab leaders, particularly if those being abused are not willing to try to protect themselves," I explained.

"I understand."

"Have any of the attacks involved the use of weapons?" asked Judah.

"A few times our people have been attacked with clubs, but usually it is just fists and intimidation," answered the rabbi." When a person falls to the ground they are often kicked and spat upon as well."

"Here is my suggestion," I said. I realized that passiveness in the face of persecution hadn't solved the problem and more than likely never would. "If you can arrange a meeting of your proti, Judah and I will try to convince them to allow us to recruit a number of healthy young men. Judah will train them in the arts of self-defense. Unless the community is willing to resist being bullied, nothing will change. Your lives will become increasingly more difficult,"

I glanced at Judah, and he nodded his agreement.

The rabbi was silent for several minutes. "I understand, but I am afraid resistance will only lead to more severe reprisal. Our sages teach passive resistance is best. I am afraid if we fight back people will die."

"So, that's your solution, to just endure? Why did you bother to write to Ibn Shaprut for help? This situation will not improve without some action taking place, in our opinion."

I looked again at Judah and again he nodded.

The rabbi's face showed puzzlement, then resignation, as he shook his head and pondered. I decided just to wait.

"I will ask the proti to meet with you, perhaps tomorrow evening? Perhaps they will agree with you. If they do, I will not oppose you."

"Tomorrow evening will be fine," I said. "Tomorrow, during the day we will present the credentials Effendi Hasdai gave us to the mayor. The credentials say we are envoys of the caliph of Cordoba and are here on a mission of goodwill to promote more trade between Panormus and Cordoba. The document we carry was written by Effendi Hasdai but signed and sealed by the grand vizier of Cordoba. We understand why you are hesitant, but it is apparent that here, as in many places in the world, Hebrews are considered inferior and weak. We, as a people, will continue to occupy that position if we don't stand up for ourselves and fight for dignity and acceptance. Some day we Hebrews might have our own nation, a haven for all Hebrews who can make their way to that place. But we cannot expect your situation here, now, to change unless you resist."

Three days later we had a politely formal meeting with the mayor of Panormus. We did not raise the issue of the treatment of the Hebrews directly, but I tried to address it in an oblique way.

"The Arab captain of the ship that brought us to Panormus claimed that dealing with the Hebrew merchants was easier and more profitable than with the non-Hebrew merchants. I wonder if that might be of interest relative to your relationship with the Hebrew community? As the documents we presented tell you, our mission here is to expedite and improve trade relations between the two caliphates and your city is the primary port of commerce.

The mayor did not respond to that piece of information but looked at Judah. "You haven't said anything, big man, what is your role in coming here?"

Judah, as was his custom, answered all questions briefly and directly. "I come as the companion and protector of Effendi Yusuf ibn Nasir."

I smiled inwardly. Neither of us felt the need to identify ourselves as Hebrews.

" What is it you want from me, Effendi ibn Nasir? I am not involved in trade," said the mayor.

"I understand you levee special taxes on only the Hebrew merchants. That means they must sell their goods at higher prices. This distorts the marketplace and has an adverse effect on trade. I am also told that Hebrew citizens have been attacked on the streets and even in their own section of town. That cannot create a healthy situation, especially for any Hebrew merchants who come from Cordoba for business."

The mayor got to his feet, a scowl on his face and took two steps towards the chair I was seated in. "The Hebrews are an inferior people. They must know and be kept in their place. I think we have exhausted all we have to talk about. I will take the proposal you brought under advisement."

During our meeting with the proti that evening I introduced Judah and told a little of his background as a soldier. Only one member of the proti evidenced interest in learning defensive skills. He was strongly built, maybe a year or two older than me. The other members of the proti were elderly, not disposed to physical activity, but two of them said they would help us recruit younger men. The others agreed not to interfere and to observe the outcome of our efforts with great interest, although they were clearly skeptical of the wisdom of resistance.

The following morning five eager young men, joined by our friend from the proti, gathered in front of the synagogue.

"We need a remote place to train," I explained to the group. "Do any of you have an idea for a place?"

One of the young men raised his hand. "My sister married an Arab farmer. Their farm is about a parasang from here. I'm pretty certain he won't mind."

"Good," said Judah. "You will need more than the self-defense skills we will teach. You will have to be in good physical shape to be able to use those skills effectively. What is your name?"

"Joshua ben Israel."

"Thank you, Joshua. We will all follow you as you jog to your brother-in-law's farm."

Judah kept up a continuous commentary as we jogged through the streets and out into the countryside. "You must increase the speed and length of your running a little each day," he explained. "We will also do some other exercises I will teach you, those you can do at home, but you must do them to gain strength. Now let's run as fast as you can for the next forty strides."

After running the short distance, I was struggling for air, as were all our recruits.

"Good, now we will continue to jog." Judah was breathing normally.

Everyone in our group was now breathing hard, except, of course, Judah, and I was happy to notice, me. We arrived at the farm and Joshua, with hands on his hips, taking deep ragged breaths. I looked around and observed tidy, well-kept fields, orchards, and buildings. As we arrived a young man left his work in an orchard and came to find out what we were about. When he recognized Joshua, they greeted each other and embraced. Joshua briefly explained what we were doing then introduced his brother-in-law, Abu Ahmadi.

I introduced myself and Judah and explained in more detail what we planned and why we needed a place to train.

"I am happy to learn that my brother-in-law and his friends are willing to defend themselves. The Hebrews must learn to do so if they ever want others to stop persecuting them," said Abu Ahmadi.

"That is exactly our message," I replied.

The first skill Judah taught was how to block, then counter, a punch aimed at the head. He worked individually with each of our recruits until they mastered the footwork and technique. The brother-in-law and I were interested observers.

"May I join your class?" Abu Ahmadi asked Judah.

"Of course," he replied. "Do you plan to help your wife's family?"

"If necessary," he said. "I think the time is long overdue for them to demand some respect."

The following day the group rehearsed all the moves from the previous day and Judah added new moves. The training continued for a week and each day another one or two men joined the class. Judah had those who had been with us teach the new men while he carefully watched, making corrections if necessary. I decided that I needed to join the class as well. I was determined to learn these skills and found that teaching the moves to those having trouble grasping them and to newcomers improved my own skill level.

As we began the training on the tenth morning, a group of rough-looking men approached. Leading them was the mayor, who was holding a club in his right hand. Judah and I positioned ourselves in front of our group of students. They all moved forward, close to our backs. Not for protection, but to take part in any action.

The mayor slapped the palm of his left hand with his club. "You told me you were here to promote trade, but it seems you are really here to promote insurrection. That I cannot and will not tolerate. These Hebrews," he said it as if the word made a sour taste in his mouth, "must continue their rightful place in our society. They are inferior, subservient to us, incapable of defending themselves. They are, by nature, a weak and pathetic people, except for their innate gift of knowing how to turn a profit."

The mayor strode towards us, stopping three feet away from Judah. He continued tapping his open left hand with the club.

"I think you will find this group of Hebrews not so meek as you imagine," said Judah, through clenched teeth.

"Is that so?" asked the mayor. "Do you think you can keep us from teaching all of you a lesson in humility?"

Judah said nothing.

"Well then," shouted the mayor and rushed at Judah, the club raised to strike.

I smiled as Judah easily side-stepped, grabbed the arm holding the club, and used the momentum of the man to twist his arm, dislocating his shoulder. I had anticipated seeing that well practiced move again. The club dropped to the ground and the mayor screamed in pain, holding his shoulder. His men rushed forward. One of them picked up the club and came at me while three others attacked Judah. Our recruits pushed into the melee, anxious to apply their newly acquired skills. I was worried that the few basic skills I had managed to learn would be enough. I remembered Judah's instruction to step forward into an attacker. I managed to twist to my right, avoiding the club aimed at my head. I aimed at the man's exposed left side hoping to contact his kidney with the punch I delivered with all my strength. The man grunted from the pain and dropped the club. I took three short, quick steps to intercept another man who rushed at Judah from behind. I stopped him with a well-aimed punch to the left side of his face, hitting him flush on the ear. A trickle of blood ran down the side of his face from the ear, he wobbled, then sat down hard. Judah had dispatched two of his attackers with well-placed blows to the face, the third man was circling him cautiously.

"Stay down," I ordered the man sitting at my feet. "If you get up, I will injure you more seriously."

When I looked over towards Judah, I saw he had the third man on the ground. Two of our newest recruits were on the ground, but the others were all still standing and ready to fight.

"I think it is time for you to take your leader for medical attention," said Judah. "You recruits should all step away now. I believe a lesson has been taught."

The mob got to their feet and departed the field of battle, two of them supporting the mayor. Our lads raised their arms in exultation shouting their excitement and joy.

"This is not over," said Judah, raising his voice to be heard. "They have been humiliated and will, most certainly return, armed and seeking vengeance. Yusuf, can we have a quick consultation?"

"Of course."

We stood close. "I think we should purchase weapons for them and teach them how to use them as soon as possible. Do you agree?"

"Yes."

He turned to address the group. "We will purchase weapons for you and teach you to use them, hopefully before the need arises. I doubt we will have enough time to teach you all the skills you will need, but any training might help. Return here an hour after the midday meal. We will get as many weapons as possible and begin your training with them."

Judah and I split up to find and purchase whatever weapons were available, taking with us those recruits who knew where to find weapons merchants. When we returned that afternoon, we found not all our recruits were willing to continue. Three of them, including the two who had been knocked to the ground, had decided risking life and limb was not something they were prepared to do and departed before our return.

Judah demonstrated basic defensive moves using the sword and shield. He then took turns sparing with each of us, correcting our mistakes until he was satisfied we had learned, if not mastered, the rudimentary techniques.

"Tomorrow at dawn we will meet here again to continue," instructed Judah. "I think we have very little time."

I was worried as Judah, and I sat eating dinner that evening at our inn. Judah, as usual was silent, stoic.

"I am afraid we might have made a mistake," I said. "They are eager enough, but I don't think you can teach them enough to protect themselves."

Judah chewed the food in his mouth and swallowed. "I cannot turn them into trained warriors. If the same mob returns, they may be able to hold against them. I doubt any of that mob have trained with weapons enough to be effective, but the mayor probably has a trained garrison of soldiers to maintain order in the city. If he describes our skirmish as a rebellion and brings trained soldiers, we are in trouble."

I remained silent, thinking hard, for some time then responded. "You are right. We can't take on trained soldiers with these eager recruits. I need to go to Syracuse to speak to the caliph about his brother, Maybe he will intervene. I hope someone knows where I can purchase a good horse."

"How about Abu Ahmadi?" said Judah.

"That's an idea. Do you think it's too late to go to him now?

"He seems willing to help, let's go wake him up."

We ran as fast as I could doing my best to keep up with Judah. Abu Ahmadi was just finishing his dinner when we arrived and explained what we needed.

"I can help with that. My uncle breeds the best horses on the island and his place is not far."

"Do you think he will receive us this evening?" I asked.

"I don't know why he would not. It is his custom to memorize poetry each evening for a couple of hours. He will still be up."

Abu Ahmadi lit a lantern and we walked quickly to his uncle's farm. We explained what we needed and why.

"I understand," replied the uncle. "If you return here first thing in the morning, I will have a strong horse saddled and ready for you. The road to Syracuse is well marked, you should not have any problems, but I would not recommend you try it in the dark."

"I must insist on paying you the full value of the horse and tack," I said. "If there are any repercussions you can rightfully say my purchase was just a business deal."

He frowned but nodded his understanding. "I have always found the Hebrews a fair and moral people. I was not surprised when Abu Ahmadi found his wife. She is a beautiful and intelligent girl, from a pious and honest family that I have known for many years. I was happy to welcome her and her family into our family."

CHAPTER EIGHT

The mare provided by Abu Ahmadi's uncle, was more than expected. He had already saddled the mare and she was munching from a bucket of oats. The animal was an outstanding example of Arabian breeding, bay with long flowing mane and tail, and a smallish head with a very slight dish. Her wide nostrils constantly sought information. Her intelligent, aware eyes missed nothing. I discovered her gait was smooth and effortless, an easy rocking motion that enabled me to become as one with her. The uncle told me she could maintain that pace for hours. The road was as described, well-marked and well-maintained. I kept the mare at a lope until she showed signs of tiring, then walked her until she regained normal breathing. She needed no more than a touch of my heels to break back into the easy lope.

I arrived in Syracuse well before sunset and asked directions. I went directly to the alcazar where I showed my credentials. The officer of the guard took my credentials and guided me to the grand vizier's office.

The guard knocked on a solid oak door with intricate carvings.

"Come," answered a voice from within.

The guard opened the door, went inside, and handed the man behind the desk my credentials. He read them quickly and looked up.

"*As-salamu alaykum*, I am Aser ibn Adheri, grand vizier to the caliph. You are the emissary of Abd Ar-Rhaman III?"

"Yes, I am Yusuf ben Ezia."

He extended the hand holding my credentials. "How can I be of assistance?"

"I would greatly appreciate being allowed to inform your caliph of the situation in Panormus, where the Hebrew community is being harassed and persecuted by a group of thugs supported by the city's government. As you may know, the caliph of all of Andalusia is very tolerant of the Hebrews. He responds immediately, and with all necessary force, against individuals or groups causing problems for the Hebrews in his caliphate. I wish to discuss with your caliph the persecution I have witnessed first-hand. I seek a solution to what I, and I am certain my caliph, consider unacceptable behavior."

"You are welcome to make yourself comfortable and wait here in my office. I will visit our caliph and find out when and if he will grant you an audience."

I wondered how long this would take and began to worry that the caliph would not agree to see me. The Grand Vizier reached the doorway then turned.

"You are aware that the mayor of Panormus is the caliph's half-brother?"

"I was informed he was a brother. I know very little else."

"Have you discussed your concerns with him?"

"In a manner of speaking, yes. My associate and I visited him in his office and explained that the caliph of Cordoba wanted to improve trade relations with Sicily, particularly via the port of Panormus. A few days later he and a group of thugs confronted my associate and myself. A physical altercation resulted."

"Indeed? Right then, please make yourself comfortable. I will have coffee and something for you to eat brought."

"That would be most welcome. I have been in the saddle since early morning."

A short time later a servant brought coffee and a platter of meats, cheeses, and bread.

"We have fruit juice if you like," he said.

"No, thank you, but some water would be most welcome."

I sipped at the coffee. It was very strong, very sweet, with no hint of bitterness. The servant returned with a jug of water and a goblet.

"Thank you," I said.

He nodded and backed out of the office.

I tasted a small bit of each of the cheeses. They were quite good, each one different in taste and smell from the others. I avoided the meats. I try to avoid eating milk and meat products at the same sitting.

Aser ibn Adheri returned and took his seat behind the desk, opposite me.

"The caliph is quite occupied," he said, "but he has agreed to meet with you tomorrow morning."

"Thank you. Perhaps you can recommend an inn close by, one that can also provide for my mare?"

"Yes, of course. I will instruct one of the guards to take your horse to the army stables and to make certain she is well cared for."

He called out and a servant stuck his head through the doorway.

"Go immediately to the Prophet's Inn and arrange for a room for Effendi ben Ezia. Tell the innkeeper I am responsible for the bill. Also tell the captain of the guard to have one of his soldiers take the Effendi's horse to the army stables and make certain it is taken care of properly."

The servant disappeared.

"Do you need instruction about our protocol when appearing before our caliph?"

"I have stood before Caliph Abd Ar-Rhaman several times. Is there something special about the protocol for your caliph?"

"Probably not, the most important thing is to never turn your back to him."

"That's always good advice." I smiled.

"Did you bring a suitable robe with you? The one you are wearing speaks of your hasty journey."

"Yes, I have a more suitable robe with me."

"Good."

The servant again appeared in the doorway. "All is arranged, Your Excellency."

"Good, please show the effendi to the inn."

He again looked at me. "I will send someone to you in the morning, allowing time for you to clean up, breakfast, and return here for your audience with the caliph."

"Thank you, Grand Vizier, you are a most thoughtful host. I look forward to seeing you again in the morning. However, I would like to visit my mare before going to the inn. I will rest easier seeing that she is being well cared for."

"Of course, I understand. Just tell the man I send with you."

"Thank you again, *As-salamu alaykum.*"

"*Alaykum salamu.*"

My mare was in a stall by herself, munching on some grain. A soldier stood outside the stall gazing at her, his admiration evident. I entered the stall, picked up her left foreleg, and saw the hoof had been cleaned.

"How much grain did you give her?" I asked. "I don't want her to founder."

"Only two handfuls, just before you arrived. I didn't know how much she was accustomed to. She is a beautiful animal, Effendi, much superior to any of the horses here, and extremely well mannered."

"Yes, thank you. I appreciate the care you have given her."

"It is an honor to be allowed to do so Effendi. I will give her some hay if that is acceptable. We have some very sweet grass hay."

"Yes, excellent, and make certain she has plenty of fresh water. I see the bucket is full. Did she drink a great deal when she arrived?"

"Yes, she drank an entire bucket and half of a second. I will make certain she has all the water she wants."

"Thank you again."

I followed my guide less than a quarter of a parasang to a large building not far from the entrance gate of the alcazar. A sign hung over the door proclaiming it as the Prophet's Inn.

As I walked through the doorway a short, stout, redhaired, blue-eyed man hurried from the doorway of what I could see was his office. "You are the emissary from Cordoba. Please follow me." He dismissed my guide with a backhanded wave. "I have reserved my best room for you. If you require anything, anything at all, please make it known to me. If you are hungry, I will have a meal prepared, is there anything special by way of a meal that you might want?"

"No, thank you. I just need to rest."

"Yes, of course. Is there a time you wish to be awakened?"

"The grand vizier told me he would send someone to fetch me, giving enough time for breakfast before my audience with the caliph. I would like some warm water, soap and towels so I can clean up."

"Yes, these things have been placed in your room. If you need more water, or anything else, just call out, I will have a servant standing close enough to your door to respond."

"You are most thoughtful."

I interpreted his smile to indicate he rarely received compliments but was impressed that I represented the caliph of Cordoba and had an audience with his caliph.

The morning brought clear skies, bright sunshine, and a hopeful state of mind. I was seated at a table in the dining room, eating a toasted roll smeared with soft cheese, when my guide of the previous evening appeared at my left shoulder. I glanced up at him. "Do I have time to finish my breakfast?"

"Yes, Effendi, I will wait at the front door until you are ready."

I finished my breakfast, and we made our way to the Grand Vizier's office where he greeted me. "*As-salamu alaykum,* Yusuf ben Ezia, I trust you had a restful night."

"*Alaykum salamu*, Grand Vizier ibn Adheri. Yes, thank you. I was quite comfortable and slept soundly."

"Good. The caliph agreed to see you. However, he had me send emissaries to Panormus to gather information about the situation there. He asks that you be our guest here in Syracuse for the next four or five days until they return. Then he will see you."

I smothered a sigh. "I understand, but I hope he sends word to them to not escalate the situation during the interim."

"That was included in my instructions to the men I sent."

"Thank you, Grand Vizier. I will happily wait for my audience as long as necessary."

Four agonizing days later I was finally summoned to the grand vizier's office. We exchanged salutations, then he got up from his desk and indicated I should follow him.

We entered a well-decorated, but smallish chamber. Several men stood in small groups conversing in hushed tones. At the far end of the room a man sat cross legged on a resplendently decorated pillow resting on a slightly raised platform. He wore a sky-blue robe with a matching turban. His reddish-brown beard was cleverly shaped to cover what I supposed was a rather weak chin. He sat quietly but his eyes darted around the room missing nothing.

He is appeared to be only pretending to listen to the man on one knee in front of him. The caliph held up his hand. The man pleading his case stopped talking, stood, moved to the side of the room, and leaned against the wall. He seemed to be relishing its support. The grand vizier motioned for me to follow as he walked up to the caliph and bowed. I followed and mimicked the grand vizier's bow.

"This is Yusuf ben Ezia, envoy of Abd-Ar Rhaman III. I spoke to you about him previously."

"Yes, thank you, Adheri. *As-salamu alaykum*, Effendi ben Ezia. I am told you came here on a very fine Arabian mare after riding hard all day to get here from Panormus. What has caused this pressing need to come before me?"

"*Alaykum salamu*, Your Excellency. I come on an errand of mercy hoping to put an end to violence against some of your subjects in Panormus."

"Is that so? I have received reports that you and your companion from Cordoba have been training a group of Hebrews to attack my brother. The brother I appointed mayor of Panormus."

"Not exactly true, Your Excellency. The Hebrew community of Panormus is being persecuted by unfair taxes and violent attacks on the people and their property. Word of this reached my mentor, Hasdai ibn Shaprut, who, as you may be aware, has the ear of Abd-Ar Rhaman. Effendi Shaprut sent me and my companion to Panormus to investigate. We found the rumors to be true. We felt the problems of the Hebrew community were exacerbated by their meek acceptance of the abuse, so we began to train a small cadre of young men in the arts of self-defense. There was an altercation, instigated by the mayor. He and his followers experienced a lesson in humility."

I took a deep breath, worried that I had said too much.

The caliph chuckled. "That story is quite different than the report I have of the altercation. My brother claims that your ex-soldier companion, along with you and a large group of Hebrews, initiated an attack on him, and a small group of his men, and that he suffered a dislocated shoulder as a result."

"It is true that my companion, an experienced fighter, dislocated the mayor's shoulder but only after the mayor rushed at him with a raised club. It was clear he meant to bash my companion's head. I stand by the veracity of my account, Your Excellency. The small Hebrew community has suffered from attacks in the streets of Panormus, including within their designated area of the city. Their synagogue has been threatened with destruction and some of their businesses have been ransacked. Their merchants struggle to pay the *kharja* and *jizya* that the non-Hebrew merchants are not required to pay."

The caliph answered. "I understand Abd-Ar Rhaman, III does not impose such taxes and protects his Hebrews against persecution. He says that his interpretation of the Quran orders this. Are you saying I should follow his example? Are you a scholar, familiar with the Quran?"

"No, Your Excellency, but my mentor ibn Shaprut is, and he supplied me with the relevant passages." I took out the sheaf of folded papers Hasdai had provided for me should the need arise.

"Never mind," said the caliph. "I know the passages of which you speak. This is what I will do. I will bring my brother here and explain to him the importance of not irritating the caliph of Cordoba. I do not know it for certain, but I imagine if the treatment of the Hebrews in Panormus does not improve, Effendi Shaprut will be able to convince Abd-Ar Rhaman to take some action that will not benefit me or my caliphate."

"That may be, Your Excellency, but please do not imagine that anything I say is threatening. I am only here to ask for your help to correct an injustice."

He grinned, ruefully. "Yes, yes, of course. I understand your companion is not only a fierce warrior, but he is also a very effective teacher who is, even as we speak, training the Hebrews in the use of weapons."

"Yes, Your Excellency."

He grinned again. "I do not want the caliph of Cordoba to think badly of me. I will protect your Hebrews."

"Thank you, Your Excellency, that is a great relief for me. I am certain the Hebrew communities in your caliphate will celebrate your decision. With your permission, I will return to my companion, and we will find our way back to Cordoba."

He said, "Go with Allah."

"And may Allah give you a long and healthy life, Your Excellency." I backed out of the chamber with a serious face, smiling inwardly.

The mare and I returned to Panormus at a leisurely pace, finding a nice inn along the way where we stayed overnight. The next day I rode directly to Abu Ahmadi's farm, where I found the recruits sparing with each other using swords and shields, under the watchful eye of Judah.

"Welcome back," said Judah. "How did it go?"

I dismounted and tied the mare to a nearby tree. "It went well," I said. "The caliph seems anxious to avoid any kind of confrontation with Hasdai and thereby our caliph."

"So, you were able to convince him that Hasdai would involve our caliph if the situation here doesn't improve?"

"I believe so, yes."

Abu Ahmadi walked over to join us. "*As-salamu alaykum*, Yusuf."

"*Alaykum salaamu*, Abu."

"Your trip was successful?"

"Yes, but I do have a favor to ask of you."

"What is it?"

"I have no more need for the amazing mare I purchased from your uncle. May I give her to you as a gift?"

"That is very generous, but why? You could easily sell her and recover what you paid, maybe even make a profit. Or I could sell her for you and donate the proceeds to the synagogue."

"I will have no further need for her and want to insure she will be well cared for. I know you will take good care of her and find use for her. By accepting her, you remove any need for me to worry about her."

"If you insist," replied Ahmadi.

By this time all the recruits had gathered around us, anxious to hear about my experience with the caliph. I told them and the relief on their faces was plain to see.

Judah cleared his throat and the recruits turned to listen to him. "Despite this good news I hope you will continue to practice the skills you have acquired. We hope you will never need to use them, but you will find great peace of mind knowing you are able to defend yourselves if the need arises."

"I agree with Judah," I added. "But you do need to practice with some regularity and maintain the physical conditioning you have achieved. If you do this, you will be able to protect yourselves and your loved ones if necessary."

The next morning Judah and I went to the docks and found a ship leaving the following day and bound for Malaga. The captain agreed to take us. I was pleased to discover I had the ability to address and resolve issues outside of those concerned with the practice of medicine. I felt more self-assured and confident. I told myself to not to forget to thank Hasdai for giving me the opportunity.

CHAPTER NINE

Four years after our adventures in Sicily I woke early and went downstairs to my office to catch up on patient notes from the previous day. Hasdai was sitting in my chair. His hands cradled his head, his elbows rested on the top of the desk. He looked up.

"You're up early," he said.

"Not as early as you," I replied.

He stood came around the desk to me and we embraced, pounding lightly on each other's backs.

"What can I do for you?" I asked. "You seem troubled."

"I am getting old, Yusuf. I am discovering I don't have the ability to find solutions that I once had. There are always new problems seeking solutions. I find that our caliph relies more and more on my unofficial advice, but I remain, officially, only the collector of duties."

"Yes, the last few years were eventful for the caliphate. Shall we sit? I will get someone to bring us breakfast and strong coffee."

I shouted for my servant who appeared almost immediately in the doorway.

"Something to break the overnight fast and strong, sweet coffee," I ordered. "How can I help lighten your burden, Hasdai?"

I sat in the chair reserved for my patients and pointed at my own chair with an open hand. Hasdai grimaced, then moved my chair around the desk so we could sit knee to knee.

"You no doubt remember Fat Sancho."

"Oh, yes, how could I ever forget Fat Sancho's long walk back into power?"

"You are aware he died a couple of years ago?"

"Yes, I heard that."

"Sancho had a son, named Ramiro, who was only five years old when Sancho died. Sancho's full sister, Elvira Ramiro, became regent, responsible for the young King Ramiro. During the early months of her regency there were increasingly frequent raids along their northern coasts by Vikings. Last year the Viking leader, Gunro, sailed from Norway with a small flotilla and established a colony on the coast of Galicia. Elvira enlisted the support of three different bishops, who led forces attempting to expel Gunro and his colony but none of their efforts succeeded. Now Elvira has found another champion, Count Sanchez, and she has asked our caliph for men, money, provisions, and arms to send the invaders back to Norway, or even better, to annihilate them."

"So how has this become your problem?"

"The caliph wants me to negotiate an agreement with the current ruler of Galicia that is the regent. An agreement that will make it worth our while to help them."

"You will go to Leon for this negotiation? Will you allow me to accompany you? I am concerned about your distress and perhaps your health. Have you been ill recently? My mentor was then only thirty-eight years old but appeared much older to my twenty-eight year old eyes.

"I seem to tire more easily. I had hoped that you and Judah would accompany me. At my quickly advancing age, I may require your professional expertise and Judah's strong arms."

"I am happy to do this, although I pray my skills will not be needed. I'm certain Judah will feel the same way. I enjoy travel, and the excitement that often comes with it, particularly when it has a defined purpose. What specifically does the caliph want you to accomplish?"

"Negotiate to obtain concessions that will secure our northern borders and reduce the need to quell incursions on our territory."

I smiled. "That's all?"

"My plan is for the three of us to go ahead to the capitol of Leon, with a small contingent of bodyguards. The caliph will send a regiment of our finest soldiers under the command of General Malik ibn Tarif al Rhaman, the fifth great-grandson of the conqueror of Andalusia. They will leave Cordoba sometime after us, making their way north leisurely. If the negotiations are successful General al Rhaman will agree to serve under the leadership of whomever the regent chooses to command Leon's forces, but with the provision that since our general is a highly decorated, gifted leader, and exceptional strategist, the leader of the Christians will listen to and follow his suggestions."

"And if you are unable to negotiate a satisfactory agreement?"

"Then we and our soldiers will return to Cordoba."

"Why is this important to you Hasdai? Why did you agree to do this?"

"If I don't continue to be useful to the caliph, I would not be able to protect our people. You, understand, don't you Yusuf, that the Hebrews of Cordoba are always at risk to a change in attitude by this caliph or the next? We are in even greater danger if the Christian nations to the north gain influence and territories of the caliphate. You know that a long succession of popes has preached hatred against us?

"Yes, I know, and I now understand your motivation. Rest assured that I share it and want to do my best to protect our people."

Two weeks later, it was then late spring of 948, the three of us, with our bodyguard of a half-dozen ferocious looking soldiers, left Cordoba.

As we left the city Hasdai swiveled in his saddle to speak to me.

"I spoke with General al Rhaman last evening. He will leave Cordoba in six days. His supply wagons will form a train he estimates will be at least two parasangs long. It will carry all the food and supplies, equipment, weapons, and armor, needed for our soldiers to campaign through the summer. He is also bringing along two dismantled counter-weight siege machines known as farangi, the machines that were known as trebuchet by the Romans."

During our journey to Leon, Hasdai tired after only three hours in the saddle. We would rest for an hour or so, cover a few more parasangs, then take a couple of hours midday to rest to eat and for him to recover enough to continue. After the midday respite, Hasdai was able to continue for another hour or so. During the midday break, Judah would ride ahead to find a suitably clean inn where Hasdai could rest for the night. Judah made certain his private room was thoroughly cleaned and fresh straw put in the mattress. He also told the innkeeper what we would require for dinner. When we arrived, I put one of Hasdai's clean blankets over the mattress and a light blanket over that. He rolled up his cloak for a pillow. We made certain he had warm water to wash himself and ate a good meal. Hasdai, ever mindful of his own comfort, had added two cases of good wine to our provisions.

After he retired, one of the soldiers stood guard outside his door and was relieved by another soldier every two hours. When I asked how they felt about this assignment, I was told it was the easiest they ever had.

Late in the afternoon of the eleventh day, we sighted the fortress of Leon in the distance. It took another hour for us to reach the gate. Judah announced us and the gate swung open almost immediately.

The fortified palace, what we would call an alcazar, was formidable. Towers at the corners guarded all the high stone walls providing unobstructed lines of fire. The main entrance was well guarded. The entry was about ten cubits long and four wide, tall stone walls surrounding it with many ports through which arrows and crossbow bolts could be fired. The construction and design were similar to that used in our alcazars. The gates could be quickly released to fall and close off the entry, trapping would-be invaders.

As we rode through this death trap, I glanced at Judah who was also studying the structure. Hasdai rode with his eyes focused straight ahead.

Judah twisted his face into an expression of grudging respect. "It would not be prudent to attack through here unless your forces were already in control inside."

We were greeted by a middle-aged man resplendent in bright red robes and skull cap.

"I am Cardinal Rossini," he said. "It is a great pleasure for us to welcome Hasdai ibn Shaprut and his companions as the emissaries of the caliph of Cordoba."

We dismounted. Servants appeared from the shadows to hold our horses.

"Allow me to introduce my associates," said Hasdai. "This is the physician Yusuf ben Ezia, my former apprentice now the leading physician of Cordoba, and this is Judah ben Shlomo, my trusted companion."

"All Jews then?"

"Is that a problem for you, Cardinal? If so, we will depart immediately."

"No, no, please don't. My king and the regent are most anxious to meet with you. I understand your caliph is very tolerant of Jews."

"Yes, he is. And I understand your church and your pope are most intolerant of Hebrews," Hasdai replied, with what I considered quite an evil smile.

"Ah, well, in some places that may be true, but we here are anxious to find common ground with Cordoba and rid ourselves of the Viking menace."

I glanced at Judah. He wasn't smiling, but I could see he was satisfied with Hasdai's words.

We were guided through a series of rooms and hallways, all ornately festooned with sculptures and paintings of people and animals, not something we would see in the homes and palaces of Cordoba. We followed the cardinal into a large room with tapestries covering all four walls. All of them depicted battle scenes with images of men and horses in the throes of agony and death. At the far end of the room a boy of about thirteen years sat dwarfed in a huge oak chair with intricate carvings. The throne was placed on a platform two steps above the tiled floor of the room. To the boy's left, sat a slightly past middle-aged woman with dark hair that hung loose to her waist. Her eyes were dark, unblinking, and intelligent. I assumed she was the regent. The location of the wrinkles on her face indicated she rarely smiled. Three men in formal uniforms displaying many medals of achievement, stood next to another priest, this one with a long, gray beard. His robes and skull cap were black.

The three of us bowed, not very deeply, our eyes focused on the boy.

"Your Highness," said Hasdai, addressing the regent, "please allow me to introduce the rest of this delegation from His Majesty the Caliph of Cordoba. This is the physician Yusuf ben Moses and my companion, Judah ben Shlomo."

"Welcome," said the regent, who then introduced the other men in the room, but not the boy. "I assume you are tired from your travels and would welcome the opportunity to refresh yourselves, eat and rest. We will make you as comfortable as we are able and perhaps, if you are agreeable, we will meet first thing in the morning and do our best to reach an agreement on matters of great importance that require joint action."

"I agree we should wait until everyone is rested. Tomorrow morning after rest and refreshment is a welcome idea for me," said Hasdai.

The second priest, who had been fidgeting the entire time since we entered the chamber, could contain himself no longer.

"He sends us three Jews. It is an insult."

"Shut your mouth, Bishop," snapped Elvira Ramiro, "These men are our honored guests. We need their friendship and help. Your bad manners and prejudice are not welcome. You can leave us now.".

The priest stalked out of the chamber, mumbling.

"If that personage is to participate in the negotiations, I think we will be returning to Cordoba very soon," said Hasdai.

"I apologize, sir. You will not be troubled by his presence; I can assure you of that. He will be told, in no uncertain terms, to stay away."

A servant showed us to two adjoining rooms. Hasdai had the first to himself, the second had two beds. The rooms were furnished very comfortably, decorated with tapestries, paintings, sculptures, and decorative vases. In our room hot water sent up a small cloud of steam from a large pitcher next to a basin on a long, sturdy table. There was a pile of towels and a bar of soap neatly arranged on the table. Four chairs stood against the wall behind the table. On the opposite end of the table from the water and towels resided a large platter of food.

Hasdai entered our room. "The servant told me there was food in your room."

"Yes." I pointed at the platter, containing a cooked meat of unknown origin, some fresh vegetables, boiled potatoes, and a pyramid of apples.

"What kind of meat do you think that is?" Hasdai asked.

"Probably pork," answered Judah.

Hasdai winked at us. "You may be correct."

We partook of the vegetables and fruit but left the meat.

The next morning, we were provided with more hot water, and another platter of food, with the same ingredients as the previous evening.

A different servant led us to the throne room. The rude clergyman was not in attendance.

Hasdai produced a sheaf of papers listing fourteen fortified towns along the border between our two states. "These are the fortified towns along our frontier from which incursions into our territory have been launched over the past several years. If we are to be friends and support each other, my caliph insists these places must all be under his control."

Elvira Ramiro's face betrayed nothing, but I assumed she had not anticipated so high a price.

"This, I assume, is open for negotiation?" she asked.

"We are open to reasonable counter offers," answered Hasdai.

"If you will excuse us, my officers and the cardinal will withdraw with me to discuss our response. Ramiro, my boy, will you agree to entertain our guests? There's a good lad."

The regent and her entourage left the room and for the first time since we were in the room with him, the boy king smiled.

"Is it true you are all Jews?" he asked.

"We prefer to be called Hebrews," answered Hasdai. "To be called a Jew is a slur. It suggests prejudice and an assumption that we are, in some way, inferior."

The boy king spoke almost perfect Latin, indicating a good education. "That is most interesting for me to learn. I have never spoken with a Hebrew before this. Do you really drink the blood of Christian infants at your Passover celebration?"

Judah snorted. Hasdai raised his hand, indicating Judah should control himself. "That is a terrible and unfair falsehood told by your priests. Many of them, the most intelligent and wise of them, know it is a lie, but the others are too ignorant to know the truth. Our people have been used as scapegoats since even before the time of the Romans. Do you know the meaning of the term scapegoat and its origin, Your Majesty?"

"Yes, in pagan times any evil was blamed on an animal that had been possessed by the devil, usually a goat. The goat was killed to make whatever evil, be it bad weather, disease, or anything else, go away."

"And do you think it was an effective strategy?" asked Hasdai.

"I don't understand how it could make any difference," answered the boy.

"Exactly," said Hasdai. "To blame the Hebrews for bad fortune is the same."

"But what about how the Hebrews convinced the Romans to kill Jesus?"

"Any group of people, Christians, Muslims, Pagans, Hebrews, will include individuals who do evil for a host of different reasons. But these are acts of individuals, even if they convince others to go along. Is it fair, or reasonable, to blame those who happen to be members of the same religion, generations later, for that evil? Prejudice is a mindset that enables a person or group of people to believe they are superior to the people they speak ill of."

The boy did not respond. He was obviously thinking about what Hasdai said. I hoped he was absorbing and considering the wisdom imparted. Hasdai watched silently as the boy cogitated. Then he spoke again. "How important do you think it is for us to help your kingdom get rid of the Viking settlers?"

The boy seemed surprised that Hasdai would ask him such a question. As was I. I wondered why he was treating the boy as if his opinion mattered.

"My aunt says—"

Hasdai held up a hand. "I know your aunt's thinking. I am interested to hear what you think."

"Nobody has ever asked me what I think about anything," said the boy king, smiling ruefully.

"But you obviously have thoughts about many things."

"Yes."

"Well, how important do you think it is to rid your kingdom of the invaders?"

"I am told they are very cruel people who do horrific things to my people. They do not believe in God. They murder, rape, and rob."

"But they come from a harsh, cold land where it is difficult to raise crops and feed their people. One can understand why they would want to come to a place where life is easier."

"So, you believe we should not try to expel them?"

"No, I didn't say that. I only suggest a reason for their actions. The fact that they murder, rape, rob and enslave the current occupants of the land they claim is the history of mankind. Your ancestors took this land from the people who were here before their arrival. Hopefully they were not as cruel to the people as the Vikings are, but they might have been. It is the conquerors who write the history. The people who occupied this land when your ancestors arrived no doubt took it from some previous peoples. I fear we learn nothing from history since it continues to repeat."

I interrupted. "I think you are confusing His Majesty."

"Exactly, that is my intention. I assume he will soon claim the power of his throne. When he does, I hope he can think through complex situations and is, at least, wise enough to surround himself with intelligent, thinking people who will provide him with good advice."

He smiled at the boy king.

The boy furrowed his brow, clearly thinking intently about Hasdai's words.

The regent, trailed by her advisors, strolled back into the room. I looked carefully, but her face revealed nothing. She stopped in front of Hasdai with the men in a half-circle behind her.

"Effendi Shaprut—is that the proper way to address you or do you prefer the title of Ambassador?"

"Effendi is fine."

"Well, Effendi Shaprut, we feel your caliph demands too much."

She extended the list Hasdai had presented to her. "We can agree on relinquishing the seven towns we underlined, but that is the best we can do."

"Then, we will return to Cordoba and our forces, already on the road, will turn back with us."

Now she was unable to hide her emotions. She bowed her head rubbing her forehead while leaning forward. Then she straightened her spine, lifted her head, and looked directly into Hasdai's eyes. "I assumed you came here to negotiate, not to deliver ultimatums."

"Our caliph has agreed to enable you to rid your country of the Viking invaders. He will not do this out of kindness nor sympathy. It is a matter of self-interest. He wants to be compensated for his support which, I must say, is sizeable."

I noticed Hasdai start to sway. I moved to him and put a hand on his back to steady him. "May I suggest we all sit down," I interrupted. "We didn't sleep well in unaccustomed beds last night and I think all of us are still quite tired from the long trip here."

The regent called for servants to bring in chairs. A few moments later we were all seated, the regent in her throne looking down at us. "What is your caliph's absolute minimum demand?" Out of the corner of my eye I could see the boy king leaning forward, listening with great intent.

Hasdai studied the list handed back by the regent. He was silent for several minutes, The only sound in the room was quiet breathing. Finally, he looked up. "It is possible I can convince my caliph to allow you to keep three of the fortresses." He read the names of three that were a little over a parasang away from the border. "However, for him to agree, we will need to add something else."

The regent allowed a sigh to escape. "What else?"

"There will be some spoils of war once the Vikings are defeated. We will want to keep all of it. It is the major reason our mercenaries fight for us, our contract with their leaders only covers the cost of maintaining them. I suspect the value of what is taken will not be large enough to even come close to covering the cost of our involvement."

The regent looked at each of her advisors and each, in turn, nodded their agreement. The boy king's eyes followed each face as they responded.

The regent spoke again. "One more thing, I want this physician of yours to train our physicians in caring for the wounded. His skill is well known here. I want him to not only train our physicians but go with the army and organize all the medical help needed."

Hasdai looked at me, and raised his eyebrows, a silent question.

I was caught off guard by the request but flattered. I had no idea I enjoyed a reputation outside of Cordoba. "I am willing to do that, but I ask that Judah go with me."

Hasdai looked at Judah. "Are you willing to go along with our physician?"

Judah's face betrayed no hint of what he thought. "That's fine with me. It might be interesting to witness this."

Hasdai turned again to the regent. "All the physicians in our army are trained in the medical academy I started and that ben Ezia now heads. I can attest to their skill. But since ben Ezia, is willing, I see no reason why he cannot serve in this way. I will ask him to write up four identical contracts of all we have agreed to. There will be two in Latin and two in Arabic. We will both sign and put our seals all four copies, one in each language for each of us. I can be back on the road to Cordoba yet this afternoon. When I reach General ibn Tarif al Rhaman and his troops, I will tell him to increase the rate of his travel and arrive here as soon as possible."

"Yes, I agree with everything," said Elvira Ramiro.

She motioned for one of the men in her entourage to stand and come forward. "This is Count Gonzalo Sanchez. He will lead the effort to rid our kingdom of Gunrod of Norway, his army, and his colony of Viking bandits that now occupy Gallaecian soil."

The count was a fearsome looking fellow, about my height but powerfully built with massive forearms. A scar ran from the top of his forehead across the bridge of his nose to below his right eye and onto a prominent cheek bone. I thought he had been quite lucky to not lose that eye. He took two strides toward Hasdai and offered his hand. Hasdai stood and shook his hand with enthusiasm.

Hasdai departed that same afternoon. Two days later General al Rhaman made camp on the plains outside the fortified capital. In the week that followed the count and our general met twice daily. The first two days they discussed tactics and strategy in general terms and then agreed on a plan. Neither Judah nor I attended any of these meetings, but the general took dinner with us each evening. During those meals he told us that he and the count agreed on most things. He believed they had worked out a method for their collaboration.

General al Rhaman told us that he and the count continued their planning but with all their senior officers present. They finalized the order of march, logistics, and the chain of command that would enable them to act as a single army. They agreed on the various drum and bugle signals that would command a wide variety of maneuvers, including which units would conduct them. Our general's command included an infantry unit of mercenary Nubians. This unit was especially effective against cavalry, but also very skilled in hand-to-hand combat. They were armed with long shields, thrusting spears, and curved swords. He also had a unit of light cavalry, mounted archers, crossbow archers, and slingers. The slingers were men trained to use a sling to throw rocks or Greek fire grenades. Additionally, there were engineers to set up and repair the siege machines and men trained as artillery to man the machines. Each unit was commanded by an experienced officer.

The count's forces consisted of eight nobles, each bringing a varying number of their own knights as heavy cavalry. Each of the nobles and their knights had a squire who could, presumably, be called on to fight, but whose primary job was to care for their knight. Each noble also brought some archers, of unknown skill, and an infantry of serfs more suited to the plow and scythe than to their shields and weapons. It was easy to understand why the previous armies sent by Leon had been unable to dislodge the Vikings who were fierce fighters, unafraid to challenge heavy cavalry, and able to make quick work of the poorly trained and unskilled infantry. The decision was made to integrate the count's infantry and archers with ours. The heavy cavalry would operate in their usual fashion, every man seeking his own success and honor.

I met daily with all the physicians, including the four assigned to the count's forces. The four accepted the principles of care established by Hasdai in his academy. After going through the recommended treatments for various wounds and illnesses I thought they should be prepared for, we spent time making lists of medications, supplies, and instruments we anticipated we might need. By the time the combined armies were ready to depart, we had four wagons loaded with chests of medications, bandages, surgical instruments, cots, stretchers, hospital tents, and everything else we thought might be needed.

Judah and I were in our room in the palace the evening before the army was to depart. We stood side-by-side looking out of the only window in the room. It was a small window, shoulder high to me but mid-chest to Judah. The shutter used to close the opening was swung inward, resting against the wall to the left of the opening. We saw many campfires out on the meadows, the combined armies spread out in a half-circle only a half-parasang from the fortress.

Judah turned away from the window. "I don't understand how this combination of armies will work. Our soldiers are organized into units that live together, train together, and know the skills needed and how to deploy them. The Christian army is composed of nobles of various rank and knights who follow their noble, each with a cadre of squires and servants to support them and care for their horses and armor. They are accustomed to fighting but are deployed by their noble as he sees fit. Their infantry is an untrained rabble. Their archers and crossbow archers seem to be skilled, but I'm not certain how well they will follow orders. Count Sanchez tells our general that all his men will follow his orders. I will believe that when I see it happen."

I laughed. "Judah, I believe that is one of the longest speeches I can remember you ever giving. I haven't been paying much attention. How many fighting men do we have?"

"Our caliph's forces are just under a thousand, but that includes engineers, artillery, wagon drivers, servants for the officers, cooks, grooms, farriers, and your physicians. The Christians have about a third that many men, including the squires who, presumably, can fight. The count says he will recruit more nobles on our way to the Viking settlement."

"Do you know where that settlement is? How far away?"

"I am told it is located about ten parasangs east of Faro. The commanders seem to believe the army can cover about ten parasangs a day. The route is to go north from here until we reach the coast, then travel east on the coastal plains. They estimate it will take twelve days. I seriously doubt we will make ten parasangs a day. There will be broken wheels and axels, horses and mules will be injured or become ill, as well as some men. If we arrive in anything under two weeks, I will be surprised."

Now I began to worry. Judah seemed to have little enthusiasm for the plan, and I now didn't have much faith in how well the two armies would function once the battle began. I wondered how much physical danger I might have to face. I was not happy that I had agreed to this. What if our armies were defeated? Would I be able to escape, even with Judah's help?

CHAPTER TEN

Twelve days later Judah and I rode behind General al Rhaman and Count Sanchez, their respective bodyguards close in front and behind us. Directly behind Count Sanchez rode a soldier with two large drums hanging from straps in front of the pommel of his saddle. The army and supply wagons stretched out behind us at least three parasangs. The coastal plain extended inland from the beaches and cliffs for at least a half day's walk. It was early summer, the weather warming more each day. Ahead of us rose a hill, no more than a dozen cubits above the plain. It was topped by a wood fortress.

Long before the fort became visible, we heard the clanging of metal striking wood, the Vikings were pounding their shields with their swords, announcing our approach. There were still workers in the fields surrounding the fortress, but the fortress itself was shut tight.

As we rode closer, I could see Viking warriors standing on the parapets, brandishing their weapons in defiance.

Tree trunks sunk into the ground vertically reached up at least fifteen cubits, the tops shaped into points. The main gate faced south. The stockade was no more than two-hundred cubits square, with towers rising six or eight cubits above the palisades at each corner. The towers provided good lines of fire along the outer walls.

The count raised his hand, and the long column gradually came to a halt. He swiveled in his saddle and pointed at the soldier with the drums.

"Sound the call for a meeting of all ranking officers," the count ordered.

The drummer beat out four loud, well separated beats followed by three, quick, short ones. He paused for ten heartbeats then repeated the signal. Within a few minutes the count and the general were surrounded by their senior officers.

"Disperse your men and set up camp," said the count in Latin. The general repeated the order in Arabic for his officers.

That evening Judah and I strolled through the encampment while the senior officers gathered in the pavilion set up for the count and the general.

"Will they decide to lay siege to the fortress or attack it?" I asked Judah.

"I think they will try to take it as soon as possible, that would be the wise thing to do. It will be difficult to supply all these men for a prolonged siege."

"Holding this many men so close to each other with the inevitable breakdown of hygiene will start an epidemic of dysentery or something worse, I said. "How do you think they will proceed?"

"I was never trained to be an officer, let alone a general. They are well schooled to deal with this sort of situation."

"Yes, of course, but you are not totally ignorant of these things. I'm just curious to see if you can think like these generals."

"The fortress is made of wood, and wood burns. I would launch fire arrows and, once the farangi are reassembled, lit containers of Greek fire against the palisades. Rather than die in the fires, I believe the Vikings will come out to fight, probably in close formation using their shields to form a moving attack force."

We stopped our ambling in front of one of the hospital tents where two of our Arab physicians were gathered around a small campfire.

"*As-salamu alaykum, ibn Achmed, ibn Chem.*" I greeted each of them by name.

"Alaykum salamu, Effendi ben Ezia," they each responded, then nodded at Judah.

"Will you take some tea?" asked one of the physicians.

I looked at Judah and he silently indicated his acceptance of the invitation.

"Yes, thank you," I said. "We welcome some tea."

We squatted with them around their fire, but not close enough to feel its heat. The summer night was still warm from the day long sun.

"All is in readiness?" I asked.

"Yes, we are ready for the onslaught of wounded."

"Good."

We talked until the moon was high in the sky, about their families, their lives in Cordoba. The cloudless sky allowed the reflected light of the moon and the brightness of the stars to create an eerie, diffuse, dawn-like illumination of the camp. The myriad of campfires reduced to glowing embers and the soldiers lay on their cloaks or blankets on the warm, sandy earth, waiting for the sleep that would allude most of them.

"Well," I announced. "We will leave you and retire to our tent. I doubt I will be able to sleep but Judah can fall asleep no matter the situation."

They chuckled at my lame jest, and we got to our feet. I had not paid attention during our wanderings to know in which way we had to return to our tent.

Judah looked to the sky and pointed to the north star, then turned. "It's this way, south."

I followed him back. Our pallets were laid side to side on the ground. We lay down and to my surprise I quickly followed Judah into a deep slumber.

Shortly after dawn we were awakened by the sounds of soldiers eating, and nervous laughter. Shortly after we got out of our tent trumpets blared and drums beat out orders. Our tent was only about five hundred cubits directly in front of the main gate. We watched as all the units of archers from both armies circled the fortress.

Judah pointed at a group of about thirty men running around the fort to the opposite side. "They are sending slingers with jars of Greek fire around to the sea to burn their boats. There will be no escape,"

Fires were lit in front of each group of archers and within moments fire arrows were launched directly into and over the palisades.

"The Vikings only have short bows," said Judah. "See, their arrows are falling short of our archers."

The engineers had been busy reassembling the farangis most of the night. They were now rolled into position about a hundred cubits on either side of the gate. Large ceramic jars were loaded into the slings and four men pulled on a rope attached to a long arm. A ratchet clicked until the long arm of the device was fully cocked. An engineer dropped a burning rag into the open end of the jar in each sling and the triggers were released. The arm of the farangi swung forward, bringing the sling up and over in a long arc. Burning jars of Greek fire smashed against the palisade on either side of the gate. The farangi were then moved and aimed at portions of the palisade not yet on fire.

I counted two-hundred and forty seconds before the next salvo was launched.

"It won't be long now," murmured Judah.

"What won't?"

"Those Norsemen won't wait to be consumed by flames. Watch the gate."

The gate swung wide framing a huge man. The muscles in his arms bulged, his neck was as wide as his head, his red beard and long hair twisted in the wind caused by the flames.

"That must be Gunrod," I said.

"I'm sure it is," said Judah.

Within moments the giant of a man was surrounded by equally fierce, if not quite as large, men banging swords, axes, or maces against their shields. They marched forward, maintaining close order.

Our archers ran to get into position to fire at the moving fort of men. The mass of Vikings formed a wall with their shields, which soon bristled with arrows. The Vikings quickened their pace, anxious to engage their enemies, but the archers retreated just as fast continuing to fire their arrows.

Loud bellows came from the moving fort, with each minute that passed the bellowing intensified. The Vikings were becoming more and more frustrated. Two units of crossbow archers moved into position. They laid prone on the ground and fired their bolts at the exposed legs and feet of the Vikings until they were out of bolts. They retreated as another group took their places on the ground and started firing.

Vikings hit with bolts from the crossbows dropped to the ground. They soon resembled porcupines, their quivering bodies thick with the missiles. Then the labdereai, huge crossbows mounted on wheels, were rolled up and their spears launched. The spears ripped open the formation. Realizing their tactic wasn't working, the bull-like roar of orders from their giant leader boomed over the tumult. The Vikings scattered in all directions looking for someone to kill.

I touched Judah's elbow. "How many of them are left, do you think?" I asked.

"Maybe a few more than fifty. We will overwhelm them with numbers. They are fierce warriors, extremely strong, and determined, and our side will endure some casualties," Judah replied.

Our archers and crossbow archers, most of their supplies of arrows and bolts exhausted, left the field to replenish them from the supply wagons. Our Nubian infantry marched in close formation, armed with their five-cubit long spears and round shields. They all also carried a sheathed sword with which they were as adept as with their spears. The Christian infantry, untrained, inexperienced, and equipped with old weapons, were easy prey for the Vikings, but the Nubians were equal in skill to the Vikings. Isolated small groups of archers returned and maneuvered to shoot the Vikings in the back or side while they fought.

The sound of drums and trumpets summoned the heavy cavalry of the Christians and our cavalry units into action. The long lances of the charging horsemen wrought havoc, although the strongest Vikings were able to deflect the thrust of the lance directed at them and often unhorsed the rider. Unhorsed knights were quickly dispatched.

Our wounded were being carried, or dragged, to the hospital tents by anyone available for the task. The unfortunate Christian serfs were more than happy to provide that service. I ran to the closest hospital tent and was soon inundated by patients with deep wounds and severed limbs.

Suddenly a Viking warrior charged through the back of the hospital tent. Cutting and slashing with his battle axe he pushed his way towards me. As his axe swung through the air, aimed at my head, he grunted, as a spear head pushed through his chest. The axe fell and he fell forward, his helmet banged on my right foot. The spear shaft stuck upright from his back. I looked up to see Judah standing with a sword in his hand.

"You hurt?" he asked.

I shook my head no.

"Sorry I was guarding the front when I saw him circling around. I'll pull him out of here and go back to guarding the entrance.

All of us worked feverishly to stop bleeding by applying tight bandages. When the lines of new wounded slowed, we were able to go back and treat the more severe wounds with the skill and medications necessary to affect a more permanent solution.

Less than an hour passed after the attack by the lone Viking. We heard the jubilant Arabic shouting heralding our victory. The man I was suturing had a deep wound to his right shoulder. He raised up and announced, "The heathens are defeated," and lay back on the cot. His pulse was strong. I finished suturing his wound, applied a poultice and a bandage and patted him on the uninjured shoulder. "You are going to heal up good as new. Just rest for the next ten days so the wound heals properly. Good luck to you." I moved to work on the next patient waiting.

The last of the wounded were treated. I walked outside the tent and stood next to Judah. A pit had been dug and dead Vikings were being dumped into it. Our own dead were being buried in individual graves with wood markers. Arabic prayers for the dead wafted through the still air. The smell of death filled my nostrils.

"How does a person become accustomed to this, Judah?"

"One doesn't. I'm going to go help with the burials."

"I'm going back in, help clean up and check on the patients," I murmured.

I didn't get back to our tent until the moon was no longer in the sky. When I entered, Judah sat up. "All the wounded cared for?"

"Yes, but several were lost before we could stem the bleeding. Were you able to witness the outcome?"

"Yes, I saw Count Sanchez finish off Gunrod with his lance but not until two of our Nubians wounded him grievously. He was already bleeding from at least five other wounds when the Nubians got to him. Sanchez charged in to impale him with his lance."

"Were any of the Vikings taken as prisoners?" I asked. "None of their warriors. They all fought until the end, shouting for Odin to take them to Valhalla. We discovered that four of their dead were women, who fought just as fiercely as the men. Some of their other women and slaves were taken. The locals, whom they had enslaved were given their freedom. There were even four local families reunited, but most had already lost their close relatives, slaughtered when the Vikings invaded."

I lay down on my pallet and rested the back of my head on my arms. "Do you know how many men we lost?"

"No, I don't know the number of dead. Do you have a count of the wounded?"

"We treated only seventy-six of close to the two thousand involved. I suppose that's a good thing. Most of the dead were Christians, their infantry. I presume that is acceptable in their culture. Some of our wounded are critical and may yet die, but all the physicians performed admirably. Some of the more seriously wounded are still being treated. I am very pleased with how all the physicians performed, they all did exactly how they were trained."

Judah grunted. "That's good to hear."

Morning came too soon for me. Judah and I sat next to our cooking fire and ate stale bread and cheese while drinking strong, sweet coffee. We watched, silently, as the smoking ashes from the Viking's fortress sent wisps of smoke straight up into the cloudless sky. The camp was stirring, as units were commanded to prepare for departure.

Shortly after the noon meal, all the tents were struck, campfires were doused, and the two armies embarked on their separate journeys home. I was ready to forego war in the future, happy to return to my medical practice and help Hasdai whenever he asked for it, but I had all the experience with war I ever needed or wanted.

CHAPTER ELEVEN

I t was 950, two years after the battle with the Viking invaders. The five of us, including Judah, were once again gathered in Hasdai's office. The tense relationship between Dunash and Menahem seemed to have been shelved. We were all anticipating a good party to celebrate Hasdai's fortieth birthday. His health and demeanor had recovered, and he seemed to be enjoying our renewed comradeship. Then he turned serious.

"You all know the caliph has been ill. I am treating him for a heart condition, but he is not improving despite my best efforts. I am more and more worried about what will happen to all of us, in fact all Hebrews of Cordoba when Abd-Ar-Rahman passes on. It is not clear what the crown prince, Al-Hakam's, attitude towards our people will be when he assumes the throne."

"Perhaps we should do more find out if the stories about the Khazar empire are true," suggested Dunash.

As long as I could remember the story had been told and retold about the Khazar empire, supposedly located somewhere north of the Byzantine and Persian empires, and south of the Rus. It was said to control a significant portion of the Silk Road and was under continuous pressure to align with either the Christian world or that of the Muslims. The king of the Khazars was also not content that almost all the tribes that paid him tribute had their own separate religions. He decided that a state sponsored religion would serve to unite his people. All he need do was to gain influence with the religious leaders to unify and control his subjects. His solution was to invite the most learned scholars, rabbis, imams, and priests to travel to his capital and, in the presence of his court, debate the merits of their religions.

After listening to all the arguments, and consulting with his advisors, he decided the Hebrew religion was the best for his subjects. He started the process by converting himself. He then encouraged all his extended family to follow his lead. Once he and his extended family converted, his administrators, and most of the tribal chiefs, did so as well. A large portion of the population followed their leadership. The unintended consequence of this conversion was that the new Hebrew nation would welcome any Hebrew emigrants escaping intolerable conditions, providing they could find their way to Khazar's borders.

Hasdai, Dunash, Menahem and I had often discussed the possibility that this popular legend was a reality. Menahem, as always, the skeptic declared that if such an Empire empire exists, and if it was true that it had converted to our religion, it was most likely because they wanted to maintain their independent status to avoid being influenced by the dictates and teachings of Christ or Mohammad. I thought Menahem's argument made sense.

Three months after we had this discussion Hasdai interviewed two recent arrivals in Cordoba, Rabbi Judah ben Meir and Rabbi Joseph ben Hegari. The two claimed they had travelled to, and recently returned from, the land of the Khazars, but had not visited its capital. Unfortunately, they were not clear about the actual routes they had followed, explaining they had been in the company of merchants who knew the way. They had not thought to make notes of the landscape or the names of significant geographical landmarks such as rivers or mountains. Hasdai was courteous to them and took note of what they said. He played the good host, but he was skeptical of their story.

A short time later, Hasdai learned of the arrival of a group of merchants from Khorasan, a kingdom north of Persia. He had them brought to his house and interviewed them. They claimed to have knowledge of the Khazars but admitted they had never been there. They did verify the story that it was a Hebrew state. Hasdai thought by saying this they hoped to curry favor with him. He felt their story was also suspect.

Only a week later, a delegation led by a new ambassador arrived from Constantinople. They brought gifts from the emperor for Ahd-ar Rhaman III and for Hasdai. After their audience with the caliph, Hasdai gained the grand vizier's approval to welcome the entire delegation to his home for a banquet. Dunash, Menahem, Judah and I were all invited.

Hasdai turned to the ambassador. "Ambassador, what, if anything, can you tell me about the Khazars?"

"Effendi Shaprut, I can confirm that somewhat more than fifteen day's travel by boat from Constantinople, depending on the weather and winds, one reaches the border of the Khazar empire. That empire is said to consist of a host of different tribes scattered over large areas of steppe. The ruling class, and most of the subjects, are reported to practice the Hebrew faith. The name of their king is Joseph. That's about all I can tell you."

"Do any of the rest of you know more about this place?" asked Hasdai, looking into the faces of other members of the delegation.

One man raised a hand even with his shoulder.

"Yes, Effendi, what can you tell me?"

"I was a customs officer for the emperor and can tell you that the Khazars trade using dried fish, skins of both domestic and wild animals, and furs of high quality. They trade some manufactured items, pots, pans, well-made knives, swords, and lances. They also produce high-quality, short, compound bows."

"What about produce and grains?"

"Very little of that arrives in Constantinople for trade from the Khazar empire."

"I should add," said the ambassador, "that there is some communication between our Empire and the Khazars. It usually involves the exchange of emissaries and mutual gifts."

"Do you have an embassy in their capital and they one in yours?"

"Not that I am aware of."

A man in military uniform spoke up. "The Khazars are quite powerful militarily. They maintain a large army and frequently dispatch troops to quell any sort of uprising or invasion. They protect their borders vigorously."

The next evening an excited Hasdai insisted that Dunash, Menahem, Judah and I join him for dinner.

"I think it is likely that this place exists and, if it is true that it follows our faith, that fact is very important for our people. It might become the haven we have all hoped for. We must learn if it is true, and if so, the route by which it can be reached."

"What do you want to do next?" asked Dunash.

"First, we need to identify someone we all trust to take a letter to this King Joseph."

"I will do it. I have hoped for a long time for this opportunity," I said. *"Please God, tell Hasdai to let me go."*

Are you certain, Yusuf? This could be a very long and very dangerous journey. What about your medical practice?"

"I must do this I will find someone to take over the practice while I'm gone."

"What are you going to say in this letter?" asked Menahem.

"We have to think carefully about that. I want input from all of you, but I think Menahem should use his skill and understanding of Hebrew grammar to compose the letter. All of us can comment on and critique the drafts until we arrive at a document that we can all be pleased with. What do you think?"

"I am happy to fulfill that role," said Menahem.

Dunash, Judah and I nodded our agreement.

Hasdai stared at me. I felt his eyes boring into my skull with the precision of a trephine. "Yusuf has volunteered for the mission. He is the messenger we can all trust with this assignment. The journey will be long and probably dangerous. We cannot allow the messenger to find some excuse to not deliver the letter."

"Judah, as is your custom you have not contributed to this discussion."

Judah's smile engulfed his face. "To have the opportunity to visit the Khazars and to map the route to a Hebrew empire? One that could provide sanctuary to any of our people capable of escaping persecution and immigrating? Do you think for a moment I would allow Yusuf to do this without me?"

"How long do you think this trip will last?" I asked.

Hasdai shrugged. "It is difficult to estimate. We don't know the route or the distances. I suspect to get there and return at least a year, maybe two. But what an adventure, Yusuf! I envy you this opportunity. If I could, I would go myself, but that is impossible."

Hasdai took my right forearm in his hand and squeezed gently. "First, you and Judah must start lists of what you will need for the trip. You will compare then combine the lists and Dunash, Menahem and I will review and help make a final list. I will finance everything you will need. Since our most reliable information comes from Constantinople, you should make your way there first. I think the most convenient way will be by ship from Malaga. I will identify a reliable ship's captain and arrange for your passage. You will need to take gifts from me to the king of the Khazars and to the Byzantine emperor since you will need his help to find the Khazars."

"While you are getting ready, I will write to our ambassador in Constantinople asking him to find out all he can about the route to take to the Khazars. I will also send him funds for you to draw on if need be. The good news is that neither you nor Judah have any family to worry about supporting while you're gone. Do you? Do either of you have wives and children I am unaware of?"

Judah looked at him incredulously. I knew he was just teasing us. I had been too busy learning, becoming a physician, and treating my patients to attend social functions or meet a woman. I was too shy to ask Hasdai's mother for help and not certain I wanted the responsibility of a family. Judah was in charge of managing Hasdai's household. Sarah was the fulltime cook, her husband the fulltime gardener, and there were a host of servants for the main house and the house next door housing Hasdai's harem. I doubt Judah had the time to consider having a wife and family either.

Dunash and Menahem burst into laughter and were joined by Hasdai. "Ah, I thought not. Do not forget a medical chest, Yusuf. I will also add some herbs that might help for sea sickness."

"Sea sickness?" I was bewildered.

"Yes, some people suffer severe dizziness, nausea and, vomiting because of the motion of the boat on the sea. Have we never discussed this malady?"

"I would have remembered if we had."

"Do not worry, I am unaware of anyone who has actually died from it."

"Doesn't mean that some haven't," interjected Menahem.

"Thank you, Menahem. I can always rely on you for encouragement." I said. I hoped

he was not oblivious to my sarcasm.

Hasdai rubbed his hands together. "One last thing. Judah, we will need someone to make maps of the route. Do you know how to make maps?"

"I can read them, but I need to be schooled on making them."

"That is easily solved. I will send you to one of the engineers in the caliph's army. I recently treated him for a rather serious illness, and he made a full recovery. I'm certain he will be able to teach you all that is needed in a relatively short time. Good, it's all set then. We have a lot of work to do, all five of us."

Over the following two weeks Hasdai, Dunash and Menahem had lengthy discussions over the form and substance of the letter to King Joseph. I was only present for those sessions when I could take time away from my practice and preparations for the odyssey. It took several sessions for them to agree on the letter's introduction. They finally settled on a lengthy letter, full of details.

"I, Hasdai, son of Isaac, son of Ezra, belonging to the exiled Hebrews of Jerusalem, in Hispania, a servant of My Lord the Caliph, bow to the earth before him and prostrate myself towards the abode of Your Majesty, from a distant land. I rejoice in your tranquility and magnificence and stretch forth my hands to God in Heaven that He may prolong your reign.

They continued the letter using what I considered to be over flowery language, a reiteration of the plight of the Hebrew people, and the nature of their suffering.

When we had transgressed, He brought us into judgement, cast affliction upon our loins, and stirred up the minds of those who had been set over the Hebrews to appoint collectors of tribute over them, who aggravated the yoke of the Hebrews, oppressed them cruelly, humbled them grievously and inflicted great calamities upon them.

Next, they described how Hasdai came to enjoy the power he had to lessen the burden of the Hebrews in Cordoba and a description of the power and extent of the caliphate of Cordoba. The letter went on to describe, in detail, the size of the city of Cordoba and the geographical location of the caliphate. It described Judah and me, in very flowery terms, while exaggerating my skills as a physician such that, if tested, I was certain I would be found wanting.

"I shall inform My Lord the King of the name of the Caliph who reigns over us. His name is Abd-ar Rhaman III, son of Mohammed, son of Abd-ar Rhaman I, son of Hakeem, son of Hisham, son of Abd-ar Rhaman II, who reigned in succession except Mohammed alone, the father of our caliph, who did not ascend the throne but died in the lifetime of his father.

A recitation of the history of the Arab conquest of Spain and the subsequent rulers until the unification by the present caliph followed. Then, the letter described the riches of Cordoba.

"This land is rich, abounding in rivers, springs and aqueducts; a land of wheat, rice, olive oil and wine, of fruits and all manner of delicacies; it has pleasure gardens and orchards, fruitful trees of every kind, including the leaves of the tree upon which the silkworm feeds, of which we have great abundance. In the mountains and woods of our country the red dye cochineal is gathered from the bodies of the insect. There are also found among us mountains covered by crocus flowers from which we gather the spice called saffron. Also, in the mountains are found veins of silver, gold, copper, iron, tin, lead, sulfur, porphyry, marble and crystal."

The letter continued to describe how healthy the economy of the country was, how wealthy the caliph was, and the many and valuable gifts the caliph received. It detailed Hasdai's responsibility to receive all the gifts in the name of the caliph and to make certain gifts of equal value were sent to the various rulers who had sent gifts to the caliph. It described how as chief of customs he controlled the business transactions of the merchants who came to Andalusia to buy or sell. The letter described the difficulties Hasdai had faced in ascertaining the truth about the Khazar empire and its exact location, and in trying to find persons who had visited and knew the routes to follow to deliver a letter from him to the king. He explained his interest in making contact and establishing a relationship with the king of the Khazars and the need for a Hebrew homeland willing to take in members of the faith.

"I did none of these things for the sake of mine own honor, but only to know the truth of whether the Hebrew exiles anywhere form one independent kingdom and are not subject to any foreign ruler. If, indeed, I could learn that this was the case, then despising all my glory, abandoning my high estate, leaving my family, I would go over mountains and hills, through seas and lands, until I should arrive at the place where My Lord the King resides, that I might see not only his glory and magnificence, and that of his servants and ministers, but also the tranquility of the Hebrews."

Finally, Hasdai questioned the king about any ideas he might have about when the Messiah might arrive.

One more thing I ask of My Lord, that he would tell me whether there is among you any computation concerning the final redemption which we have been awaiting so many years, whilst we went from one captivity to another, from one exile to another. How strong is the hope of him who awaits the realization of these events! And oh! How can I hold my peace and be restful in the face of the desolation of the house of our glory and remembering those who, escaping the sword, have passed through fire and water, so that the remnant is but small? We have been cast down from our glory, so that we have nothing to reply when they say daily unto us, 'Every other people has its kingdom, but of yours there is no memorial on the earth'.

When they finally were satisfied with the letter to King Joseph, Hasdai, Dunash and Menahem presented me with a long list of questions I should find the answers to. What was the nature of the Khazar government, and the nature of the land within the empire? What were it's boundaries, its length and breadth? What tribes were part of the empire? How did kings succeed one another—were they chosen from a certain tribe or family or did sons succeed their fathers as was customary among our ancestors when they dwelt in their own land? How many walled cities and open towns were there? Did they have to irrigate their crops? I should ask about the number of armies and the training of their leaders—but I should be careful with this question and make certain I tell the king that Hasdai's only interest in this was to rejoice when he learned of the strength and power of the Khazars. How many provinces did he rule? What amount of tribute was paid to him? Did his people tithe to him? Did he stay in his royal city or visit all regions of his empire? Were there any tribes or areas in his empire that did not follow the teachings of the Torah? Did he judge his people himself or appoint judges? Did he attend synagogue? What peoples did he wage war with? Did he allow war to set aside the observance of the Sabbath? What were the names of the kingdoms or nations on his borders? What were the routes that traders from the east travelled to arrive at his empire? How many kings had ruled before him? What were their names, and the length of their rule? What was the current official language of his empire?

When I saw the length of this list I had to sit down. I backed into a chair then read through the list quickly. I looked up at Hasdai, then looked down and read the list again, carefully, shaking my head. "You really want me to ask the king about all of these things?"

Hasdai's face was serious. "You and Judah should find out all the answers you can from just paying attention and talking with the people. Some will best be answered by the king, yes. But I know I can trust you to be discrete and diplomatic. I would not be sending you otherwise."

It took longer than any of us anticipated to collect everything we would need for the trip and to arrive at an agreement for the content of the letter. It took even more time to make all the arrangements. Meanwhile, Judah became expert in the making of maps.

A month and a half after the initial decision to embark on this trip we were once again all together in Hasdai's office when he announced, "It seems we are dependent upon weather and winds to make the voyage from Malaga to Constantinople. From May to October the prevailing winds, called the levant, blow from west to east. Since we are still in the month of March, we have time to identify a reliable captain and ship for your voyage. I sent letters to the leaders of the Hebrew communities here in Cordoba, Seville, Malaga, and other port cities seeking a merchant-trader who travels regularly to Byzantium and who is reliable and honest. All have responded and several recommended the same man, a fellow Hebrew named Abraham ben Moses. I was able to communicate with him and it happens he is a co-owner of a sturdy cargo ship. He is currently purchasing trade goods to sell or barter at various ports between Malaga and Constantinople."

"Will Judah and I have the opportunity to meet this man and judge him for ourselves?" I asked.

"Of course, that is what I have arranged."

"Where is he now?"

"He is purchasing merchandise in Jaen but plans to be in Cordoba the middle of next month. I will arrange for you and Judah to meet with him as soon as he arrives here."

The time passed quickly, but we still had much to do in preparation. Judah and I met with Abraham ben Moses for dinner at Hasdai's house inside the Alcazar. Hasdai was not present. He was busy attending one of the caliph's ill children. Abraham was a slight, wiry sort of man, small in stature and somewhat abrupt in manner. He seemed especially anxious for Judah and me to join him and his partner on their voyage.

Abraham told us about the co-owner of his ship, the *Fair Winds*. "The captain of the ship is my partner, a Greek. He designed and helped build the ship and is, appropriately, very proud of her. He is very experienced and cautious, and we have made many successful voyages together."

"Good," I said. "That's reassuring. What is the name of this experienced yet cautious captain?"

"Stephanopulus."

"How long will the voyage take?" asked Judah.

"It will take several weeks depending upon wind conditions, weather and how quickly we can complete our business in each port."

"How many ports?" I asked.

"Half a dozen, maybe more if we get delayed. In each port we will take on fresh water and provisions, as well as disposing of trade goods and purchasing others that will turn a profit along the way."

"How long will we be in each port?"

"That depends on the tides, the weather, how long it takes to complete our business. This is our life. Stephanopulus and I share the philosophy of taking as much joy as possible from each day. There is no rush. Profit comes to those who take time and care about quality. Plus, we enjoy the best that each port has to offer."

"You value a good life as part of your business then," I commented.

"Exactly. I should add that Effendi Shaprut has already paid handsomely for your passage, more than I asked for or expected. I assured him we would take very good care of you both."

Judah smiled. "Effendi Shaprut is a very generous man."

"He is indeed. He explained to me that your mission is to deliver a letter to the king of the Khazars. I have had dealings with two merchants from that empire, both devoutly committed to our religion. They didn't divulge much about where they came from. They seemed reluctant to talk about their home. It is my understanding that you will still have an arduous journey ahead of you after reaching Constantinople."

"I think we are both aware of the dangers involved, but" I looked at Judah for affirmation, "we are resolved to complete our mission."

The following week Judah and I departed for the port city of Malaga. Each of us had gold dinars sewn into our garments and cloaks and carried leather pouches of coins secured to our belts. There were more coins secreted in our luggage.

Judah drove us in a wagon pulled by a strong team of horses. Our baggage included many gifts for King Joseph and for the Byzantine emperor. We were both well supplied with sturdy travel clothes and garments suitable for audiences with the rulers we hoped to meet. We carried a generous supply of dried fruit and salted, dried meat, packed securely to prevent spoilage, to use in case of emergency. The distance from Cordoba to Malaga was approximately thirty-seven parasangs. Always efficient, Hasdai had reserved rooms for us at three comfortable inns along the well-travelled and safe highway between the two cities.

Upon reaching Malaga at midafternoon on our fourth day of travel, we went to an inn adjacent to the port where Abraham had reserved a large room for us. He also arranged for a buyer for our horses and wagon.

After closing the deal, Abraham handed me a heavy bag of coins. "It was a fair price. The buyer was happy. I hope you are as well."

"I will take your word for it. I haven't the slightest idea how much Hasdai paid, so I am in the dark," I said.

"Effendi Shaprut told me how much he paid, and I have managed a slight profit for him," said Abraham.

"I'm glad you have looked after his interests. I am a novice about the details of commerce. Although my father was trader, he died when I was quite young. During the voyage I would appreciate that you educate me about the value of the things you purchase and how you determine that value."

"I will be happy to do so."

We had dinner that evening with Abraham and Stephanopulus, an average sized man with bulging forearms and a face darkened and wrinkled by too long exposure to sun and wind. While Abraham was mostly quiet and introspective, Stephanopulus regaled us with an endless supply of sea adventures.

The next day Abraham was off making final arrangements for the delivery of leather items he had previously purchased. He was also making certain they were packed in crates with adequate protection against dampness. He explained that leather goods would develop mold if exposed during the voyage. He told us the items purchased were made by very skilled Hebrew craftsmen. The market for their work was very good in Constantinople.

We accompanied Stephanopulus to the docks. "Here she is. *Fair Winds*," he announced proudly.

"Abraham told us you not only designed, but helped build her," said Judah.

"That is true. She is based on the old Roman cargo ships called corbitas but sized to carry as much as a hundred tons of cargo. She is forty-seven cubits bow to stern and seventeen cubits midships. She has two tons of ballast and a deep, wine-glass shaped keel. She is the most stable ship I have ever sailed, even in the roughest weather."

He stepped on the gangplank and motioned for us to follow.

"Ships built in the north were originally modeled after those used by the Vikings. The Roman style of building was to lay each plank flush with the next. The shipbuilders of the Baltic and North Seas used a building method for the hull that overlaps each board with the bottom edge of the next higher board. It is called clinking; those boats are known as clinkers. A more recent improvement is to join the planks using mortice and tenons held in place with plugs. I believe it is a much more secure method of construction that allows less leaking. However, it is significantly more time consuming and requires much more skill by the carpenters. That is the method we used to build *Fair Winds*."

"How many men do you need to sail her?" I asked.

"You see she has a single mast and square sail. The square sail allows us to raise it to various heights, we can reef it—that is change the angle to catch the wind—all from the deck. We don't have to send anyone up into the rigging unless a repair needs to be made of the rigging itself. That means we only need a small crew, no more than four sailors. Larger cargo ships with multiple masts and sail sets require a large crew to operate. Warships and cargo ships with oars, require men to man the oars as well as sailors."

"So, the design of the ship saves money to operate it, meaning more profit," observed Judah.

"Indeed, but we save in other ways as well. While sailing, Abraham acts as our cook and is, I should add, quite a good one. My crew has sailed with us for several years, We feed them well and they are happy. If any repairs are necessary, I can manage to get them done myself."

"Since you helped build her, I expect so," I observed.

Stephanopulus motioned for us to follow him. "Come, I'll show you around. Aft, in this structure above the deck, are the galley and dining room, my captain's berth and an identical berth that Abraham usually occupies."

He opened the door, and we descend four steps into a small room with a table and benches on either side of it. Forward but off to the side was the galley, small but efficient with a coal burning stove, sink, and storage for cooking and eating utensils. Smoke from the coal fire was vented out through a metal chimney penetrating the side of the galley. At the end of the room were two narrow doors. He opened the one on the left and showed us his berth. Crammed into it was a small desk with charts neatly rolled and stowed in slots, a chair, a hammock slung from the ceiling, and a single bunk with storage below. There was a small window aft to allow air and light into the room.

"During this voyage, Abraham and I will share this cabin and you will share his next door. You can decide for yourselves who gets the bunk and who sleeps in the hammock. Effendi Hasdai has paid handsomely for your comfort. Have either of you ever slept in a hammock?" he asked.

Judah and I shook our heads. I wondered aloud how long we could exist in such a small space.

"Well, one of you will get used to the hammock in short order. It saves a lot of floor space. I think you can find room for some of your luggage in your cabin but there is additional storage in a separate compartment below where we stow our food and water."

Back on deck, we maneuvered around the ropes that held the mast upright. These ropes extended to the top of the mast and were secured at the bottom to smooth holes cut through the thick top rail all along the sides of the boat. There were two other lines attached to the top of the mast, one attached to the bow of the ship, the other to the stern. The stern rope was attached to the peak of the roof of the cabin.

I stopped to look at the sail. It was made of a heavy weave of alternating cotton and hemp twine. I was pleased to note that it appeared to be very sturdy.

Stephanopulus unrolled a corner of the sail. "These are called brail rings. They can be made of wood, lead or horn. I prefer the horn. They are more expensive but smoother and last longer. They are sewn onto the face of the sail, the side that faces the wind. The brail rings guide a series of ropes that are manipulated from the deck. We use them to change the shape of the sail, reduce its size as the strength of the wind dictates, or furl it, that is roll it up, when it is not needed."

We continued to the bow where a small, very cramped shed-like structure was located. I glanced inside to see a box with a hole cut in the top, the water visible below.

"That's the shit hole. Try to not piss on the seat. Until you get your sea legs best to sit for whatever needs you have."

"Lovely."

I thought to myself.

"That hatch leads to the crew's quarters. It's called the forecastle. There is room for the men's sea chests and hammocks. No need for much more than that. Any questions?"

He looked first at me, then at Judah. We both shook our heads.

"We're waiting to load the rest of our cargo in the next couple of days. The dock fees are accumulating. Once loaded, we will get towed into the harbor where we'll anchor to wait for the winds to arrive, and the tide to go out. While we're waiting for that, you can use our lifeboat to row to shore and enjoy Malaga. But stay close, if you aren't ready to sail when we are, you will be left behind."

I turned to Judah and smiled. "I doubt we will allow that to happen. We've prepared for this and looked forward to it for too long to miss the boat."

"Ship," Judah corrected.

CHAPTER TWELVE

The following day *Fair Winds* was loaded. One of our crew cast a hawser with one end attached to the bow. A man standing in an open boat with four oarsmen caught it and secured it to a post in the center of the tug. With all four men straining at their oars the tug slowly pulled *Fair Winds* around to face the mouth of the harbor. Once she was moving, they rowed easily until Stephanopulus hollered at his crew to lower anchors fore and aft.

We sat at anchor for three days as the breeze from the west strengthened slightly each day. Judah and I rowed the lifeboat to shore on the second day.

"You told me you wanted to learn to defend yourself beyond what you learned in Panormus," he said. "We will start by getting you in physical shape. We are going to jog through the city."

Although I considered myself still young, and in reasonable physical shape, after less than an hour I was breathing heavily. I convinced Judah to stop and take some refreshment and a light meal. He smiled indulgently.

Just after sunrise on the morning of the fourth day, our captain announced the tide was running out. He ordered the crew to hoist anchors and raise the sail. Our adventure had finally begun.

The wind stayed steady from the west. We sailed east until passing Almeria, then steered northeast, keeping the coast of Andalusia on our left always visible in the distance. At night, we steered further from the shore and Stephanopulus used the stars to set the course.

At each four-hour shift change the captain emerged to check our course and instruct the new man at the helm how to maintain it. Stephanopulus estimated our speed to be a little under a parasang every hour.

The waves were not large and *Fair Winds* cut through them with surprising ease. From what Hasdai had told us, I had anticipated a lot of up and down, and side to side motion, but it was smooth and steady and neither Judah nor myself suffered any dizziness or nausea.

We reached Cartagena the morning of the third day, gliding into the harbor with the sail furled. We dropped anchors fore and aft. Leaving the crew on board, Abraham, Stephanopulus, Judah and I rowed to the stone wharf. While Abraham made the rounds of the merchants he expected to trade with, Stephanopulus arranged for *Fair Winds* to tie up at the dock the following day.

Judah and I explored the seafront then, asked directions to the Hebrew section of the city. The synagogue was near the center of the separately walled neighborhood. The rabbi, of course, had corresponded with Hasdai. He welcomed us with enthusiasm and invited us to the patio entrance of his home to share cups of an excellent local wine.

"Effendi ibn Shaprut wrote that you were on your way to visit the land of the Khazars. Do you really think they are Hebrews? Will they be willing for oppressed Hebrews to find sanctuary with them?"

"That is what we are going to find out, Rabbi," I said.

As well as being knowledgeable about religious teachings, Rabbi Shmuel knew a great deal of local history and seemed anxious to share this knowledge with us.

While Hasdai developed an interest in language as a student, my obsession was history. I was determined to learn as much of the history of the places we visited as I could, therefore the visit with the rabbi.

"This city was originally named Mastia and has been important for a very long time because of the excellent harbor, one of the best in the western Mediterranean. The Romans found silver in the nearby mountains and established mines, some still yielding today. The region is also well known for its excellent esparto grass which has been, and still is, used to make all manner of baskets, ropes and more recently paper."

"The Carthinian general, Hasdrubal, rebuilt and expanded the city a couple of hundred years before the Christ child was born, intending to use it as a gathering place for the conquest of Iberia. After the Western Roman Empire weakened, the city was occupied and ruled by the Vandals, then the Visigoths, then Byzantium, then re-conquered by the Visigoths and finally, praise God, by the Muslims. The small Hebrew community, here since the original Roman era, were often persecuted, but persevered. When the Muslims assumed control, our lives improved significantly especially since Hasdai ibn Shaprut became influential. When you next see him, please tell him that all the diaspora appreciate what he is doing for our people."

"Of course, we will do that," I answered. "I have several small, waterproof containers made from esparto. I use them to store liquid medications. Do you think they came from here?"]

"Yes, most likely. On the outskirts of the city, large plots of several different varieties of esparto are cultivated. It is a major product of this area. The newly harvested leaves can be left to dry in the sun until they turn a yellowish color. This raw esparto is used to make baskets of many different styles, size and quality."

"Yes, we've seen them in your markets."

"Another technique is to soak the leaves in water for about a month, then they are dried and crushed. The crushed esparto is stronger and easier to weave and to manipulate to make rope. My father, may he rest in peace, made esparto canteens, waterproofing them with pine pitch. I'm certain the small containers you use were made using the same techniques."

"We were told there is an old Roman theater as well as some partial and even a few complete buildings from the Phoenician, Roman and Byzantine periods," interjected Judah. "Can you find someone to show us these?"

"I didn't know you were interested in artifacts from the past Judah." I said, I was surprised.

"I am interested in many things," he said, his face unreadable.

"Yes, of course. If you return tomorrow morning, I will have one of my sons guide you," said the rabbi.

We found Abraham and Stephanopulus at the inn at the end of the stone wharf where we had agreed to meet before returning to the ship. We explained our plans for the following day and Judah secured a room for us at the inn for the night.

"That's interesting, so you want to learn more of the local history of all the places we visit?" said Abraham.

"Yes, good idea, but watch yourselves," added Stephanopulus. "Don't display that you have money. There are many criminals and cutthroats who haunt these docks and the seaport hunting for easy pickings. I will bring *Fair Winds* to dock at the wharf tomorrow so you can come aboard after sightseeing but be careful this evening."

After our dinner Judah and I, while sitting in the inn's front patio, heard music coming from the main plaza of the city. We had strolled through that plaza in the afternoon looking at the wares of the vendors stands set up around its periphery. It wasn't far from the inn.

"Should we go see what the celebration is?" asked Judah.

"I don't see any reason not to. Let's go."

We reached the plaza to find a dozen musicians playing for a group of dancers. The performance was ringed by onlookers clapping their hands in rhythm.

"Keep one hand on your purse," instructed Judah as we joined the crowd.

The music and dancing continued without interruption for almost an hour. When the music stopped, the onlookers started to disperse. Several men tried to press past us at the same time and I felt a tug at my purse.

"Hey," I shouted, and grabbed the hand on the purse. The owner of the hand jerked it out of my grasp and ran off. I wasn't fast enough to see his face.

"Did he get your purse? I told you to keep a hand on it," admonished Judah.

"No, he didn't. I think we should get back to the inn."

"Good idea. Please stay close. We have to pass through that narrow, dark street we came through on the way back."

We entered the darkness. The only light visible coming from our inn at the far end of the dark street. Then a window opened, casting a thin bit of lamplight into the street. At the same time two men materialized from a shadowed doorway to block our path. Each held a knife; their blades reflected the light from the open window. They circled to get on either side of us. I felt a third man at my back.

"If you are looking for trouble, you've found it," said Judah as he unsheathed a short, straight sword from under his cloak.

Another surprise from Judah. I had no idea he was armed.

I heard the man behind me scurry away.

"I believe you will find those knives very little defense against this sword, but if you insist, I will provide a demonstration," whispered Judah.

The man on the left lunged, his knife thrust out at arm's length. Judah's sword flashed and the knife fell to the cobble stones.

"I could just as easily remove that hand as knocking the knife out of it."

He glanced at the other man, who was still holding his knife, then kicked the knife in the street over to me.

I bent, grabbed the grip of the knife, and took it from the cobble stones. I held it out in front of me, waist high, as though I knew how to use it.

Judah's voice was low, but it cut through the darkness with an edge as sharp as the blade of the sword he held. "I warn you it will cost you a hand, maybe an arm, if you decide to be brave."

The two turned and fled.

"Well, that was entertaining," Judah said.

"Entertaining? We could have been killed! Where did that sword come from? How did you hide it so well? I had no idea you were armed."

"Effendi Shaprut instructed me to protect you. I am always armed."

He pulled aside his cloak and replaced the sword in a sheath attached to the inner lining.

"What kind of sword is that?"

"It is modeled after the old Roman swords. I had it made specially because it's easy to conceal. It's good for both slashing and stabbing."

He pulled up the sleeve on his left arm to reveal a steel cylinder fastened around his forearm. "This is called a vambrace. I use it to deflect blows. It is also useful as a club."

I shook my head. "You never fail to surprise me, Judah. I am thankful for your friendship and protection. You must teach me how to defend myself. You might not be there to save me the next time."

"We will begin in earnest tomorrow; I have been wondering if you were truly ready."

For a quarter of an hour Judah and I ran in place on the deck of *Fair Winds*. The crew formed an audience, obviously enjoying my discomfort as I struggled to keep up with Judah's pace. Each time I managed to match him he went slightly faster.

"I thought . . . you were . . . going to . . . teach me . . . how to . . . defend myself." I panted and fell further behind.

Judah slowed his pace, still breathing normally. "Keep going, Yusuf. An unfit man is incapable of defending himself. Lift your feet. Lift your knees. You're shuffling in place, not running."

I stopped running and bent over, trying desperately to catch my breath.

"We will increase the time by a fraction each day, Yusuf. The next exercise is called a push-up."

"What is it?"

Judah laid on the deck, his feet stretched out, his hands and his toes anchored to the deck. He lifted himself up with his arms outstretched then touched his chest to the deck and lifted again ten times, quickly, without effort.

"Now you try it."

I got flat on the deck, as he had, and tried to push myself up. Nothing happened.

"Try it bending your feet up and putting your weight on your knees."

I pushed up until my arms were half bent then collapsed.

The crew, joined by Stephanopulus, bent over laughing, slapping their legs. Abraham, bless his kindness, looked on, his face betraying no emotion.

"We will do these, and other exercises, three times a day. Have faith." said Judah softly. "In a week you will be much stronger and maybe, in six months, you will be able to keep up with me."

"When will you teach me to use a knife and sword?"

"You are more than a month away from that. You must be strong enough not to have a weapon taken away from you. First, you will learn how to fight without a weapon."

"Maybe I should reconsider my request to learn to fight."

At the end of my first day of training, every muscle and joint in my body ached. I thought I would not be able to fall asleep because of the pain, but as soon as I fell into the bunk I passed out. Judah fit the hammock better than the small bunk where his entire lower leg hung over the end, so we had agreed I would have the bed. In fact, he seemed to adapt to almost any situation much easier than me.

The next morning, as I tried to get out of the bed, I experienced severe cramps in both calves. I was immobilized until Judah managed to massage out the cramps. I found the balm containing eucalyptus oil in my medicine chest and rubbed in on my calves, then most of the rest of my aching body. When I slowly lowered myself to the bench for breakfast in the main cabin, Abraham and Stephanopulus sniffed, and burst out laughing.

"So, Judah, what prompted this sudden dedication to exhausting exercise on the part of our physician?" asked the captain.

Judah looked at me but didn't answer.

I put down the spoon I was eating with. "The night before last we were attacked by three thugs. Judah ran them off in short order, but I realized I would have been at their mercy. I was paralyzed. I reminded Judah he promised to teach me how to defend myself. I didn't realize I would have to be tortured by exercise before I could be taught the necessary skills."

Stephanopulus smiled. "Judah is quite correct. You must be physically fit to be able to use any kind of fighting skill. Don't worry, in a week or two the aches and pains will abate."

"If I'm still alive"

A day later, Abraham had concluded all his trading, including the purchase of a large number of esparto ropes in a variety of diameters. He explained that some would be used to replace rigging on *Fair Winds*, but most would be for trade.

"The rope makers of Cartagena are renowned for the quality of their work," he explained.

"Yes, Rabbi Shmuel told us."

We weighed anchors and sailed out of the harbor east to our next destination, Cagliari on the island of Sardinia. The caliphate of Cordoba was now behind us. I felt vaguely ambivalent about leaving the relative safety of Cordoba but still excited about our mission.

"This will be the longest leg of the voyage," explained Stephanopulus. "It is roughly one hundred and eighty parasangs. However, at sea we calculate distance in nautical miles. It is about five hundred and thirty nautical miles to Cagliari. A nautical mile is, roughly, two thousand cubits. We will be out of sight of land, so we'll navigate by the sun and stars. If this breeze holds, will make about three to four nautical miles in an hour. In a day we will cover about eighty-four nautical miles, as long as we don't have to do much tacking."

"What do you mean by tacking?" I asked.

"Tacking is going at an angle relative to a straight line to the destination. If the wind is not blowing directly from our back, or up to about a thirty-degree angle from either port or starboard we can move the sail to catch the wind. If the wind is not within that sixty-degrees, we must sail back and forth across that direct line. Obviously, that makes the distance and time necessary to reach our destination longer. In six or seven days, if we don't encounter any storms or adverse winds, we should reach Cagliari."

Judah punched my shoulder. "You should be able to run in place for half an hour and do at least ten pushups by the time we reach Sardinia—without collapsing."

CHAPTER THIRTEEN

T he second day after sailing out of Cartagena's harbor, the wind grew stronger, blowing from the northwest. Stephanopulus ordered the sail set to catch the wind, *Fair Winds* heeled over and picked up speed, slicing through two-cubit high swells.

I took a firm hold on the top rail and considered offering a small prayer for our safety. I didn't really believe God worried about the safety of every individual, but who would a prayer hurt?

"Now we are making good headway," said Stephanopulus. "Eight or more knots is my guess. Don't worry, Yusuf, we won't tip over. We'll take advantage of this fresh wind as long as possible, but my knees are telling me we are in for a serious storm."

Just then a sudden strong burst of wind made *Fair Winds* heel over further, the top rail just skimming the water. My hand on the rail slipped and I fell to my knees. I whispered my prayer.

Stephanopulus shouted for all hands-on deck and calmly gave curt, definite orders in Greek. The four seamen responded immediately. Demitri and Georgy reefed the sail so only two-thirds of it was set to catch the wind. The ship reverted to its normal, slightly heeled, position and I was able to stand upright. Galen and Cletus disappeared into the hold and reappeared carrying coverings for the two hatches. They secured both hatches tightly, covered them, and lashed the coverings down with rope.

"Look there." Stephanopulus pointed north as a heavy line of blue-black, low-hanging clouds made an ominous appearance on the horizon.

"That is a major storm. Yusuf, you, and Judah best go to your cabin to ride this out. It's going to be quite rough. Pop your head in on Abraham and let him know what's happening. My crew knows what to do in a blow like this. We don't want either of you to get in our way. Go now."

I had no idea a storm could materialize that fast. As soon as Judah and I reached our cabin we were thrown to the floor as the ship lurched to one side, then shuddered and seemed to come to a stop before moving forward again. Judah climbed into his hammock, and I managed to crawl into my bunk. For what seemed like hours we were tossed up and down, back and forth, side to side. Abraham had told us early in the voyage that in a storm the most important thing was to keep the ship pointed into the wind and to cut through the waves as much as possible. If the ship was caught sideways by a large wave, it could capsize.

I had no way of knowing our captain was able to keep the ship facing into the wind, As would any sane man, I prayed that he would and made a long list of impossible promises to God if He would see us through the ordeal.

Heavy rain, then hail, then sheets of rain sounding like a waterfall, pounded the roof over the cabins. This was followed by more hail. I caught a glimpse of Judah's face in a flash of lightning. He was smiling, completely relaxed in the hammock.

"Why do you have that stupid smile on your face?" I shouted over the roar of the storm. "Why are you smiling? We are in danger of drowning."

"Don't be so negative, Yusuf. This is nothing compared to a battle with comrades and enemies being killed and maimed on all sides. Enjoy the ride. I expect this ship has weathered far worse storms than this one."

After four, or maybe six, hours the wind died, the ship stabilized, and we seemed to be moving steadily in one direction.

"Let's go on deck and find out how well we got through this," said Judah.

We found Abraham in quiet conversation with Stephanopulus. Demitri was resetting the sail, Galen was at the helm.

"Where are Georgy and Cletus? Were they lost overboard?" I asked.

Stephanopulus chuckled. "No, no. They went below to get some rest for a couple of hours. They will relieve Demitri and Galen. All of us weathered the storm without serious injury, including *Fair Winds*."

"I see Demitri is favoring his left shoulder. I should have a look at it."

"Good idea, Yusuf. He lost his balance and was thrown hard into the top rail. Almost went over, but Georgy held him. Demitri, let the physician look at your shoulder," he ordered in Greek.

He went over to help Galen with the sail and Demitri came and sat down on the hatch cover near where I was standing. I examined his shoulder and found it bruised, but not dislocated or broken. I tried to get him to wear a sling, but he shook his head no. I gave him some extract of willow leaves to relieve the pain and inflammation. Stephanopulus came over to interpret. He explained what I had found, and the treatment given. None of the crew spoke anything but Greek so it was impossible for me or Judah to communicate directly with them, except for hand signals, smiles and shrugs. Abraham had told me he had a working knowledge of spoken Greek but couldn't read or write it.

"Are we back on course?" I asked.

"Not for a while," answered Stephanopulus. "We were blown far south. I must adjust our course. It will probably cost us a day or so extra to reach our destination. Did you and Judah enjoy the ride?"

"Judah seemed to," I answered. "I don't have any desire to experience anything like that again."

"When you travel by sea, it's just part of the experience. That wasn't the worst I've been through, but it was exciting for what it was, short lived."

A week later we finally came in sight of the headland, the sheltered eastern boundary of the port of Cagliari.

Abraham asked if Judah and I wanted to learn about the history of the port we were entering.

"I am always interested in history. I don't know about Judah."

Judah shrugged and we made our way slowly into the harbor.

"This port affords good anchorage sheltered from storms, and the markets here have been active since long before recorded history," explained Abraham. "The Phoenicians took control of the island seven or eight centuries before the birth of Christ, displacing or absorbing the previous occupants. Two or three centuries later when Carthage took over, Cagliari experienced a growth surge. Next came the Romans. It seems Cagliari has always been the capital city of the island, most likely because of its excellent harbor."

"What things do you trade for here?" I asked.

"They have a good appetite for the dried fruits and meats of Andalusia. These are light to carry and keep for a long time. Anyone traveling into the interior mountains uses them for rations. They are especially popular with the shepherds. There is always a good market for good rope. Also, a market for silver and gold ingots. because some of the jewelry craftsmen here do exquisite filigree work. I will trade ingots for jewelry that I can easily sell in Constantinople. There is also a good market in every port we stop at for the sheep cheeses, especially the pecorino, produced here. There are probably a hundred different cheeses made here, all unique. They have been making these cheeses since the time of the Carthaginians. They also produce some excellent wines. I will try to obtain some amphora of wine, also very popular in Constantinople. They also make excellent knives here, perhaps you should shop for one. There are jewelers who craft in coral and one family I know that crafts extraordinary embroidery. I always try to purchase some of the jewelry and embroidery for resale."

"Will you sell some of the baskets from Cartagena?"

"No, they do excellent basket work here, a long tradition. They weave using straw, willow, and a wide variety of reeds. They create vivid colors by staining with plant dyes. They also make mats, trays, and other items. In Assemini, a small village just outside the city, there is a group of artisans who create ceramic work of exceptional beauty, prized by the knowledgeable. Perhaps you will accompany me when I go there?"

We dropped our anchors in the well-protected harbor, and leaving Demitri and Galen to mind the ship, Georgy and Cletus rowed us to the wharf.

"I will make arrangements for dock space," said Stephanopulus. "I assume you two will want to stay ashore with Abraham. His favorite inn is that one at the top of the street, up the hill."

"I will leave you to explore," said Abraham. "I will reserve rooms for us at the inn and then contact some of the merchants to let them know we've arrived, although they all know our ship and will be expecting me. We can meet for aperitives, good wine and snacks, on the patio of the inn this evening, just as the sun starts to set. It's a Sardinian custom, and one I find both enjoyable and civilized. They don't eat dinner until very late here, a light meal. The main meal here, as it is in Cordoba, is after midday."

Judah and I explored the area around the wharfs, watching as workmen toiled on a ship resting in dry dock. Then we wandered up into the city. Following Abraham's suggestion, we shopped for my knife.

"I don't have any idea of what to look for," I told Judah. "I will rely on your judgement to select one that will serve."

He carefully examined several knives, testing their weight and balance. "Hold this one, Yusuf. How does it feel in your hand?"

The knife was heavy, the handle had small, raised pimples that, I presumed, made it easier to hold onto. "Fine, I guess. What should I be deciding about?"

"Just the comfort in your hand, how the grip feels, how well you think you can hold onto it when you stab or slice. Here, compare it to this one."

"The first knife felt solid, my grip on it secure. I felt I could easily lose hold of the second one."

"Good, let's get that one and a sheath for it as well. You will also need a belt so you can always carry it with you. You should feel undressed unless you have it on your person."

We stopped to eat a meal at a busy restaurant where the sign was in Arabic. Only Arabic was spoken inside. As soon as we sat down a basket full of bread was placed on the table with a container of olive oil and another with sweet vinegar. The waiter explained the bread was called daily bread, baked in a wood oven, and could be found in any bakery on the island. It was crusty, full of large holes inside, soft, and slightly salty. It turned sweet in my mouth.

After a discussion with the waiter, we ordered culurgionis. He explained it was a pasta filled with potato, mint, garlic, and cheese served with a plain sauce of ripe, fresh tomatoes. The owner came to our table to question where we were from and to complement our ability to speak grammatically correct Arabic. He recommended a main course of dogfish cooked in white wine vinegar with walnuts. He said it was the most typical dish of Cagliari.

We wandered the city until late afternoon then found our way to the inn. Abraham and Stephanopulus were already occupying a table on the patio. They waved us over. On their table was a large platter, somewhat picked over, that still held dry sausage, pancetta, ham, and at least eight different kinds of aged and semi-aged pecorino cheeses. There was also the ubiquitous basket of bread. As soon as we sat down, a waiter appeared with wine glasses for us and poured red wine from a clay jug.

I raised my glass. "What are we drinking?"

Abraham took a sip of the wine from his glass. "This is called Nuragus. It is a very local wine, not enough of it made to export. I find it dry and light-bodied, with a hint of acidity."

Stephanopulus took a sip. "Abraham says he tastes citrus and plums, but when Abraham talks about wine, he speaks with an overactive imagination. He considers himself a wine expert. I just decide if I like it or not. This one I like."

While in Cagliari, Judah continued my training. Morning and evening we ran up and down the hills outside the town. Each day Judah increased our distance and speed. He introduced me to a new array of calisthenics. Unfortunately, we did not abandon the push-ups or jumping jacks, the new torture he demonstrated by jumping up, spreading his legs to the side and his arms over his head then jumping again and returning arms and legs to their original position. I was still tired to the point of exhaustion after each session but recovered more quickly each day.

"You are making good progress, Yusuf." Judah said. "Probably because, unlike me, you are still relatively young."

I looked at him, surprised. He was tall and muscular, very fit, a fine physical specimen. I had never considered his age or asked about it. I thought he was no more than five years older than my thirty-five. "You don't have any gray hair."

"Not yet, but it won't be long. I will be forty-eight soon. Tomorrow we will run a longer distance. If you keep up with me and complete your push-up goal, it will be time to start teaching you how to defend yourself."

"Finally," I said.

We left Cagliari in the evening of the seventh day, starting a three-day journey to Panormus on the island of Sicily. The next morning Judah and I were on the deck early. After half an hour of running in place and another half hour of calisthenics, I finally reached the twenty-five push-ups Judah had set as a goal before I could begin training lessons on self-defense. I was elated.

"There, that's twenty-five." I was upright, fully extended resting on my hands and toes.

"Let's see you do one more," said Judah.

I let myself down and struggled to complete one more, but managed it.

Judah nodded. "Good, now we begin the serious training." He demonstrated five different methods of countering a knife thrust to my chest. Demitri and Galen glanced repeatedly over their shoulders as they fussed with the sail. Judah corrected my mistakes. I was determined to show the crew I could do this, irritated that they were amused. Stephanopulus stood with arms carefully folded, watching Judah easily block my initial feeble attempts at stabbing. Finally, Judah grabbed the piece of wood we were using as a fake knife, stabbed at me several times and corrected my responses. This was repeated many times for each different type of blocking maneuver until I was able to do each one correctly.

Each day while sailing we had little else to do so Judah intensified my instruction. I was gradually teaching my muscles how and when to respond. We repeated each skill over and over, faster and faster.

After watching us silently for three days Stephanopulus finally spoke. "You have a good teacher there, Yusuf," he said. "Judah, I would like you to teach me that counter of a knife thrust to the groin. I think that might prove handy."

"Of course, my pleasure."

After Stephanopulus joined the class, I had another person to spar with. One skill we practiced relentlessly was taking a fall to avoid injury.

Judah taught us that rolling with the punch or blow was an important skill which we had to practice. I had bruises from falling to match the bruises from being hit.

While I fussed over my training injuries, Abraham, our history tutor, continued our education as we sailed toward the harbor of Panormus, now renamed Balarm by the emir of the emirate of Sicily.

"As the Roman Empire evaporated, the island of Sicily was occupied by the Vandals under the rule of their king, Gerseric. After occupying North Africa, they acquired Corsica, Sardinia, and Sicily. It wasn't long until they lost all their territories to the Ostrogoths under Theodoric the Great. That happened in 488. Next, the Byzantines defeated the Ostrogoths under General Belisarius and Byzantine rule was solidified by Justinian I. The Arabs took control in 904 and Balarm, I still think of the place as Panormus, replaced Syracuse as the capital of the island. The Arabs introduced a wide variety of agricultural crops to the island and those products now form an important part of the cuisine."

"What will you trade for in Sicily?" I asked.

"I have barrels of wheat flour, coal and crates of iron bars. All these items are in great demand. They don't grow sufficient wheat to meet their demand. I will purchase the Sicilian anchovies preserved in olive oil and almonds. These are both in great demand elsewhere."

"Will   we   be   here   long?"
"No, I should be able to conduct all my business in a couple of days, then we'll be off again. I assume you are becoming anxious to complete your mission."

"Yes, but I need to check in with the Hebrew community here and make certain they are all doing well. Judah and I were here a few years ago and helped them resolve some issues they were having with the government."

I was happy to find the rabbi and his congregation were all doing well. Judah and I were invited to a dinner at the home of Joshua ben Israel and were able to catch up with the friends we made on our previous visit. They reinforced my thinking that showing they were capable of resistance reduced the attacks on the community, if not the prejudice.

Abraham was true to his word. Judah and I only had two mornings and evenings to run the hills of Sicily. Fortunately, although I was becoming more proficient at defense, we had no occasion to test my skills.

Once we returned to sea, Judah told me it was time to start perfecting offensive moves.

"Finally," I sighed.

Three days later we arrived at the port city of Chandax on the island of Crete. I was weary of four hours of exercise and two hours of combat training daily, but my endurance and ability to control my body and reaction times had measurably improved.

I already knew a significant amount about the history of Crete. After Abd-ar Rhahman III defeated the forces of Ibn Hafsun, that rebel, and a large group of his followers, fled to North Africa where they joined forces with several fundamentalist Islamic tribes to conquer Crete. For several years the Byzantine Empire tried to dislodge them but were unsuccessful. The Muslims established their stronghold and capital on the northern coast of the island and named that place Chandax. The Muslim control of Crete was problematic for Byzantium because it threatened their control of the Aegean Sea, allowing raids by Muslim fleets. Just last year the Byzantine general, Theoktistos, made a serious attempt to reclaim Crete from Muslim control but was unsuccessful in conquering the entire island. He returned to Constantinople and the outposts he left were soon reconquered, the soldiers killed or captured as slaves.

Abraham said he had purchased a large variety of spices in Andalusia, especially saffron. All were in high demand and would be sold in Crete. The local merchants would resell them at a good profit to traders from all over the Aegean. He also still had iron, silver, copper, and tin to sell. He told us these goods would be sold only for coin because most of the merchandise for sale on Crete was commonly traded throughout the Aegean region. There was not much profit to be made from the products of Crete.

We were only in Chandax only to replenish our fresh water in case we were delayed by storms. We stayed on board *Fair Winds* finding nothing of great interest in the town. Abraham was not able to sell any of his goods for coin, so we were done. The sail from Chandax to Smyrna took just under three days. Smyrna has been in existence for many centuries, but I didn't find much to interest me about it. The city is located at the head of a gulf, well sheltered from the storms of the Aegean. Judah's and my overriding interest were to get on to Constantinople and find our way to empire of the Khazars, we were tired of the slow pace and many stops, but I realized the purpose of this voyage was for Abraham and Stephanopulus to make a profit. We were just passengers they had agreed to take along.

Abraham conducted all his business in Smyrna in one long day. We caught the tide out that night and wound our way through the many islands to the Dardanelles and into the Sea of Marmara.

Five days later, we tied up to the wharf in Constantinople, the capital of Byzantium. Abraham supervised the unloading of our baggage and arranged for a coach to take us to the Cordoban embassy. We thanked Abraham and Stephanopulus for all they had done for us and said goodbye to the crew. There were hugs and backslapping all around and admonitions from both Abraham and Stephanopulus to find them if we needed help with anything more.

A short time later we were ushered into the office of the ambassador. The room was functional, neither overly large, nor opulent. I doubted the ambassador needed to impress visitors who wanted something from our caliphate. He welcomed us, anxious for news from Cordoba. I gave him the letter Hasdai had entrusted me to deliver to him

He read both, slowly, then looked up. "I have already made preliminary contacts for everything Effendi Shaprut requires of me. The building next door has excellent apartments. I have arranged one of them for you and staffed it with a cook and a servant. You will have full use of it while you are here. I will do my best to secure an audience with Emperor Constantine VII Prophyrogennetos as soon as possible, but I think I can arrange for you to meet with the foreign minister tomorrow or the next day."

"Have you found someone to take us to Khazar?" I asked.

"No. Unfortunately, there seem to be wars and skirmishing along all the routes to the Khazars. It may be possible for you to get there by boat but finding someone willing to make that trip will be difficult. When you meet with the foreign minister, perhaps he will be able to provide more information."

Two days later we were shown into the elaborate offices of the foreign minister of the Byzantine empire. All three walls of the office were covered with detailed tapestries depicting hunting scenes. On the other wall was a large map of the territories controlled by the Byzantines. The minister's desk was gigantic, elaborately carved in dark mahogany. There were four chairs for visitors but, although he was seated, he made no indication that we should sit, so we stood. My mouth was dry. I grasped my hands behind my back. Judah seemed unperturbed. On the way to this audience, I had tried to remember how Hasdai handled this sort of situation. I had decided to be brave, direct, confident.

"Your Eminence, I am the physician Yusuf ben Ezia ibn Nasir, and my companion is Judah ben Shlomo. Here is a letter from our benefactor, Effendi ibn Shaprut, a senior diplomat for the caliphate of Cordoba. The letter describes our mission and asks for your help getting us to the empire of the Khazars. We also bear gifts and a letter from Effendi Shaprut addressed to your emperor."

"Yes, your ambassador told me you were on the way. I have been expecting your arrival, Physician. I will ask the prime minister to receive you within the next few days. He will accept your gifts for the emperor and will transmit the correspondence. How else may I be of assistance?"

"Our desire is to reach the capital of the Khazar empire as quickly as possible. We have gifts for their king and a very important correspondence from Effendi Shaprut. We will greatly appreciate any aid or information you can provide so we can complete our mission."

"The news I have for you is not good. The land route which goes north along the western shores of the Black Sea is closed. Various tribes along the way, especially in the region of the Donau River, are fighting for control of disputed territories. It will be extremely dangerous for you to take that route from here to our port of Chersoneses. That port is also under almost constant attack by pirates. There is also a long time, ongoing war for control of trade amongst the towns of Chersoneses, Kersh and Samkarsh. That is the most current information I have. Perhaps you can learn more about the situation by talking to people who deal with the traders coming from the Khazars. I can give you the names of only two of our merchants who trade with the Khazars, but I will do my best to identify others. Perhaps there are traders from there who are in our city now, if so, I will try to find them for you."

He stood, pushing his chair back, then walked to stand in front of the map. He used an inlaid pointer to show us the three port cities and the sea route to Chersoneses.

"Thank you, Excellency, any help you can provide will be greatly appreciated," I said.

A week passed with no message from the foreign minister. Judah and I continued to run twice daily, learning the city. We also sparred a minimum of two hours each day, perfecting my fighting skills. During our sparring sessions, we were using wood swords Judah had made for the purpose. I deflected Judah's thrust aimed at my chest and touched his neck with my sword.

"You are starting to push me, Yusuf. I will have to work harder so you don't continue to best me."

Thirty minutes later I was bent over at the waist, panting. I looked up at him, standing quietly, breathing normally and shook my head. "When you are as out of breath as me after a session, I will start to believe you."

We had found the two traders the ambassador had told us about, but they hadn't had any interaction with traders from Khazar for the past three months. We asked for help finding Abraham's home, but the ambassador could only provide directions to the Hebrew ghetto. After finding and gaining access, we asked a young student coming out of a yeshiva for help. He led us to a street with larger houses hidden behind tall stone walls. We followed him into a large courtyard full of fruit trees and flowering bushes. The young man opened the front door of the house and called out for his father. Abraham appeared in the doorway within a minute.

"I did not expect to see you so soon, but this is a pleasant surprise. Come in, come in. Follow me to my study and we'll talk. The young man who brought you here is, in fact, my eldest son, Yacob."

We told him of what had transpired since our arrival three weeks earlier. "Yes, I wondered if you might discover all the routes to the Khazars, for all practical purposes, closed. But, enough of your problems. Let us talk about possibilities. More importantly you must stay for Shabat dinner. My wife always makes extra. Please join us. All are welcome at our table on Shabat."

We spent the evening praying and eating with Abraham's family and agreed to attend Shabat services with him the following day.

After dinner, Abraham pushed away from the table and motioned for us to follow him into the adjoining room. The floor was covered with a large, multicolored, oriental rug. Large cushions were scattered about. Abraham plopped himself down on one and indicated with a wave of his hand that we should join him. "As you well know, I am not very devout when travelling, but Rachel insists I behave myself and become a practicing Hebrew when at home. It's not very onerous. I believe the teachings of our rabbis and the precepts of our religion are helpful as a guide for correct and honorable living. That is important for our two sons and daughter to learn. Do you agree?"

Judah, always stingy with words, remained silent.

I decided it was necessary for me to assert some sort of role in this discussion. "Yes," I said. "I agree. Morality is the basis of our religion and an important aspect, maybe the most important, to living an honorable life."

Abraham changed the subject. "I must tell you both that anyone leaving the ghetto after dark is in some danger. I hope you will accept our hospitality and spend the night with us. Even though, after watching you two train on the ship, I know you can take care of yourselves, there is no need to tempt fate by risking injury."

I looked at Judah. He shrugged.

"We can defend ourselves," I smiled, "but thank you, Abraham. We will stay and take advantage of your hospitality. It will save us getting up before dawn so we can attend services as we promised."

CHAPTER FOURTEEN

· ·

The next morning, Abraham took us aside. "I have spoken with some of the other traders this morning. Perhaps I can help you get to where you want to go. I found some merchants who have had dealings with the Khazar traders. If you wish, I can introduce you to them, but not on Shabat.

"It would be helpful, Abraham. Maybe essential. Judah and I have begun to feel as though the Byzantines don't really want to help us reach our destination."

"That's possible. They have their own agenda for almost everything. I will talk to the men I mentioned and find out when and where they are willing to meet with you. Perhaps they will put you in touch with the Khazar traders. I will let you know what I learn. It may take some time, but perhaps they can be of assistance."

A week passed, then another. Abraham visited us twice during that time, but he reported that all trade with the Khazars seemed to be at a standstill. To make matters worse, we were experiencing an unusually stormy period and travel on the Black Sea was problematic even without the pirate activity. Because of the bad weather and the threat of being stopped by ships from one or more of the three feuding cities no traders from Khazar had appeared in Constantinople for the past three months.

Another month of frustration passed. Judah and I haunted the seaport trying to find anyone with a ship who would agree to take us to the

Khazars, without success. Another frustrating week passed, and we received a message that the prime minister would meet with us the following day. We arrived at the palace at the indicated time but were told to wait. The prime minister would see us after he had completed some urgent business. After at least an hour, one of the prime minister's clerks motioned for us to follow him.

Our footsteps on the terrazzo floor of the long hallway echoed off the marble-clad walls. We passed several closed doors before arriving at the end of the hallway where the door to a large anteroom was open. We followed the clerk to the opposite side of the room where he knocked on a heavy oak door. A voice called out from behind the door. The clerk opened it and motioned for us to enter.

A stout man was seated behind a huge desk. He was swaddled in heavy robes and a wool scarf, despite the roaring fire in the fireplace behind him. He motioned us forward and pointed to two chairs opposite him.

"Come in and sit," he croaked. His voice was raspy, his eyes red and watery. His face had a very unhealthy pallor, and there were beads of sweat running down his face from his forehead. I had to lean forward to hear what he said.

"You are the emissaries from Cordoba, yes?"

"The gifts Effendi Shaprut sent for the emperor are in that chest." I pointed to the large, locked and sealed, ornately carved chest on Judah's shoulder.

I reached into the pocket inside my best robe extracting a key and the letter Hasdai had sent for the emperor.

"This is the key for the chest, and this is correspondence for the emperor."

"Just put everything on that empty corner of the desk," rasped the Prime Minister, deliberately taking a slow, painful breath, between each spoken sentence. "I will make certain the emperor receives everything and he will, . . . no doubt, have a response for you to take with you on your return to the caliphate. . . . . My understanding is that Ibn Shaprut sent you to travel to their capital city, Atil, of the kingdom of the Khazars to meet with their king."

"Yes, that is our mission, Excellency. We hope that you might be able to expedite our journey."

"That will be . . ." He produced chest-rattling, non-productive coughing that lasted several minutes, while holding up a hand to halt conversation, "difficult. "The unusual weather has halted all travel on the Black Sea. . . . I assume you have been informed of the dangers of the land route." He coughed again. . . . "I am afraid you may be stuck here for some time."

Another coughing spell ensued, this one lasting longer than the previous one.

His coughing spell suspended. He wiped his nose and mouth with a cloth taken from his sleeve then stared into my eyes. "I understand Ibn Shaprut is a renowned physician and is the personal physician of the caliph."

"That is correct, Excellency."

"And you were his student?"

"Yes."

"You follow his precepts and teachings?"

"Absolutely. If you wish I would be happy to examine you and prescribed appropriate treatment Your Excellency."

"Do you think you can cure me?"

I glanced at Judah and he gave me a be careful of what you promise look. I nodded as my heart rate increased. Then I relaxed feeling I was on solid ground and confident in my medical training and knowledge. "I would have to do a thorough examination and some tests to arrive at a diagnosis. The effectiveness of any treatments I might prescribe would depend upon the correctness of my diagnosis and the progression of the disease. What treatments have you received thus far?"

"All my physicians seem to know how to do is bleed me."

I raised my eyebrows marveling at the magnitude of medical ignorance. "How long have you had this cough?"

"Over three weeks, it hurts rather much when it takes over me."

"Were you ill before the cough developed?"

"Yes, I was nauseated, and my stools were very loose for several days before the coughing started."

"With your permission, Excellency?"

His pulse was fast and thready. His forehead was abnormally warm. I convinced him to allow me to put my ear to his bare back and chest, listening to the sounds of breathing and to his heart.

"You are more ill than you think, Excellency. Your lungs are very congested and are consolidating. That means you will have more and more difficulty breathing. If you don't follow my instructions exactly, there is a very good chance you will die within the week. Even with my treatments it might be too late. The bleedings must stop, they have weakened your system. You must return to your home and stay in bed. Complete rest is essential. You must drink as much fresh fruit juice and water as you can. I will prepare several different medications to be taken as teas and in broths. Any kind of broth, chicken, beef, veal, duck, whatever your cooks can devise, but the broth must be strong. Do not try to walk to your home. You must be carried in a litter. No walking at all."

The prime minister looked stricken. "I have an apartment here in the palace. I will send a messenger to the emperor and inform him of my situation. I will do as you say."

"Good. I will go and prepare the medicines then return here. Will you have someone here who can take me to your apartment?"

Now he appeared to be frightened. "Of course, how long will you be?"

"Not long. I have most of what I need in my medicine chest. As your treatment proceeds, I may have to find some ingredients in your local markets. However, the most important aspect of your treatment is bed rest. The medicines I give you will help control your coughing, lower your fever, and make it possible for you to sleep."

I returned to the palace less than an hour later that same afternoon and was escorted directly to the prime minister's apartment. My patient was in bed, still coughing. I dosed him with royal honey to sooth his throat. I ordered that a container of burning coals be brought with an open basin of boiling water. I added some eucalyptus leaves to the boiling water, had the prime minister sit on the edge of his bed with a large towel engulfing his head and the basin, and instructed him to inhale the steam. While he was thus engaged, I made a tea using willow twigs for his fever.

When the steam treatment was completed, he looked at me and smiled. "My chest is much less painful, and I can breathe easier."

"Good, that's why I wanted you to do it. Unfortunately, the effects don't last long, and you will have to repeat it often. I will leave a supply of the eucalyptus leaves so you can repeat the treatment as often as you feel it is necessary. No harm can come from it." I gave him some of the tea along with a healthy dose of Therica explaining that what I was giving him was the long-lost formula Hasdai ibn Shaprut had rediscovered, and that it was effective for many different types of illness. Whenever he tried to talk, I waved for him to be quiet.

"Talking will only stimulate coughing, Your Excellency. You must try to avoid talking."

Before I left, I administered a dose of the poppy extract, hoping he would sleep through the night. I then turned to the servant who was hovering nearby. "Watch him closely. Do not allow him to get out of bed for any reason, including to urinate or defecate."

The servant looked puzzled.

"You don't know the words urinate or defecate?"

He shook his head no.

"Pee or shit."

He covered his embarrassed smile with his hand.

"Good. Now before I leave, I want you to go to the kitchens and find a shallow pan large enough for the Prime Minister to sit on while still in bed. That's how he must relieve himself. If his condition becomes worse, or he has other problems, send someone for me immediately. I will return early in the morning to check on him and continue his treatment."

The next morning the same servant reported that the Prime Minister slept soundly the entire night and had urinated—he smiled when using the word—but not defecated—another smile. He was apparently not as dense as I had first thought.

I listened again to my patient's heart and lungs. I thought the lungs might be slightly less congested. He was coughing again, but his fever was down. His heart rate was still quite rapid and his pulse the same as the day previous. I repeated all the treatments from the previous day and added a small dose of an extract made from the foxglove plant.

"This medication will slow your heart and make each heartbeat stronger," I explained. "I think you are slightly improved this morning, Your Excellency. However, you must remain in bed, rest, and drink as much fluid as you can. I will have some strong broth brought for your midday meal, but only fruit juice this morning. I understand from your servant that you have not vomited."

"No, I have not. How long do you think I will have to remain in bed?" He coughed again. "As you might imagine I have a great deal of responsibilities. I cannot abandon them."

This time his coughing was more severe. He grimaced and put a hand to his chest. His pain was reflected in his eyes. "Your Excellency, no talking!"

I turned to a hovering servant. "Please get someone from the prime minister's office to bring him a quill, ink and paper so he can write questions and orders."

Suddenly a disturbing thought occurred to me. *What if my treatments are unsuccessful and he dies in spite of my best efforts? I better talk to Judah about how we can leave this place in a hurry if we have to.*

I turned back to the bed. "We must try to prevent you from coughing. The only possible way for you to recover is complete bed rest, along with the medication to control your cough. I'm certain you must have trained many reliable assistants over the years. Let them assume some responsibility. If you don't do as I say and subsequently die, they will have to keep the business of the empire going anyway."

He listened to me and frowned but stayed silent. A short time later a clerk arrived with a hand full of sharpened quills, ink and paper, and a large board to put across his lap to write on. He waved the clerk over and took everything from him. Leaning over the board he scrawled a message.

"I suppose you are correct. How long?"

I stifled a smile. "I will know more in a few days. I will be able to better evaluate the efficacy of my treatments then."

He groaned as he smudged the ink while writing something more. Then started over and scratched out something and threw the quill down on the board.

I read the note aloud. "Yes, Your Excellency, it will have to do."

Fortunately, my patient made steady progress. After two days I suggested the cooks add some boiled rice to his broth. He continued drinking a lot of juices and his urine became more diluted, a good sign that his kidneys were functioning. The cough gradually became more productive. He was bringing up a lot of phlegm, another good sign. His heart rate was slower and his pulse stronger, because of the foxglove. His demeanor improved, probably due to the Therica.

On the fifth day I helped him out of the bed and steadied him while he took a few steps, but he tired quickly. He was, by then, able to talk without coughing.

"I feel very weak, Physician."

"It's to be expected, Your Excellency. You have been extremely ill and in bed for some time. It will take a while for you to regain strength. You must not overdo. If you suffer a relapse, it will be very bad. If you want, you can summon one or two of your assistants to attend you here, but they must not stay more than a quarter of an hour at a time. Save your voice and write your instructions to them. If you start coughing again, no more visitors. Your assistants must be aware of the constraints and must prepare succinct summaries for your disposition."

He smiled and waved me closer. I leaned into him as he whispered. "Physician, I will require that you stay here and organize my office for maximum efficiency. You obviously know what is needed."

This raised a significant problem. If I did as he requested, our mission would be delayed significantly. *Now, how do I handle this. Should I tell him that your mission must be our priority? No, for now I will hold my tongue, say nothing. Just nod.*

He leaned toward me, wrapped his fingers around my forearm and fixed me with a stare. "Get me back to work as soon as possible. I will make an extra effort to assist you."

"That would be much appreciated, Excellency."

He held up a finger. "After you return from the Khazars, perhaps you will agree to stay a while and organize my office, but more importantly, you should start a medical school to train young physicians in your methods. If you do that, I will make you a very rich man."

"When I return, we shall certainly discuss it, but you could also choose some of your brightest medical students and send them to study in our medical academy. Effendi Shaprut has resumed heading it after sending me on this mission. I'm certain, if they arrive with your endorsement, we will make them welcome."

"That is an excellent idea, but I still want you here, at least for a time."

"Thank you, Excellency. I am honored. Now, let's give you this next round of medications."

A week later the prime minister was back in his office. I did manage to convince him to only work half days for another week to make certain he didn't suffer a relapse. The day after his return to work, I declared him fit for service.

"Excellency, I think you have made a remarkable recovery. You should continue to take the medicine for your heart each day. I suspect you feel stronger now than you have for some time."

"That is correct, Yusuf. Do you mind if I use your name? I feel better now than I have for years."

"Please do use my name, I consider it an honor."

"I would like you to come with me now to meet Constantine, he asked me to bring you to him after your visit with me today."

"I don't know what to say. Perhaps I should go home and change into more suitable clothing first?"

"No need, the emperor dislikes people attempting to impress him in any way. Come along now."

We took a surprisingly short walk down two different corridors before entering the throne room. The emperor was in military uniform seated at a not very imposing desk. He looked up when we entered and stood.

"This is the physician?"

"Yes, Your Excellency, this is the physician Yusuf ben Ezia ibn Nasir," said the prime minister.

"Physician, you are a miracle. The small army of physicians that treated my prime minister previously all assured me he would not survive. I was already interviewing possible replacements. I understand you were apprenticed to our good friend Hasdai ibn Shaprut."

"Yes, Your Excellency."

"And all you know you learned from him?"

"From him and a multitude of medical textbooks he made me study."

"Admirable. I understand you and your companion have been tasked to deliver a letter to Joseph, King of the Khazars."

"Yes."

The emperor paused, collecting his thoughts, I presumed, then gave me a long, discerning look. "And you are experiencing difficulties obtaining passage because of the unseasonable bad weather and the irritating, and inconvenient, border wars taking place along the land route skirting the east coast of the Black Sea."

"That seems to be the case. Also, the fear of being intercepted by ships of the three feuding cities."

"Perhaps I have a solution, but it could be dangerous."

"I will be happy to consider any possible solution, Your Excellency."

"There is a man currently held in one of my prisons because he attacked two of my officers when they accused him of smuggling. My authorities have, apparently, been aware of this man's illegal activities but were not able to collect the necessary evidence to convict him. He is a dangerous rascal, but very clever. I suggest you visit him. If you decide he can be relied upon to help you arrive at your destination, I will release him to your custody."

"That is an interesting idea," I replied. "I will be happy to meet with him. Will I be allowed to bring my companion along? He is probably a better judge of character than me."

"That will not be a problem."

The next day Judah and I were admitted into the prison after showing a letter bearing the seal of the prime minister. We waited in the small office of the warden until two guards brought in a man in his mid-thirties, bound hand, and foot in chains. The guards pushed him roughly down on a chair. He was filthy dirty and smelled of feces and urine.

Judah and I had agreed beforehand that he would conduct the interview. We spent the previous evening deciding on the questions to be posed. I wanted to be able to observe the man's demeanor and body language more than his answers to the questions.

"What is your name and why are you here and in chains?" Judah asked, in Arabic.

"I am Hamza ibn Kafeel. I am here because two of the emperor's minions accused me unjustly and moved to confiscate my boat. During the inevitable argument and struggle I inflicted some minor damage to one of them with my knife. I assume I am in chains now because I did not allow other prisoners to dictate to me." He allowed himself a thin, brief smile. "I don't allow anyone to tell me what I can and can't do."

Judah looked at me. I gave a slight nod of my head. He turned back to the man in front of him. "Your name means strong and steadfast. Are you?" He asked.

"I can be," he replied.

This man could be the answer. He is very sure of himself. But can we trust him?

"My companion here, is a renowned physician. He and I are on a mission to deliver important correspondence to the king of the Khazars. We are told that you are an experienced smuggler and know the way to the Khazar capital."

"I have never been convicted of smuggling or anything criminal."

"Not the issue. Are you capable and willing to take us to the capital city of the Khazars, Atil?"

"Depends. My boat has been impounded by the authorities. I would need it back. What can I expect by way of compensation?"

"The most important compensation is that you will be released from this hell hole."

Hamza shrugged, clearly not impressed only by the offer of his release. I could sense that he was a skilled negotiator, looking for more than his freedom.

"We will also provide a significant compensation in gold coin," said Judah.

"That sounds interesting. How much is a significant compensation?"

I decided to enter the discussion. "What was the value of your last successful endeavor?"

Hamza smirked. "Almost a hundred gold dinars."

I motioned to Judah, and we huddled in a far corner of the room, whispering.

"Do you feel we can trust him?" I asked.

"He is obviously quite intelligent, but I don't know if I trust him to keep his word."

"Well, we don't have a host of options. Should we take a chance?"

"I am willing if you are," said Judah.

"I presume that a hundred gold dinars a greatly inflated number," I said, "but we will ignore the truth and pay you a hundred gold dinars, one fourth before we depart and the rest upon our safe return."

Hamza's expression turned to puzzlement and disbelief. "You can get me out of here and get my boat back?"

I smiled. "Yes, we can, plus we will pay all of the expenses incurred on the way to Atil and our return to Constantinople."

"Remarkable. I accept."

Judah spoke up. "You will be able to get us to Atil safely given the current situation?"

"Of course. My own safety as well as my compensation depend on me performing that successfully."

Neither of the two guards in the room with us had moved nor made any indication they understood the conversation. I don't think either of the guards understood Arabic or what had just transpired. I addressed the guard closest to me in conversational Latin.

"If you will be so kind, please ask the warden to join us. I have documents from the prime minister to secure the release of this prisoner into our custody."

"Yes, sir," he said and left the room.

Just a few moments later the warden arrived. The previous correspondence I had given him when we arrived contained information on why we were there. I reached into my robe and extracted a second official document also secured with the seal of the prime minister. The warden took it, broke the seal, and read it quickly.

The warden looked pleased. He held out the document I had just given him. "If you will also sign this document, you can have this troublemaker. I am happy to be rid of him."

I signed. Hamza's chains were removed, and he followed us out of the prison, into the sunlight and our waiting coach. We stopped at a market. I handed Hamza some copper coins and told him to purchase new clothing. Next, we stopped at a bath house where we availed ourselves of the opportunity to see Hamza scrubbed clean and the three of us enjoyed the relaxing warm mineral water pool. After the bath, we stopped at a restaurant where Hamza ate ravenously.

"I take it you weren't fed in the prison," I said.

"Not for the last four days." Hamza mumbled with his mouth full. "They were punishing me for defending myself."

Judah and I watched in amusement as the hungry man stuffed more and more food into his mouth.

"You best stop and rest," I said. "If you continue stuffing yourself, you will become very ill. I promise you will not go hungry while you are with us."

Hamza refused wine from the jug Judah, and I shared but did not refuse orange juice. All the dishes he ordered were vegetables.

"You are a devout Muslim?" I asked.

"Not as devout as my mother wished me to be."

"But you only eat halal."

"If possible."

"Neither Judah nor I are devout Hebrews, but we try to follow the dietary laws."

"Good. That will make life somewhat easier. Now, about my boat," said Hamza.

"Ah, yes, your boat." I patted my chest where another official document resided in the commodious pocket inside my robe. "I have the necessary papers to release it at the dock where she currently resides. Shall we go?"

Hamza was already on his feet. I read him another note telling where his boat was. His smile lit up his face.

"Yes, I know the place. I am anxious to make certain she is secure and safe."

We found the dock without difficulty, but access was blocked by a locked gate. Hamza started to climb over the gate, but Judah restrained him.

"Let's not cause more problems with the authorities," he said. "Be patient. We will take care of this."

In less than half an hour we located the guard with the key to the gate at a wine shop nearby. I showed him yet another document, also signed by the prime minister, authorizing the release of the boat. A short time later we untied the hawsers securing the boat to the dock and the three of us got on board.

Hamza took control. "Judah, will you take the tiller and guide the boat towards the open water? I will raise the sail."

"Do you need me to do something?" I asked.

"Just stay out of my way."

He raised the lanteen sail to half-mast and it caught the evening breeze, moving us away from the dock. He scrambled back to take the tiller from Judah.

I had learned from our experience on *Fair Winds* that owners of boats have a love affair with them. I knew Hamza would, no doubt, be as well. "Hamza, tell me all about this boat. I notice the name *Shabh* on the stern, why 'Ghost'?"

A huge smile engulfed his whole face. "She's a felucca, a type of boat favored and built by the Egyptians. She has a single, triangular, lanteen sail, as you see. She is twenty-seven cubits bow to stern and only four cubits midship. She is named Ghost because she is like a phantom, quickly sliding past anyone I don't want to see her, from land or sea. Most importantly, she is very fast, long and lean like a sight hound. With just the main sail, she will outrun almost all other craft, but I can also rig a jib. With two sails there is not a boat on these waters that can catch her. She has a deep keel and is very stable even in a strong blow. As you see, she has an open deck, no cabin, but I have a tarp I put up when the sun is too hot or for protection during a storm."

I interrupted his monologue about his boat. "I hope you are not planning to begin our trip now! We have preparations and obligations before we can depart."

"No, Effendi, I'm just going to drop anchor out in the harbor. We will take that small rowboat on the deck to go to shore. I must find Achmed, my mate. He will be in one of a half-dozen wine shops."

"We'll leave you to find your mate and get him sober. Judah will find you tomorrow and make certain you have all the water and supplies necessary for the trip. Also, you need to check *Shabh* for any needed repairs to her hull or rigging. I noticed a small tear in the sail, that needs to be repaired. If the sail is too old and fragile, we can purchase a new one. Better to be detained here while she is made whole than to be stuck in the middle of the Black Sea trying to make temporary repairs."

"As you say, Effendi. I will expect Judah tomorrow and we will make a meticulous inspection of *Shabh*," responded Hamza.

The next evening Judah returned to our apartment after spending the afternoon with Hamza. He told me *Shabh* needed a new sail and new rigging. There was also a leak near the rudder that needed to be repaired. Hamza had assured him that once the necessary repairs were completed, the boat would be ready to sail.

"How long?"

"He said if we were willing to pay top price the new sail could be made in a week. He and Achmed would take care of the other repairs. I agreed that we would cover the cost of materials."

"Good. Then we have a week to get ready."

"I suggest we visit some sword makers and find you a sword. We can also find a leather worker to affix a scabbard for it inside your travel cloak, like mine."

"All right. Maybe if we find a suitable sword in the next day or two you can start teaching me how to handle it. I assume it will be heavier and more difficult to maneuver than our wood practice swords."

Ever taciturn Judah didn't bother to respond.

The following day we visited five different armories looking for just the right sword. It had to fit my hand, feel correctly balanced, keep a sharp edge, be correctly forged and tempered, and short enough for me to conceal. At the last armory we visited, we found a sword meeting all those requirements. It felt good in my hand, so I made the purchase. After examining Judah's vambrace, the blacksmith took measurements and said he would have one ready for me in two days. We asked the blacksmith about a leather worker who could make a scabbard like Judah's. He sent us to his brother-in-law who examined how Judah's was made and affixed to his cloak. He also examined Judah's vambrace and how it was attached.

"This is not a problem, leave the sword with me. Return in two days and I will affix the scabbard to your cloak. I will also have straps made for the forearm protector my brother-in-law is making for you. I have never seen this method of hiding a sword or a forearm protector like this. Very interesting."

Three days later we met with Hamza. *Shabh* was tied to a more distant, private dock. "There is a delay with the new sail, but the rope to replace all the rigging is ready. If you will come with me, you can pay the merchant for the rope. We will bring it back and get everything replaced."

I heard a pounding and looked up to see a man on top of the mast hacking with a knife at the knots securing the old rigging to the top of the mast.

"I presume that is Achmed."

"Yes," Hamza answered, "it took only a day and a half for him to sober up enough to be able to work, but he is fit enough now. He knows *Shabh* almost as well as I do."

We had been in Constantinople too long. It was mid-August, *Shabh* was fully repaired and loaded with supplies and our baggage. The previous week our morning and evening runs were each followed by an hour of intense sparring. Judah taught me the mechanics of using my new sword and arm protector for both offense and defense. I was still clumsy with the sword, but more adept, because of my previous hand-to-hand training, with the knife, and my new vambrace.

Throughout my training Judah constantly harangued me about the importance of going forward as a means of defense. "If you step forward when your opponent is attacking, it puts a question in his mind. Then you need only to step aside to avoid his weapon while using his forward momentum to throw him off balance. Your defense becomes offense. Let's try it again."

"The tide will go out three hours after sunset tonight," said Hamza, "We should depart then."

Judah clapped me on the back. I grabbed his arm and squeezed. "Finally," I shouted, raising my arms.

CHAPTER FIFTEEN

W e sailed steadily northeast. I don't know if we were going any faster in *Shabh* than when we sailed *in Fair Winds* but, because we were much closer to the water and *Shabh's* design was longer and sleeker, it seemed much faster. Judah and I volunteered to make necessary sail adjustments according to Hamza's or Achmed's directions. Hamza and Achmed split four-hour watches on the tiller. I wondered aloud if all ships had a four-hour sandglass. Judah shrugged, disinterested.

That first day Judah and I continued our twice daily calisthenics and sparring with sword, knife, and bare hands.

Achmed evidenced no interest in our antics, but Hamza watched closely when we sparred. "Effendi Yusuf, I see Judah could take you at any time, with or without a weapon, but you are not unskilled. I thought I was pretty handy with a knife but watching you two I'm happy to be on your side in a fight."

I flashed him a grin. "From the report we had about you from the prime minister, that sounds like a compliment. It is my fervent hope never to put these skills to the test."

"If we have to defend ourselves, you will be ready," assured Judah.

"It is more likely to be when than if," said Hamza.

The second day mirrored the first, with steady, continuous progress in my fighting skills. On the third day Achmed pointed out a craft with two sails east of us. Both sails were full of wind.

"They are on the same tack as we are," said Hamza. "We will watch to see if they try to come closer."

They did not but fell behind quickly still sailing parallel to our course. I accepted Hamza's claim that we could probably outrun another ship on that sea.

Hamza was at the tiller a week later when dawn broke. Judah made some adjustments to the sail; the wind was strong from the southeast. We stretched prior to starting our routine of calisthenics.

Hamza interrupted our stretching. "Late this afternoon, if this wind continues, we will approach Chersoneus. We should take on fresh water and, perhaps, some vegetables and fruit."

"Is it safe to stop there?" asked Judah.

"The Byzantines believe Chersoneus, and in fact the entire peninsula, is under their control. That is an illusion the native inhabitants are happy to allow. They are interested to trade with both the Khazars and the Byzantines and profit from both. However, there is a lawless element that resists paying import and export duties to either."

"Therefore, a lot of smugglers," I observed.

Hamza smiled. "I know most of them. Some I occasionally partner with. Some of the others I distrust, and the rest I do my best to avoid at any cost."

"If we stop there, can we be assured that neither you nor Achmed will say anything to anyone about our mission?" I asked.

"We know nothing, is that correct Achmed?"

Achmed put both hands out from his sides, palms showing, and shrugged.

"What do you think Judah?"

"I think we should stop, fill our water barrels, get some fresh food and bread, and depart as soon as possible."

"Is that agreeable to you, Hamza?"

"Certainly."

A couple of hours before sunset we entered the small harbor of Chersoneus and tied up to the wharf.

"Hamza and I will go ashore," said Judah. "We'll arrange for barrels of fresh water to exchange for our empty ones. Once that is taken care of, we'll shop for the food we need. Are you comfortable to stay with Achmed and *Shabh*?"

I felt a vague uneasiness but couldn't describe why. "Yes, just get done as quickly as possible."

"I share those feelings. Probably because it is so quiet and seems deserted. We'll be back as soon as possible," said Judah.

Hamza and Judah were gone less than a quarter of an hour when three determined, rough looking men strode purposefully down the wharf.

They were only a short distance away when the scruffiest looking of the three spoke in Latin. "This is *Shabh*. Where is Hamza?"

My skin prickled. His tone of voice was ominous. I could sense these three had bad intentions. I wondered if they were among the men Hamza did his best to avoid. I decided to answer the question. "He and my partner are acquiring some fresh provisions. They will return quite soon."

"Well, we have business to discuss with Hamza. We'll come aboard and wait for him."

"I think not," I said. "I would prefer that you stayed where you are to wait for his return."

"That's not very hospitable. Do you think you can prevent us coming on board?"

His tone of voice raised the hairs on the back of my neck. I reached inside my cloak and held the grip of my sword, regretting that I had neglected go strap on my vambrace after Judah and Hamza departed. "I suppose if all three of you want to force the issue you will manage it, but at least one of you will be seriously injured, maybe even two of you. If I am injured or killed my partner is a very skilled warrior. He will most certainly seek revenge."

The three huddled together in animated discussion. Achmed appeared at my left shoulder grasping a belaying pin in his right hand, his fingers blanched from the strength of his grip.

"Thank you, Achmed," I whispered in Arabic.

He answered. "I don't like the odds, but Hamza would not allow any of those three to foul *Shabh's* deck."

"You know them?"

He nodded. "Hamza has never associated with them, that I know of, but he pointed them out to me one time in a wine shop. He said they were to be avoided, if possible."

The three all took a step towards us. The one I thought the most dangerous of the three, the same who spoke previously, sneered. "So, Achmed, you are willing to risk injury?"

Achmed remained silent.

"Oh, I forgot, you don't understand Latin, do you? Perhaps your friend will interpret." The same man was doing all the talking.

I put my left hand on the handle of my knife.

The three huddled together again. Then, as if they had practiced the coordinated move, all three drew knives. The spokesperson took a large step forward and the other two followed his lead. All three were no more than two cubits from the edge of the wharf but spread out with about three cubits between each other. *Shabh's* deck was at least a cubit below the wharf. The boat was gently bobbing with the waves. I drew my sword with my right hand, my knife with my left. Achmed and I stood with legs apart, balancing easily with the movement of *Shabh*.

I remembered Judah's often repeated instruction. "The most important aspect of any fight is moving your feet," he had said, "making certain you are always balanced, and your body is in position to move in any direction necessary."

We had spent many hours practicing how and when to put my feet in the proper position.

"The time to attack is immediately when they jump to the deck," I whispered again in Arabic. "They will be off balance."

Achmed nodded his understanding.

I decided to try once more to attempt to avoid the confrontation. "I don't know why you insist on boarding *Shabh,* but I'm certain Hamza will be returning within the hour. What is your objection to waiting for him on the wharf?"

"That is for us to know and no business of yours. Do you even know how to use that sword? You look uncomfortable," said the leader.

My heart rate doubled as the output from my adrenal glands reached it. "Set foot on this deck and your question will be answered," I replied, trying to make my voice menacing.

"Now!" shouted the ringleader, and all three jumped to the deck.

I took a quick step forward. My sword connected with the wrist of the man closest to me, the one who had done all the talking. Blood spurted and his knife fell to the deck. I spun to the side and took a half-step toward the man on my left. As Judah had predicted, he hesitated, not expecting me to move toward him. I slashed at him, but he managed to avoid it. In my peripheral vision I caught a quick image of Achmed bringing the belaying pin down hard on the head of the third man. The man whose wrist I had slashed, jumped back onto the wharf, whimpering, blood leaking between the fingers of his left hand. The third man bent at the waist; his feet were spread too wide as he jabbed in my direction with his knife.

I smiled. "Do you really want to try to fight a man with a sword with that puny looking knife?"

He lunged at me. I moved my feet and jabbed him in the right shoulder with my sword. His knife clattered to the deck. I took two quick short steps moving in close to him and held my knife to his throat. "Now, I suggest you lift your unconscious friend there to the wharf and follow him up."

As he was pushed onto the wharf the unconscious man roused, moaned, and tried, unsuccessfully, to get to his knees.

Achmed collected the three knives from the deck. "Should I keep these?" he asked.

"If you have use for them, why not?" I replied.

He tossed all three into the water.

The man Achmed had knocked unconscious struggled to get to his to his hands and knees, shaking. The first casualty sat on the wharf whimpering, bright red blood dripping from between his fingers.

"I am a physician," I said. "You best apply a very tight bandage to that man's wrist, or he is likely to bleed to death. His artery has been severed."

The man who had been unconscious managed to stand upright, still wobbly. He tore off a portion of the bleeding man's shirt and bound the wound, helping the man to his feet. The third man, clutching his injured shoulder, supported their leader on the other side. The three shuffled slowly toward the town.

I turned to Achmed. "Are you injured?"

He shook his head. "I came quite close to pissing my pants."

We laughed. I grabbed his hand and shook it.

"I did as well," I admitted.

"I wish I had something more than water to drink."

"I would join you if we did," I said.

The sound of wheels rolling on the wood planks of the wharf interrupted us. I looked up to see a man coming towards us. A mule pulling a cart filled with water barrels followed him. Achmed opened the hatch then rigged a system of pullies from a boom he lashed in place over the open hatch. He went down into the hold and secured each of the three empty water barrels with rope. Next, he attached each empty barrel to the rope from the pullies. I hoisted the empty barrels up to the deck. While we were thus engaged, the water vendor maneuvered three full barrels to the back end of the cart. He jumped down, released the back gate of the cart, and lowered the top edge to the wharf as a slide. He slid each of the barrels to the wharf then rolled them to the edge of the wharf just above *Shaba's* deck. Achmed and I helped lower them to the deck. From there we rolled each of them to the hatch then lowered each, in turn, into the hold.

I confirmed that he had been paid in advance. We helped him load the empty barrels and watched as he led his mule back toward the town.

A short time later I spotted Judah and Hamza coming toward us, each carrying two baskets. When they came even with Shabh they put the baskets down and applauded.

"We passed three injured men as we approached the wharf. They didn't have anything nice to say about you two," said Judah.

"They wouldn't tell me what they wanted," said Hamza leaping to the deck and reaching out his hands for one of the baskets, "but they appeared no longer interested in whatever it was. No loss, I'm certain. They claimed you two attacked them on the wharf. Obviously, a lie." He set the basket about a cubit away from the dried blood on the deck. "Judah, either you are a successful teacher, or your pupil has been hiding his real skills from you."

Judah managed a quick smile. "I never thought being proud of a student would feel so rewarding."

As the sun set, we glided out of the harbor and Hamza set our course. "I will take us out to the south to avoid any boats coming or going to Chersoneus, Samkarsh, or Kersh. People from those two cities have had an ongoing dispute for a generation and it frequently flares into violence on the water that separates them. After we are well out, we'll turn east. We'll pass the Straight of Kerch far enough out to avoid any problems, then come to Samkarsh harbor from the south."

On our third day of sailing the sun was directly overhead. Achmed pointed at the Caucasus Mountain range a long distance east of us. Rugged peaks reached to the sky.

Hamza recited their names. "The tallest is Elbrus, next is Dykh-Tau, then Shkhara, Koshtan-Tau and Janaga. They are much further away than they appear. They will be a useful landmark for us after we leave *Shaba* and cross the steppe from Samkarsh to Atil. We will keep them in sight to the southeast while we travel east and slightly north."

Each day Judah made notes of landmarks relative to our position on the water and explained how he was using that information to make maps. He told us he would do the same as we travelled the steppe to Atil.

On the evening of the fifth day after leaving Chersoneus we anchored in Samkarsh harbor and rowed to shore, leaving Achmed to guard *Shabh*. Hamza suggested we wait to dock the morning of our second day in Samkarsh then unload. "We will spend the day procuring riding and pack horses. I suggest you purchase rather than rent them. When we return you will be able to sell them, perhaps even at a profit."

"How long will it take to get to Atil?" I asked.

"Again, it depends on the weather and if we encounter any problems along the way. The distance is only about seventeen parasangs, but two full days of travel, unless you want to push on all night. We will have to rest the horses at some point."

"No need to exhaust ourselves, or the animals," I said. "Is there a road, with inns along the way?"

"There is no road, more of a track. There are no inns that I am aware of. Despite their conversion and supposed assimilation, the Khazar people are still a host of many different Turkish tribes, all of whom are devoted to their use of horses. They rarely use carts or wagons, preferring pack animals. We will have to purchase food, a pot or two to cook in, and maybe a tent, if you don't want to sleep under the stars. This time of year, rain is rare, but you never can count on that."

We set out to purchase horses. Judah negotiated for the animals and the necessary saddles, packs, bridles, halters, and hobbles. He carefully examined at least two dozen different animals, looking at their teeth to age them, their hooves to make certain they were in good shape, and palpating their lower legs for any swelling. After that he carefully observed them front and rear and from the side while I led each in a walk and a trot to rule out any lameness. After more than three hours of this, he selected three riding horses and three packhorses. Then he haggled with the horse trader for another hour before settling on a price for all six and the tack. I paid the agreed price in gold dinars.

The horses were not the stately, smooth coated, long-legged, elegant Andalusian/Arabian horses we were accustomed to. These were descendants of native Przewaski ponies cross-bred with the Akhal-Teke from Turkmenistan or the Buryat or Altai breeds to obtain larger animals. The resulting animals were still small, only about twelve to thirteen hands at the withers. All had thick, shaggy coats, even in the summer. I would find out the following day that they covered the ground in a bone jarring trot, their normal gait.

"Why don't they don't have shoes?" I asked the trader.

"These horses have been selectively bred for centuries for their thick hooves. Their hooves are tough, resistant to injury. There is no need for horseshoes. They also can survive on whatever grass they find. You don't need to feed them grain. In winter they can uncover snow a cubit deep with those strong hooves. They always find something to eat."

We left the horses with the trader and found a market to purchase our supplies for the trip. We found an inn near the harbor and after a satisfying meal had a full night of uninterrupted sleep. The next morning, Hamza made the necessary arrangements to dock, then, we took our horses to the dock, loaded the pack animals with our supplies, luggage, and the two ornate chests containing Hasdai's gifts for King Joseph.

When we were ready, Hamza grabbed Achmed by the arm. "Achmed, we will anchor *Shabh* in the harbor. Then you will row me back. I want you to stay on *Shabh*. Only come to shore when you need something. Yusuf will give you some coins for your expenses. Don't spend it on wine. If you value our friendship, do not allow any damage to *Shabh*. Understood?" "I will take good care of her. How long do you think it will be before you return?"

I answered. "The king may not be in his capital. If not, we will have to wait for his return or try to find him. There could be a long delay before we can obtain an audience with him. Once we meet with him and present Hasdai's gifts and letter, we will have to wait for an answer, if he chooses to answer. Once that is done, we will return here as soon as possible. I hope no longer than a month, less if all goes well."

After Hamza returned, Judah mounted his horse holding the halter rope of one of the pack horses. Hamza and I followed his example and mounted our riding horses. Our small caravan left the wharf, Hamza in the lead. We wound our way out of the city, soon emerging onto the steppe, the mountains in the far distance on our right, to the south.

Once on the steppe, our horses broke naturally into the jolting, ground-eating trot they were bred for. The grasslands spread out before us, the breeze making waves of the long grass, a sea of undulating hills. There was a track going east but it was wide, not marked in any way. Apparently, travelers just spread out while going in a general direction. The monotony of the undulating sea of grass and the hot sun beating down on us quickly induced drowsiness.

We stopped for a mid-day meal before continuing across the seeming endless expanse of tall grass. I caught myself falling asleep and started to fall out of my saddle, despite the uncomfortable gait of the horse.

Hamza stopped his horse until I came up next to him. "By this evening we will arrive at a nice stream, it's a good place to camp. Unless you want to press on through the night. How do you feel? These horses can keep up this gait for a long time, they are bred to do so. In a day they can easily cover twelve parasangs. If we camp overnight, we will still be in Atil tomorrow afternoon."

We reached the top of a larger than average hill, then rode down into a small canyon. There were trees along the stream at the bottom, but we didn't see them from the steppe, only when we reached the top of the hill. I saw a group of men camped on the far side of the stream. They were on a level area about four or five cubits above the gently flowing, almost soundless, water.

"There is another level spot on this side of the stream, maybe three hundred cubits downstream of that camp," said Hamza. "Should we set up camp there or continue until we reach Atil?"

"I am quite tired of bouncing on this horse and my rear end is sore. I need to stop, apply some balm to my chaffing, and get some rest," I said.

"I think we should talk to that group of men first," said Judah. "Find out who they are and why they are here before we become neighbors. Do you recognize any of them, Hamza?"

"No."

We rode across the stream and stopped our horses. I counted five men and a dozen horses. Packs were scattered around their camp and two fires were blazing. They were all reclining, resting with their backs supported by packs. I assumed they were waiting for the fires to reduce to coals before using them to cook.

Judah greeted the men in Hebrew. One of them responded in kind but it was obvious his command of the language was rudimentary. Judah switched to Arabic. Not one of the men seemed to understand him.

I addressed them in Latin and smiles of understanding appeared.

"We are on our way to Atil to learn more about the Khazars," I told them, and waited for them to tell us why they were on the steppe. Nothing.

"Have you been travelling long?" I asked.

A large man stood up while the others remained on the ground. I assumed he was the leader of the group. He responded to my question. "We came from Sarkel on the Don River. The people from there trade with the Rus. We acquire furs from them."

"Ah," I said, "where is Sarkel in relation to Atil? Is Sarkel part of the Khazar empire?"

The standing man folded his arms over his chest. "Yes, it is north and west of Atil."

As we were talking, one of the other men got up and sauntered over to one of our pack animals. He lifted a corner of the tarp covering one of the gift chests. Judah pushed his horse between the man and the pack horse but said nothing. The man backed away. All the men were watching Judah.

The man I had been talking to faced me again. "Sorry, my companion has an insatiable curiosity, my apologies."

"Yes, I understand curiosity. If you have no objection we will camp further down on the other side of the stream. Perhaps we can visit after the evening meal," I said.

He smiled and nodded, then waved an arm to include all the men in his party. "Yes, perhaps, but we have travelled far today and are tired, we might just go to sleep early."

We recrossed the creek and found the place Hamza had described. We took the packs and saddles off our horses, hobbled them, and turned them loose to graze. Judah thought they wouldn't wander far from the water. There was plenty of grass for them to graze on close by.

"Did you notice all five of them were heavily armed?" Judah asked.

"Yes, but so are we," I answered. "I expect it's common to travel this country with the means to protect oneself."

"The Don river does not originate from the Rus territory," said Hamza. "Maybe the Rus come to that town to trade their furs, but they would have to do so by land. Their story sounds very contrived to me. Most of the Rus traders I've met come down the Volga. Atil is where the Khazars can make it difficult for any trader from the north to go further downstream. In this way they control the trade with the Byzantines and the Muslims. Most of those northern traders just sell or trade with the Khazars then return to where they came from. I don't trust those men; they are a rough and dangerous looking bunch."

"I agree we should be on guard," said Judah. "One of us should stay awake and watch for anything untoward. Two-hour watches?"

Hamza and I agreed.

"I will take the first watch, Hamza the second. Judah will take over after Hamza. Is that agreeable?" I asked.

We talked for a while after eating the stew Judah prepared. We ate directly from the pot, dipping bread in for the soup and using our spoons to fish out meat and vegetables. After the meal we talked for a short time, then Hamza and Judah were asleep within minutes after wrapping themselves in blankets. I sat by our fire, my sword in my hand, listening intently. I judged time by the position of the moon in the clear, starlit night, as Stephanopulus had taught us to do. The stars were so bright that, with the light from the moon, it would have been possible to read. After two hours, I woke Hamza and squirmed to find some comfort on the ground in my blankets.

"Who comes?" shouted Hamza.

I was awake and on my feet in an instant, sword in hand. I felt Judah next to me.

Five men materialized from the dark and spread out to encircle us.

"We just want to find out what is in those well-crafted chests you carry," said the same man with whom I had spoken earlier.

"And you expect to learn that by simply asking?" Judah replied.

"If we have to come through you to find out, we will."

"Stand back-to-back," Judah whispered. "Wait for them to make the first move."

The five slowly circled us. All held swords in their right hand, two also had knives in their left hand. Hamza had his knife in his right hand. Judah and I had not removed our vambraces after eating. I was glad I was fully prepared to fight this time. Our swords were drawn, our knives in our left hand. Two men lunged at Judah. He took a step forward and deflected the downward slashing sword of the man to his left with his vambrace, then stabbed the man in the abdomen jerking out his sword before the man fell. He swiftly side-stepped the stabbing sword of the other man and slashed the wrist of the hand holding the sword. The other three men were dumbstruck by the swiftness of Judah's attack. Hamza seized the advantage, stabbing the man closest to him in the neck while that unworthy stood with his mouth open trying to understand what had happened to his two companions.

Judah faced the remaining two men still standing. "Now the odds have changed. Do you want to continue this?"

The two fled into the darkness of the trees, two of the wounded followed, while stumbling and groaning. The man with the throat wound sat on the ground, his feet out straight. He was struggling to breathe while choking on his own blood.

"Hold him still, Judah. I will see if there is anything I can do for him. I am disappointed though. You didn't give me the opportunity to strike a blow."

"Maybe next time," Judah said.

Hamza's knife had nicked the man's left jugular vein, but the wound was not deep enough to reach the carotid artery. I applied pressure with the hem of his own cloak.

"Will you bring my medical kit please, Judah?"

I applied the poultice I use to stop bleeding and bandaged the wound. "If you go for treatment in Samkarsh for this, you will have a terrible looking scar, but you should recover."

I helped the man to his feet. "Let's help this one back to his camp and see if the other two wounded can be helped."

"Thank you," the wounded man mumbled.

"Why do you do this?" asked Hamza. "These men would have killed us without hesitation a few moments ago."

"I am sworn to help anyone who can benefit from my knowledge and skill," I answered.

"It's just the way he was trained," said Judah. "Come help me with this one and we'll see about the others."

As soon as we came to their camp the two uninjured men disappeared into the night. The one with the abdominal wound was on his back, close to the fire, holding both hands over his wound and groaning. The other one sat on the opposite side of the fire, rocking back and forth, grasping his right wrist with his left hand.

"Let me see your wrist," I told him, pulling away his hand. The wrist was bleeding, but it was not bright red arterial blood. "You are lucky. I can stop this bleeding, but I doubt you will ever regain full use of that hand. Some tendons have been cut."

I applied a compress and bandaged the wrist. "Now I need to check on your companion."

The abdominal wound was the most serious of the three. I cut away the man's blood-soaked clothing. The wound was deep and dark blood flowed freely from it. His pulse was already very fast and weak, and his mucous membranes were colorless. He looked at me for a moment, pleading silently, then his eyes rolled up towards his forehead.

"The liver is punctured. He is in deep shock and will bleed out soon. There is nothing I can do for him. I will put a splint on the one with the wrist wound, then we can leave these bandits to their devices. I suspect they don't have enough morality to even bury the one that will soon be dead. I doubt the two faint hearts will even help their comrades. When I finish treating the arm wound, let's return to our camp and pack up. It will soon be daylight."

I nudged the now lifeless form of the man with the toe of my boot. There was still blood oozing from his abdomen. I felt for a pulse. There was none.

We returned to our camp. I was surprised, but all three of us were hungry, so we ate bread and cheese. We retrieved our horses, packed up and rode to the bandits' camp. It was empty, except for the unburied body. We dug a shallow grave. Judah and I recited the Kaddish, then we filled in the grave.

Hamza helped with the burial but refused to offer the Muslim prayer for the dead. "If he was Muslim, he didn't lead a Muslim life. I don't think he deserved a Muslim burial. Let's move on."

Now I have to reconcile why I was so anxious to participate in this fight despite my oath and obligation to do no harm. Why is it possible for me to assume these two, very different personas? When we return to Cordoba I need to speak, at length, with Hasdai on this subject.

CHAPTER SIXTEEN

bout two parasangs from the city the topography changed from steppe to irrigated, well-cultivated, fields, vineyards, and orchards. All comprehensible shades of green dominated the landscape. The people we rode past were well-dressed in sturdy work clothes. They answered our waves of greeting with waves of their own, smiles on everyone's faces. We entered Atil in the mid-afternoon, passing well-tended fields, farmhouses, and barns. Closer to the fortress visible in the distance, the houses were grouped closer to each other.

We finally approached the large fortress that filled a small island between the two rivers. "I thought the city was on the Volga. Are there two rivers?" I asked.

Hamza explained. "The Volga river splits into two branches many parasangs upstream. The eastern branch splits again south of the city and further south there are many divisions of both branches that spread out into the delta emptying into the Caspian Sea."

We rode slowly up to a huge military garrison situated on our side of the river. I dismounted and approached the two sentries at the gate. "We are envoys from the caliphate of Cordoba. Will you direct us to the palace of King Joseph?" I asked in Hebrew.

"The king and his senior ministers are not in the capital now, but his administrative center is in that large fortress on the island," one of the guards, answered pointing east. "There you will find many assistant ministers able to help you."

I thanked him and remounted. After riding about half a parasang I noticed that the bridge over the river seemed to be moving with the flow of the water. "Is that bridge moving? It seems to be floating on the water," I said.

Hamza dismounted and walked over to study the bridge. "This wasn't here the last time I passed here, several years ago. That bridge must have been washed away in a flood. This one is held up by boats. They seem to be anchored firmly to the river bottom. The chains holding them appear to be long enough to account for the spring floods as well as when the water flow is low," he announced.

"So, the bridge floats downstream when the water level is low and moves back upstream when the water level is high," I said.

"Ingenious," said Hamza. "I wonder how it is anchored to the shore to allow that much movement."

He examined the bridge's attachment to the shoreline and scratched his head. "I don't understand this. Before we leave here, I will find someone who worked on this bridge and get him to explain how it was accomplished."

Our horses refused to step onto the bridge. until we reassured them, dismounting and leading them across.

The center island was completely occupied by the limestone and fired brick fortress and the king's palace. A series of ramparts and towers reaching to the sky lined all sides of the divided river. The towers, laced with slender ports from which arrows or crossbow bolts could be launched, provided absolute control of boat traffic in either direction. The divided, swift flowing river prevented any direct attack on the ramparts.

"It seems clear they mean to control all river traffic," I said.

"No doubt," Judah replied.

I had another question. "I wonder how far downstream before the river reaches the delta?"

"Another fact to discover," said Hamza.

As we came off the bridge, we stopped in front of a deep entryway not visible from the road or the bridge. Four sentries in battle armor, holding spears, stood in front of a massive, closed gate. A small door, low enough to require anyone going through it to bend over, was set into the gate. Each sentry also held a round, convex shield, and wore a sheathed sword. They all snapped to attention when they saw us.

One of them, whose armor and weapons were of higher quality, stepped towards us. "Do you have business in the fortress?"

I gave him my name and those of Judah and Hamza, showed him the credentials Hasdai had given me, then explained our mission. The same guard knocked three times on the door then unlocked the small gate. "Please go through one a time."

I turned to Hamza. "Will you stay with the horses, please?" I was secure in the knowledge that he would get as much useful information from the sentries as possible.

I went through first and found two more guards, one on either side of the door, both with swords in hand, ready to remove the head of anyone coming through the door without proper authorization. I presumed the three knocks announced we were not enemies. Judah came through after me. I looked around the empty brick courtyard. The buildings surrounding the courtyard all had slits for archers. The outside sentry called out and another guard came running from what I presumed was a barracks in the building directly opposite the gate. The guard who had escorted us through told the new man where to take us.

The empty courtyard and strict security seem ominous. Why are such measures necessary? Could it be King Joseph feels threatened? If so, why? Maybe the situation here is not as stable as we imagined.

"Does this lack of activity in the palace seem strange to you? I asked Judah in Latin.

He answered with a nod.

Our footsteps echoed as we followed our guide into the largest of the buildings, located on the right-hand side. He stopped at a closed door and knocked. A voice from within called out in Hebrew for us to enter. The sign on the door of his office identified him as the prime minister's administrative assistant. The young man who was sitting behind a desk in the office got to his feet.

I extended Hasdai's document, but he didn't take it. "I am Yusuf ben Ezia, and this is Judah ben Shlomo. We were sent by Hasdai ibn Shaprut, the physician, diplomat, and customs officer to the caliph of Cordoba. Our mission is to bring salutations and gifts for King Joseph from the caliph."

"Welcome, welcome he was effusive, and his smile lit the room. I am Itzhak ben Yusuf. Of course, we are aware of the importance of Cordoba and your caliph. You are very welcome here. I must explain, however, that every year our king and his senior ministers travel to their estates to supervise the planting and cultivation of their fields, orchards, vineyards, and gardens, and the welfare of their many animals. After that, they travel east to the Aran river, conferring with all the tribal chiefs of the region. From there, they make a big circle of our northern, eastern and southern boundary regions prior to returning here in the fall."

"How long before they return?" I asked.

"Always late in the month of Elul, before the month of Kishrei, in time to celebrate Rosh Hashana here in Atil."

"We have been travelling a long time. We left Cordoba the first of Siven and have lost track of the calendar," I explained. "What is today's date?"

"Today is the fifteenth of Elul. I expect the king and his ministers back here within the next week to ten days."

"That is welcome news," I said. "Can you recommend a suitable inn where we can stay until King Joseph's return?"

"I will make arrangements at the finest inn of the eastern city, our commercial center. It is also where the palace of the queen, her maids, her attendants, and all their young children reside. In that section of our city there are many inns, shops, and baths. Did you come here from Samkarsh? That is the western portion of our capital city."

"Yes, we did, and crossed the floating bridge. We had never seen anything like that, nor had our horses. They were very apprehensive.

"I expect they were. Our horses become accustomed to it with, experience."

"Yes. We were wondering about why the security is so robust here in the palace?" I said.

He nodded his head. "I agree, it seems excessive to me as well, but the king ordered it so before he left, and so it is maintained. We are, in fact, at war with the Rus to the north and have sent an army, under the command of our most able officers north, to deal with them."

"What is the war about, what brought it on?" I asked.

"The Rus want to gain easy access to the Caspian Sea. King Joseph is intent on not allowing that to happen. We gain considerable income by taxing the goods they want to sell to our southern natives."

"So, it's all about money," said Joseph.

The administrative assistant nodded. "What isn't in the long run? I will send someone with you to show you the way to the inn of my father. I assure you it is the finest in the city. I'm certain the prime minister will cover the cost of your stay. I will send a note to my father to inform him you are on the way."

"We have six horses to take care of," interrupted Judah.

"That will not be a problem. My father will arrange to stable them with a reliable person. They will be well cared for and kept close to the inn so you can check on their welfare."

"Thank you, Itzhak ben Yusuf. You have been most helpful," I said.

"It is my great pleasure, Yusuf ben Ezia." He was writing the note to his father while standing and continuing to talk to us. "If you need anything while you are with us, please allow me to assist you. As soon as the prime minister returns, I will inform him you are here and wish an audience with the king."

He finished the note, called out for a junior clerk, and sent him on his way with the note. Then he called another young man into the office.

"This man will guide you to the inn of my father," he explained.

Our guide held on to my stirrup as we moved past the fortress. He was full of questions about Cordoba and the caliphate. I admired his enthusiasm and interest in our culture but soon wearied of his non-stop questions.

"How far down river does the Volga divide into the delta?" I asked our guide, mostly to interrupt his questions

He was overjoyed to provide the information. "The branch we will cross next divides no more than a half parasang downstream, then the water spreads into many channels not far after that before emptying into the sea."

We crossed the slightly narrower branch of the river on a bridge of familiar Roman design. We encountered more and more people as we entered the eastern city. Our guide knew many of them by name and was quick to explain who we were and where we were from.

The bridge into the commercial portion of the city spanned the slightly narrower branch of the river. It also was a familiar Roman design.

Our host, a man in his mid-fifties, short, well-built, with graying hair and beard, was standing in the doorway smiling. He welcomed us with great enthusiasm. He had already made arrangements for our horses. Two of his servants quickly unloaded our pack animals and carried everything to our rooms. One of them led all six horses away to a stable. The innkeeper assured us they would be nearby.

"I will follow and make certain the horses will be well cared for," said Judah.

"After you are settled in your rooms, I presume you will want to bathe," said the innkeeper. "One of the finest baths in the city is only four houses down the street." He indicated the direction with a wave of his arm.

The innkeeper was courteous, gracious, and welcoming. He explained that his wife did all the cooking and was well known for her skills. If we wanted anything special for a meal all we had to do was tell him, with enough advanced warning so he could obtain what was needed, and she would prepare it. I could understand why Itzhak ben Yusuf was proud of his family's inn.

While we waited for the king to return Judah and I established a regular routine of exercise and sparring. We found interesting places to run outside the city. For entertainment, we walked the streets of the neighborhoods on both sides of the river. We discovered many houses of worship, Hebrew synagogues, Muslim mosques, Christian churches and even a cathedral. One house of worship we could not identify with a sect. Back at the inn we asked our host about it, describing where it was located.

"Oh yes, that one is for those who believe in shamans. There are also some other pagan religions practiced in the kingdom and even here in the capital."

"Really," I mused, as Judah and I sat down on chairs in the courtyard of the inn. "So, all religions are tolerated."

"Yes, as long as they don't preach against the order of things."

"Ah, I see. What is the order of things?"

"Our government follows the teachings of the Torah, with a bit of liberal interpretation. We don't stone people to death for example. But there are some who believe the words should be taken literally. There are always those that complain about taxes or the need for almost constant wars to maintain our borders."

"What many of the people have converted and follow Hebrew teachings and how many practice it because their ancestors converted?"

"I don't know the answer to that, but I suspect a bit more than half of the total population say they are Hebrews although many do not practice it faithfully."

"Interesting. What about the judicial system? Do all follow the rulings of the Talmudic scholars and rabbis?"

"Ah, that is distributed," replied our host. "Here in Atil there are seven judges to settle all disputes. Two are rabbis, two are imams, two are priests, and one is Shamanist."

"Very ecumenical," I said. "So, petitioners follow the teachings of their respective religions. What happens when the petitioners are of different religions.?"

"Then a judge from each hears the arguments. Any decision they cannot agree on is referred to the king to settle. He first demands that a mediator be consulted. He believes solutions should found by common consent. Criminal cases are handled by judges from the religion of the accused. In severe cases where the state is the injured party, the king presides."

"And how does this work? Do you think it is fair, well-accepted by the citizens?"

The innkeeper took a chair opposite us. He sat thinking for some time before speaking. "I think most are happy with it, except maybe those who are ruled against."

During the following eight days Judah, Hamza, and I sought out people on the street, or guests in the inn, to ask their answers to the long list of questions Hasdai prepared for us. Hamza was particularly effective questioning the Muslim men he met at the largest mosque in the city where he made it his habit to attend daily prayers.

On the ninth day after our arrival, we received a summons from the prime minister. Judah and I went to the bath, put on our best robes, and arrived at the prime minister's office at the designated time. I carried one of the chests with Hasdai's gifts, Judah carried the other.

"Gentlemen, I have spoken with our king. He is very anxious to meet you and learn everything possible about your travels, your caliph and his caliphate."

"Thank you, prime minister. Here is Hasdai ibn Shaprut's letter that he ordered us to deliver. The chests contain his small gifts to the king."

He held up a hand, not taking the letter. "No, please, I prefer you give King Joseph the correspondence directly."

"As you wish."

For the next hour or so the prime minister questioned us closely about our voyages on the sea and our travails on land. I told him about the storm and the encounters that had required our fighting skills.

"I am most pleased you have prevailed despite the obstacles and are here with us safe and sound. I pray that your travels home will be more tranquil," he said.

Then the prime minister called for two of his assistants to carry the chests as he led us to the throne room. The prime minister whispered that we should hang back. He walked forward to hold a quiet conversation with the king. He turned and motioned me forward. Judah hung back while I approached the king and bowed.

"Your Majesty, I am the physician Yusuf ben Ezia ibn Nasir, former apprentice to Abu Yusuf Hasdai ben Ishaq ibn Shaprut, who is physician to our caliph, the head customs officer of the caliphate, and special confidant of our caliph, Abd-Ar-Rhaman III. My companion," I indicated Judah, "and I were sent to establish correspondence with the king of the Khazars. Here is a letter from ibn Shaprut addressed to Your Majesty."

I extended the letter that had required so many hours of debate, refinement and thought by Hasdai, Dunash, Menahem and, to some extent, me.

"Thank you, Yusuf ben Ezia," said King Joseph. "I am told your trip here was long and not without danger. I thank you and your comrades for your efforts. Please excuse me while I read what Hasdai ibn Shaprut has written and absorb its meaning."

It took him considerable time to read the long letter. Then he read it again. Twice he brought the prime minister close to him to point to a particular passage. The prime minister then consulted with two assistants. I assumed the consultations were about the meaning of a phrase or the definition of a word. While this was happening, I looked around the throne room. It was spartan, at best. The walls were bare of paintings or tapestries. The throne was not overly large nor was it covered in carvings.

Finally, the king pressed the letter to his chest. "This is a most interesting and thought-provoking letter from your world, Yusuf ben Ezia. Thank you again for journeying all this way to bring it to me. I will confer with my advisors. We will prepare a response for you to take back with you."

"That is our fervent hope, Your Majesty."

I pointed to the two chests on the floor between us. "These chests contain gifts sent by Hasdai ibn Shaprut."

The king clapped his hands together, the single clap reverberating in the room. "Oh, good. I am very fond of gifts!"

I unlocked each of the chests, opened their lids and took items out to show the king. I held up finely wrought drinking cups and serving plates, two in silver and two in gold. I handed him several pieces of elegant jewelry, some with precious stones. There were also items made of leather and ceramic as well as several containers of our most rare spices. Those containers I opened and held out for the king and his ministers to smell.

The king wore an ear-to-ear smile. "These are wonderful gifts, Yusuf. Do you mind if I address you thus?"

I was much relieved. The king seemed very open, warm, and welcoming. Perhaps this realm could become a safe haven for persecuted Hebrews.

"Where in the caliphate do all of these items originate, exactly?" Asked the king.

"Just a moment Your Majesty, I think there is a map of our caliphate with the locations of our rivers and cities in one of these chests." I rummaged through a chest and found it. "Yes, here it is." I handed the map to him. He spread it out on his knees. I did my best to explain where in the caliphate each item was produced, and the skill needed to produce it, turning a few times to check with Judah who nodded his agreement.

The king looked up from the map. "I can see some of those waiting to talk to me are beginning to fidget. Perhaps I should no longer ignore them."

"Of course, Your Majesty. I wonder if I could ask one question?"

"What is it?"

"The purpose of this visit is to ascertain if your empire would welcome persecuted Hebrews who could find their way here. Will your war with the Rus influence that?"

The king's face became very serious, he frowned. "You know of our war? That is interesting. We must have some loose lips. Who told you?"

"My colleagues and I have spent the time since our arrival talking to people and learning all we could about your kingdom. Several spoke of their sons who are with the army in the north. There was no indication " I thought it wise not to implicate our young man from the palace, or put his family in danger.

"I see."

Our audience with the king lasted for at least an hour and a half, during which time the throne room had filled with people intent on their pressing business with the monarch.

"Thank you for your time, Your Majesty. If you will send word when you have finished your response, we will return to collect it. I can say with certainty that my mentor is very anxious to read your responses to his questions."

He was now all business. "Yes, yes, of course. This will receive my attention as soon as possible. We will inform you when we have the response ready."

Judah and I returned to the inn and resumed our daily activities. We split up the rest of the long list of questions Hasdai wanted answers to and separately engaged the people we encountered with many questions about their lives and their attitudes about the government and the king. Very few had any complaints they were willing to share with foreigners.

We learned that the country was divided into many provinces, usually bounded by the historical borders of tribes, big or small. Each province elected a chief who handled day-to-day problems and reported to a member of the king's extended family who was responsible for that province. The prime minister, also a family member, oversaw all government activities and worked in close collaboration with the king.

The kingdom included mountain ranges, irrigated river valleys where crops were raised and huge areas of grass lands, the steppes. The role of king was passed from father to eldest surviving son. The prime minister gave us a map of the empire, showing its boundaries, distances in parasangs, and naming the adjoining kingdoms. The map also showed the trade routes from the east, a major source of customs income. His young administrative assistant, the same we first met was able to provide a listing of all the walled cities and open towns and located them for us on the map. While we were with him, I asked the young man about the leadership and size of the Khazar military.

"I am very sorry Yusuf," I had insisted on a first name basis, "I cannot provide that kind of information. You must understand that sort of thing is confidential."

"The knowledge about your military strength will allow Hebrews from the diaspora to immigrate with the confidence that they would be protected," I explained to no avail.

We learned there were many conquered tribes that had been assimilated and paid tribute each year to the king. Taxes were collected from all his subjects to support the government and military. There were property taxes, customs taxes, and taxes on the sale of all goods excepting food and medicine. The official language of the empire was Hebrew and almost all citizens spoke it to some degree. We learned that when engaged in a war the Sabbath was set aside for the army, so troops could move about and fight as necessary. His warriors fought primarily from horseback and were very adept using their short, compound bows, in the manner of all Turkish tribes. The administrative assistant also provided a history of the ruling family with the names of prior kings and how long they ruled.

"Until 852 the Slavs ruling from Kiev paid tribute to us with swords. That indicates they were defeated in our war with them, but they did not have to pay with furs and/or silver. That would have indicated a subservient position."

"So are they now your allies?" Judah finally spoke up.

Itzhak smiled. "When it serves their purpose."

A week later I received a summons from the prime minister. I was ushered into his office. He stood, picked up a document from his desk, and extended it to me. "Here is King Joseph's response to ibn Shaprut's letter.

He has considered all the questions and provided the most honest answers possible."

I took the document and secured it in the pocket inside my robe.

"Thank you, Your Majesty. We will arrange to depart tomorrow. I want to thank you for all you have done to help us and for your hospitality."

"I am happy to do so. I hope we will have another opportunity to meet you in the future. I'm afraid the distance separating our nations is so great that regular communication will be problematic. However, we are open to an exchange of representatives, perhaps even embassies. Perhaps that will be the subject of future correspondence and negotiation."

"I understand and I will most certainly convey the idea to Effendi Shaprut."

"Yes, thank you. Please do so." He stood and extended his hand. "Have a safe journey home and thank you again for undertaking this assignment."

"Thank you, Your Majesty, I believe we have accomplished what we were sent to do. We have discovered a strong and viable nation that is open to welcoming Hebrews who can immigrate here looking for a haven amongst their own people."

We decided not to stop during our return to Samkarsh. We pushed our horses at a steady pace along the track. After we arrived, Hamza went to the harbor to check on Achmed and *Shabh*. Judah and I found the horse trader who was happy to purchase back the animals and the tack for twenty percent less than we had paid him originally. Judah negotiated and settled for fifteen percent off the original price. I considered it inexpensive rental for the length of time we had kept them.

While we were still on our way to Samkarsh. Judah, and I discussed the possibility of making engaging Hamza, to take us all the way back to Cordoba.

"To do that we will have to renovate *Shabh* to deal with the rougher seas of the Mediterranean."

I told Hamza our plan and offered another hundred gold coins for his time and trouble.

"We will need to add a cabin so we can travel more comfortably. The open deck and tarp will not suffice for that long a voyage and rough seas," said Hamza. "We will also need to add ballast to sail the Mediterranean. The most skilled people to accomplish this will be in Constantinople."

"I was hoping you could find someone in Samkarsh," I said. "The prime minister of Byzantium wants to keep me in Constantinople to organize his office and train their physicians. That would delay my return for a considerable time. I do not want to do that. It is important I return to Cordoba and report what we have learned about the Khazars and how to get there. I was hoping we could just sail past Constantinople without stopping. I was given a letter by the prime minister of the Khazars. In that letter he asks anyone in the kingdom to provide us with whatever we may need. Maybe the letter will enable us to enlist the needed craftsmen in Samkarsh."

"Perhaps," said Hamza, "if there are people with the necessary skills to do it for us. We won't be able to bypass Constantinople completely, though. The customs people will want to board us to make certain we are not smuggling goods. They know *Shabh* and many of those men have tried to catch me smuggling in the past."

"We won't have anything on board except provisions for the trip," said Judah. "So, we shouldn't have anything to worry about."

Hamza shook his head. "They are perfectly capable of planting something on us just to get even with me for all the times I was able to outsmart them."

I decided to end the discussion. "Let's not worry about getting past them now. The first order of business is to renovate the boat so we can sail all the way back."

The prime minister's letter worked. Several shipbuilders were able to make the renovations we asked for, but the sailors and fishermen we talked to all agreed one of them was, by far, the most skilled. We found the man. After reading the letter he agreed to delay work on the boat he was then building. His price for adding the cabin to *Shabh* was, in my opinion, unreasonably inflated.

"Did you not understand what the prime minister asked in his letter?" I said. "Let me read it for you out loud." I read the paragraph where the prime minister suggested we be supplied with anything we need. "I am not asking you to provide materials and labor gratis. I will pay a reasonable price."

He grumbled, I negotiated. The negotiations dragged on for over an hour. He and I finally reached agreement when he told me he could arrange to bring stones for ballast and would secure them below the flooring of the hold for the price we had agreed upon.

The shipbuilder's property included a wharf next to his dry dock. We sailed *Shabh* and secured her to the wharf. Hamza found a modest inn nearby where we secured rooms and meals. The three of us spent the days assisting with the work to speed the process. To my surprise Hamza, amongst his many other attributes, possessed good carpentry skills.

After thoroughly inspecting *Shabh* and making measurements, our contractor agreed to cut through the deck forward of the stern. He designed a cabin and galley that dropped two and a half cubits below the deck, with two and a half cubits of storage space below the floor of the cabin. That storage space was accessible via a trap door in the floor of the cabin. The lower edges of the peaked roof were one and a half cubits above the level of the deck. The cabin was cramped but provided shelter and enabled us to prepare simple meals. The contractor also secured a small, coal-burning stove and installed it in the narrow galley. The cabin was outfitted with two hammocks and a low table. Several large cushions provided seating for the table and could be used as a bed, if needed. We would eat, sitting on the floor, from a single pot. As promised, the changes were finished in eight days of work with the intervening Shabat not defiled.

While we were still in Samkarsh, Hamza took the opportunity to talk to some captains who had experience sailing the Mediterranean. He learned that weather conditions in the fall months were quite unpredictable but winds in the Black Sea and into the Aegean were, predominantly, from the north which would be advantageous for our journey.

We purchased food that would keep; cheeses, grain, dried meats, dried fruits, and salted fish. We departed Samkarsh late in the afternoon of the tenth day after our arrival. Achmed set both the main sail and a jib. We again agreed that Hamza and I would share one four-hour shift while Achmed and Judah took the other. The wind was steady. Hamza agreed that *Shabh* seemed to power forward with more stability but without losing speed, despite the added weight of the modifications and ballast. We were soon in a regular schedule of sailing, resting, and eating. Sixty watch changes later, we entered the Bosporus Straight and a little over four hours later we were in sight of Constantinople.

As Hamza had predicted, the customs officers insisted upon boarding us. As they boarded, they pushed Hamza aside.

"Where are you going? what is your cargo? Don't I know your face?" one said to Hamza.

"I don't think you know him" I said. "We hired this man in Samkarsh to take us to Malaga, it is a port city in the caliphate of Cordoba. We are emissaries of the caliph of Cordoba and have been on a diplomatic mission to the Khazar empire."

"Is that so? Show me your credentials."

Fortunately, I had not discarded the credentials. I removed the sheath of papers from the inside pocket of my robe, sorted through them, and found what I was looking for. I handed it to the officer. Who read the document and handed it back to me.

"I remember now. This man is a known smuggler."

"I have never been convicted of anything illegal," said Hamza.

"That's because you are too sneaky."

While this was happening, the other agents were looking into every possible hiding place on the ship.

"We are carrying only our supplies for the trip," I said. If you destroy any of them while searching, I will lodge a formal complaint with your government."

The agent sneered. "I will not be intimidated. If you want, I will take you in, I am just doing my duty."

How much can I push. Should I tell him I have been of some service to the Prime Minister and will report him? If I do that the Prime Minister will detain me to start his medical school. I will have a most difficult time returning to Cordoba.

"If that is what you want to do, so be it. I think you will live to regret it."

He stared at me for what seemed like five minutes, but was, no doubt, less.

"Let the devil take you. Come on men, they have nothing to tax on this sorry excuse for a ship."

Achmed was told to watch them carefully to make certain no contraband was planted. I looked at him and he shook his head.

Hamza set our course and we entered the Sea of Marmara, passed through the Dardanelles and were then into the Aegean Sea. By then both Judah and I felt ourselves accomplished sailors, able to man the helm as well as set the sails properly and efficiently. We even mastered some ability to use the stars and the position of the sun to keep on course.

"On a clear day I will be able to navigate by the position of the sun and landmarks on the shoreline. In Samkarsh was able to purchase maps of landmarks on Crete and Sicily. Once we near the coast of Andalusia, I presume you will be able to identify where we are," said Hamza, but, but we need to find maps of the north Mediterranean coast.

"Once we get to Barcelona, I have a good idea of the topography from there to Malaga," said Judah.

The prevailing wind from the north, except when it died down about sunset, enabled us to sail with the Greek coastline to our west. Three and a half days and nights of sailing brought us within sight of the port of Athens. By then we had been at sea for over nine days. Our supply of fresh water and food was low.

We spent a full day in Athens replenishing our water barrels and acquiring some fresh food. The following day we rode the tide out and were on our way to Crete. Only a day and a half later we identified the headlands marking the harbor on Chandax where we anchored and rowed into town to purchase additional water barrels for the longer distances of our sea voyage ahead of us.

We were negotiating for the water barrels with a merchant, while standing on the wharf. Suddenly the sky darkened. Within a few minutes the wind came up and rain started to fall in torrents. We were soon soaked, water dripping from our cloaks, the wind shrieking in our ears. We ran, following the merchant to his warehouse.

"This storm looks as though it could last," observed Judah.

The barrel merchant nodded his assent. "This time of year, for storms from this direction, it could last several days. Sailing in this weather will be treacherous and quite dangerous."

"We would be wise to arrange accommodations in an inn and wait out this storm," I suggested.

Judah and Hamza agreed.

We went to the inn suggested by the barrel merchant and managed to secure two rooms.

"I will go and fetch Achmed," said Hamza. "We'll secure *Shabh* and wait this storm out." He ran out into the wind and rain.

The storm continued, mostly unabated, for five days. Chandax was no more interesting than on our previous visit. During that time Judah and I discovered a bookstore that had a large collection of maps of the Mediterranean coastlines. We purchased maps of the Greek coast, the Lombardian east and west coasts, Sicily, Genoa, southern France, and Andalusia.

Eventually the storm passed. We questioned every sailor and fishermen we could find. They seemed to agree that the good weather would hold for the next few days. We docked *Shabh*, loaded the additional water barrels, along with the ones we already had filled, then set sail northwest to intercept the Greek coast at or near the southernmost tip of the peninsula.

Half a day out of Chandax we were beset by another storm perhaps more intense than the one we had just waited out. Achmed, Judah and I struggled to furl the sails, barely managing to stay on our feet.

"Leave the jib at half-mast," shouted Hamza, but we couldn't hear him over the shrieking wind. I crawled back to him at the tiller and shouted that we couldn't hear what he said.

"You must leave the jib just below half-mast, otherwise I won't be able to aim her into the wind."

I nodded to tell him I understood and crawled back to tell Judah and Achmed.

Once the sails were furled, I retreated to the cabin. *Shabh* pitched and rolled and Hamza, fighting the tiller with all his strength, was having difficulty keeping her headed into the wind. Judah went to help Hamza with the tiller. I watched from the doorway to the cabin as Achmed tied a length rope around the waist of Judah and another to Hamza, securing the free ends to the top rail. He then fixed another rope around his waist and the end to the main mast.

"Achmed," I shouted, as loud as I could into the howling wind, "why don't you come into the cabin?"

He shook his head and held both arms out at his side, palms toward me. He couldn't hear me. Just then *Shabh,* riding the top of a huge wave, was twisted violently by an even stronger gust of wind. She lurched sideways and dipped down, water pouring washing over the deck. I was thrown into the cabin, my head hit the door, then the floor. Bright flashes of light swirled against my eyelids, and I groaned, for nobody to hear. I managed to roll over onto my stomach then raise myself up until I could stand. A wave of dizziness caused me to stumble forward two steps until I managed to balance. There was another crash as *Shabh* fell into a huge trough between waves and hit the bottom. I lost my balance again and fell into one of the bunks.

After what seemed like several hours of being tossed and battered the wind abated and we seemed to be making headway in a constant direction. I decided to leave the cabin to find out if everyone was safe. It was well after dark. The wispy clouds allowed just enough light to filter from the moon and stars so I could make my way towards the tiller. I found my three comrades laughing.

"You three seem to be safe and sound. Did *Shabh* sustain any damage?"

"Nothing serious. There is a tear in the jib but that's easily mended," said Hamza. "What happened to you. Hamza said he saw you fall, then manage to get up and fall again into your bunk."

"Yes, well I hit my head and have a nasty bump to show for it. I have a headache, but it will pass. Was that the worse storm you have ever been through?" I asked Hamza.

"Probably. I have no desire to go through anything worse. But this ship is amazing don't you think?"

"I thought we were going to get swamped, and all go down with her," I said. "I was certain we would all die."

Hamza was able to get us back on course but what should have been a day of easy sailing took the better part of two days before we were within sight of the port of Achaia at the bottom of the Greek peninsula. We continued to sail northwest until we sighted the heel of the long peninsula belonging to the Lombards. We skirted the heel to the south. A day and a half later were in the straight between Sicily and the Lombardian coast.

Ten days after leaving Crete, we were making good headway still sailing northwest while the Lombardian coast passed slowly on our starboard side. Hamza was at the tiller, and I had been making adjustments in the main sail. Judah and Achmed came out of the cabin.

"We left some food on the table for you," said Achmed.

I went to where Judah and Hamza we standing at the tiller.

"Just keep her on this same compass course," he instructed as Judah took the tiller, "but don't stray too close to the coastline, stay in deep water."

"Before you go to rest, Hamza, can we have a talk?" I asked.

He stopped and turned. "What about? You sound very serious."

Hasdai promised us handsome payment upon our return from this trip to the Khazars. He also told us we could keep any funds we did not expend during the trip. We had been reasonably frugal, and Judah and I have agreed on what to do with a portion of our new wealth.

"How does this sound, Hamza?" I asked. "Judah and I will have capital to invest at the end of this adventure. We propose a partnership. We will supply funds for you to purchase goods in Andalusia that you can trade in the port cities of North Africa. If necessary, we will supply more funds to purchase goods in North Africa that will find a good market in Andalusia. We would share equally in the profits from the enterprise."

"You would trust me to do this?"

I smiled. "We think you have proven your loyalty many times during this adventure. Yes, we trust you. We want to make you an honest man and hope for all three of us to become well off, if not wealthy.

"Even though you know I am a smuggler?"

"We offer you the opportunity to be an honest trader," said Judah. "Is that not something to aspire to?"

"What about necessary repairs and upkeep for *Shabh*?"

"We'll all share equally in those costs," I said.

"What if she goes down in a storm?"

"Ah," smiled Judah, "then you will, no doubt, be lost with her and won't have to worry about it."

"Can I think about this. It's something I have never considered."

"Of course, I said, "but you must make a decision by the time we reach Malaga."

We continued until we reached Corsica. We had no need to stop so circled the north side of that island and set our course toward the kingdom of the Franks. Once a major landmark of that country was identified, we turned west, staying well off the coastline but keeping it in sight during the day. At night we headed further offshore, to avoid shallows and rocks. We used our sounding line with its lead weight to make certain we stayed in deep water, a skill Judah and I learned early in our progression as sailors.

Several more days and nights of sailing brought us past the port of Perpignan in the northeast corner of independent Barcelona. Another two days, battling winds from the wrong direction and needing to tack back and forth to make headway, we spotted the port city of Barcelona but did not stop.

That evening Hamza told me he had discussed our offer with Achmed. "If you and Judah are still willing to form this partnership, we want to do it.

From Perpignan we sailed passed the port of Tarragona, belonging to those Islamic states not part of Cordoba. We continued sailing with the coastline to starboard, south past Murviedo, Valencia, Denia, and Alicante. Then the sea demonstrated in case we hadn't forgotten the dangers of this mode of transport. She wasn't done with us.

Achmed pointed to the north. "Look a waterspout, heading toward us."

We had seen them previously, but none had threatened us. Judah pounded on the door of the cabin. "Hamza, a waterspout is heading towards us, should we alter course and try to avoid it?"

"Wait, I'm coming," came from the cabin.

He grabbed the tiller from Achmed and turned sharply west, but the waterspout seemed to follow us, as though it was intent on capture. Hamza swerved to one side then the other, but our speed couldn't match that of the water tornado. Within minutes it was upon us. *Shabh* twisted violently making a full circle. We heard a huge ripping sound as the mainsail tore and the ship made another twisting revolution. We were all thrown to the deck, but Hamza retained one hand on the tiller. We were spit out, the ship came to a halt in the water, rocking from side to side with the waves.

"Bring the main sail down and raise the jib so I can gain control," ordered Hamza.

We did so and were on course again. Achmed, Judah and I sat on the deck sewing the mainsail back together. When done we raised it again then looked at Hamza.

"That will probably serve until we reach Malaga. It appears we will have to invest in a new sail before the partnership can even begin."

We continued, bypassing Cartagena and, turning west, past Alicante. We finally arrived at Malaga, where we anchored.

Hamza and Achmed stayed in Malaga while Judah and I rode to Cordoba.

On the ride back to Cordoba I had time to think.

Well, this has been an amazing adventure. It appears the Khazar empire might well be what we have been hoping. I wonder how Hasdai will react. What will he do to encourage migration of our people to a safe place? Perhaps he will offer to support Hamza and enlist him as transport of immigrants to the Khazars. That would be an interesting idea. Or, maybe purchase a larger ship for that purpose.

CHAPTER SEVENTEEN

We were anxious to get home. The year was 953 and we had been away for well over a year. We pushed on without stopping after acquiring horses and leaving Malaga, except for short breaks to rest the horses. We arrived at Hasdai's house at dusk of the second day. He peppered both me and Judah with questions.

"Tell me what you found out from this list of questions I gave you." He handed both of us copies of the list.

We took the list and went through each item, alternately telling him what we had gleaned from talking to people on the street and with officials. With each answer his face brightened, then he asked more questions. "Tell me more about the people who told you that. What is your impression of that person? Did both you and Judah agree on the conclusions made from the answers given? How did the citizens you talked to feel about an influx of Hebrews fleeing from persecution?" He didn't stop until my eyes could no longer remain open. The grey light of dawn filtered through the window of his office.

I was dozing, Judah was stretched out on the couch, sound asleep.

He looked up to see my eyes closed. "I'm sorry Yusuf, I see you are both exhausted. If you want, you can take one of the bedrooms upstairs and sleep.

"I will go home and sleep in my own bed. I have been looking forward to that luxury for weeks. However, I have a letter of response from King Joseph, don't you want to read it

"Yes, yes, of course. Let me have it."

I took the letter from the inside pocket of my robe where I had kept it safe for the entire journey home wrapped in a water-tight pouch to protect it. I handed it over.

"Do you know its contents?" asked Hasdai as he broke the seal.

"No, we did not dare to read it before it was in your hands."

"Well then, the three of us will read it at the same time."

I reached over and touched Judah's arm. He immediately came awake and sat up. Hasdai spread the letter out on his desk, smoothing it with both hands. Judah and I crowded in to read over his shoulders.

"Most esteemed Hasdai ibn Shaprut.

I wish to tell you that your most revered letter was safely delivered to me by your disciple Yusuf ben Ezai ibn Nasir and his companion Judah ben Shlomo. We were overcome with happiness by receiving it and impressed by the learning and wisdom apparent in its composition. We were most pleased to find your description of the lands of your caliphate, its length and width, and the rise to power of your caliph, Abd-Ar-Rhaman. We were particularly pleased by your description of your caliph's universal respect and adoration by his people and how, with God's guidance, he conquered his enemies and secured unto himself an empire that encompasses all of Andalusia, and how his fame spreads all over the known world and all kings fear and respect his power.

He went on to inform Hasdai that the Khazar empire was real, how it came to embrace the Hebrew religion, and how it enabled his ancestors to defeat their enemies. He assured Hasdai that he would welcome an ambassador from Cordoba and would happily exchange ambassadors. Then he emphasized that there is a kingdom of Hebrews, and it prospers. All Hebrews should know this and be proud.

We are delighted you are so wise and will answer each of your questions as truthfully and completely as possible. We are happy that you wrote, in detail, about your lands, your caliph, and his family. Our ancestors have corresponded by letters with rabbis in Israel and elsewhere. There are records of this in our archives and the elders of our community speak of it.

"You asked of what people, families, and tribes we came from. The genealogical books of our ancestors say we descended from Japhet, through his son Togarma. Togarma had ten sons named: Agijoe, Tirus, Ouvar, Ugin, Bisal, Zarna, Kuzar, Sanar, Balgad and Savir. We all descend from Kuzar. Our history books tell us that Kuzar, and his decedents, were few but our God honored them with fortitude and the power to overcome their enemies that included many powerful nations. They expelled all their enemies from our lands and even pursued them across the Danube River.

"Concerning the questions about the extent of our kingdom. Our capital is Atil and sits on the banks of the Volga River not far from where it empties into the Caspian Sea. We extend to the east a journey of four months."

I spoke up. "He is speaking of a very leisurely journey with full retinue, travelling only during daylight hours and stopping frequently to confer with the leaders of the tribes in the part of the country he is travelling through. The traders and administrators we spoke with confirmed that their eastern boundary is no more than one hundred and seventy parasangs from Atil. We easily covered thirty-five parasangs in ten hours on horseback."

"Yes, I understand," said Hasdai, and we continued reading.

"All along the Volga River there are many populous tribes: as well as villages, towns, and some fortified cities. All pay tribute to our government. South of my kingdom are fifteen large tribes. Their lands extend as far south to Bab al Abwab. These tribes dwell in the mountains of that region. Also to the south are tribes that inhabit the lands of Bassa and Tagat, the way to the Black Sea. From there our boundaries turn north to the Don River. All the peoples of those lands live in open, unwalled towns and occupy the whole of the steppe, as

far west as the boundary of the Hungarians. There are very many tribes of these peoples and are all tributary to me.

"My capital spans the Volga near the delta. I prevent the Rus from passing to the south, but I also prevent their enemies from going north to their lands. This policy is not without danger, and I have had to instigate terrible wars with the Rus as well as with their enemies to maintain this balance. If I did not prevent the Rus from going south, they would, no doubt, put to fire all the lands of the Muslims all the way to Bagdad.

"There are no oppressors in my lands, no enmities, or arguments. When we leave our fields my family, nobles, and ministers travel twenty parasangs to the great river called Aran. From there we travel, meeting with the heads of the various tribes, until we visit almost all our borders.

"Our country experiences rain infrequently, except in the mountains, but it has rivers and streams containing many varieties of fish. We also have many springs, and our land is fertile, rich in fields, vineyards, gardens, and orchards watered by irrigation. Our orchards have fruit-bearing trees of every kind and produce in abundance.

He went on to describe the extent of the lands he controlled and its borders to the east, south, west, and north.

"Now, I turn to your question concerning the coming of the Messiah. To answer that question, I must rely on the words of our Lord, as repeated by the wise men of Israel who dwell in Jerusalem and Babylon. Though we are a great distance from Zion, we are told that the various computations offered are all in error, but we have no direct knowledge of these matters. However, we believe that if the Lord pleases, he will send the Messiah. He will do so for the sake of his great name. The desolation of His house, the abolition of His service, and all the troubles that have beset the Hebrew nation will be repaired when he fulfills His promise to us when saying; "The Lord whom ye seek shall suddenly come to His temple, the messenger of the covenant whom ye delight in: Behold, he shall come, saith the Lord of Hosts." Other than this we know only the prophecy

of Daniel. May God hasten the redemption of Israel, gather the captives, and dispersed, you and I, and all Israel that love His name in our lifetime.

"*You say you desire to see my face. I, as well, long and desire to see your honored face, to bask in your wisdom and magnificence. I pray for the day that we will be united so that you might be as a father to me and me as your son. All my people would pay you homage. I bid you peace and happiness.*

Farewell.

Joseph, King of the Khazars"

"This is everything I hoped for," said Hasdai. "Do you think what he says is all true, Yusuf? What is your impression of the man?"

"Please Hasdai, I will return tomorrow, after I get some rest and have discovered how my practice fared and if there are any matters I must tend to immediately."

"I'm sorry Yusuf. I forgot you are now an adult with your own life. Go,"

"Judah was with me each time I met with King Joseph. I'm certain he can fill you in, but

I didn't have a great deal of time in direct contact with him," I replied.

"Yes, of course. Judah, please go to bed then come to see me after you awake and have eaten."

"Of course, Effendi."

"Please, no more Effendi, you have certainly earned the right to be my friend."

The next afternoon I returned to Hasdai's house and office just in time to hear Judah speak.

"The ministers with whom we interacted and the citizens with whom we had conversations, all said he is a wise, honest, and fair ruler. Neither Yusuf, Hamza, who I told you Yusuf and I have formed a partnership with, nor myself experienced anything to indicate otherwise."

"Good morning, Yusuf. I trust you slept well, and all of your affairs are in good order. I only had to collaborate with your assistant, I presume you will make him your partner, a few times. He is very competent and did well with your patients."

"Yes, everything seems to be running smoothly, including my household."

"So, what have you learned about the history of the Khazars?"

"We were able to piece together some of their history," I said. "For many years they have dominated the steppes of South-Eastern Europe and much of the steppes of Western Asia. They control several important trade routes and thus serve as a channel for ideas, technology, and other cultural influences. They achieved dominance in the 600's and then expanded to incorporate a host of other cultures and peoples. They were, originally, Turkic. I discovered they first brought the partially nomadic Alans, who speak an Iranian dialect, into their control. They conquered the Bulgars who were still Turkic. Next, they were able to convince the Burtas and the Finno-Urgrian Mari of the mountains, forest, and river planes as well as the semi-nomadic Magyars to accept their rule and protection while maintaining their own culture. This was all in place when Joseph assumed the crown. However, both Judah and I heard rumors that not all of these tribes are content to be subservient to the Khazars and from time-to-time rebel groups need to be suppressed."

"We also learned that the Khazars, at some time not too long ago, formed an alliance with the Varangian Rus, reported to be fierce warriors in the mold of the Vikings. They are a different tribe, separated from the Rus that Joseph denies direct access to the Caspian. The alliance is in almost continuous strife with tribes of the southern Caspian, ostensibly to counter the Islamic threat but it seems most likely to purpose is to gain booty."

"There is another reality that I hesitate to bring up, but it might prove useful."

"Go ahead."

"As you are aware from the sixth century until now Jewish merchants engaged in the slave trade, called Rhadhonites, have traded across much of Europe, the Middle East, Central Asia, and North Africa. I know what they do is an abomination to you and to all thinking Hebrews, but it is a fact of life. Although distasteful perhaps we could make use of them to carry correspondence between us and the Khazars."

"I will share the letter with Dunash and find out what he thinks of it. I will tell him you both feel the information is reliable," said Hasdai.

"What about Menahem?" I asked.

"Things have changed since you left. Dunash was the successful suiter and married Rebecca ibn Hanoth. No doubt by virtue of a series of love poems he wrote for her. Menahem tried to counter with lectures on the importance of grammar and the exact use of words, as well as his love of learning and literature, but, not surprisingly, Rebecca chose poetry over philology. Menahem was not a gracious loser. He also felt that I somehow supported Dunash over him, which was not the case. I kept my distance during the whole affair. In any case, Menahem is no longer interested in collaborating with me."

"Do you think it would be appropriate for me to visit him and try to bring him back?" I asked. "This news is very disquieting to me. The three of you have been such close friends and Menahem was not only one of my tutors, he became my friend as I grew up."

"I doubt you would be successful, but you can't make matters any worse than they are."

"I will use the pretext of telling him about our adventures. Perhaps I could also show him the response letter from King Joseph."

"Yes, it may be worth the effort, but I don't want the original of the letter to leave my house. You can make a copy of the letter to show him."

"If that is what you want, I will make a copy now, if that is convenient."

The following day I went to Menahem's yeshiva wondering what had happened that he would sacrifice his friendship with Hasdai. Hasdai had supported him by purchasing the building that housed his yeshiva, plus he paid Menahem a monthly stipend to finance his work. It seemed to me those actions should have engendered loyalty.

I arrived at the house Menahem had converted for his yeshiva and living quarters. I knocked on the closed door and it was answered by a young man with ink stains on the fingers of his right hand.

"I am Yusuf ben Ezia just back from a long trip to the Khazar empire. Is Menahem ben Saruq home?"

"Yes, please come in. Menahem is with some students. Please follow me."

Menahem was talking quietly with four students when we entered the room. He looked up, saw me, stood, and walked quickly to give me an embrace. "So, Yusuf was your trip successful? Did you reach the Khazar empire? Did you talk with King Joseph? Talk to me, tell me all about your adventures."

It took me over an hour to briefly summarize what Judah and I experienced, but Menahem grew increasingly impatient with the story.

"Do you want to read King Joseph's response to the letter that you created?" I asked.

"Indeed, that will be interesting. Is he educated enough to write grammatically correct Hebrew?"

"Yes, I believe he is a very intelligent and well-educated man, but he, no doubt, had help composing his answer."

"Is the letter in his hand, or that of a scribe?"

"I cannot say for certain. The signature looks to be the same as the calligraphy. I assume he wrote it himself, but maybe not."

I handed him the letter.

He glanced at it, then looked directly into my eyes. "This is your calligraphy."

"Yes, I made this copy. Hasdai insisted he keep the original safe."

He scowled. "Typical. He doesn't trust me enough to even hold the original in my hands."

He took his time, reading the letter slowly, thoroughly, then handed it back to me. "Do you think everything he says is the truth?"

"Yes," I said, "Judah and I talked to many of his subjects, and administrators. All seemed content with his rule and his policies."

"So, you would not hesitate to recommend to any of our people who are persecuted and have the means to travel to the lands of the Khazars that they should do so? You think they will be welcomed?"

"I believe so, yes."

Menahem paused holding his head between both hands. "Maybe . . . maybe . . . time will tell, I suppose."

I tried to shift the conversation. "So, are you working on anything new?"

"No, I am still working on the dictionary. It will be, when finished, my most important work."

I was having trouble maintaining the conversation. I sensed that although when I left on the journey to the Khazars I thought our original relationship of tutor to student had changed to friendship, Menahem considered me somewhat beneath him. Now, after my experiences and successful mission, he had to considered me his equal and he was having a problem with that.

"And how does the dictionary progress?" I asked.

"Slowly, too slowly. I am hampered by students who prove to be too slow, too uninterested, not overly intelligent, and not motivated."

I refrained from suggesting his role should be to motivate his students. "If you wish I can leave the copy of the letter with you."

"No need. I suppose you were careful to copy it exactly. I now know what he said."

I ignored the implied insult. It was just Menahem being Menahem. I felt his mood and attitude even more testy, even confrontational than it was prior to my going to the Khazar empire. The falling out with Dunash had spilled over to bad feelings for Hasdai as well.

"I must return to my own life and my patients, assuming they still want me as their physician. Perhaps Hasdai will host a dinner and we can all catch up and be together again soon," I said.

"Not likely."

We shook hands, embraced, although our chests never touched, and I left, wondering if the previous close friendship that Hasdai, Dunash and Menahem had could ever be repaired.

Several months passed quickly. my medical practice was not quite as robust as when I left, but before long-lost patients returned, and new ones came to my door. My associate had been conscientious and done his best, but any medical practice relies a great deal on the personality of the practitioner. Hasdai made good on his promise of financial reward and gave me title to the house, so I no longer had to pay him rent. I left it to Judah to handle the details of our partnership with Hamza. The first trip Hamza made to Tunisia and back was a financial success. All three of us agreed to put additional funds into working capital from our profits. Judah and Hamza worked hard to determine which trade goods we would become known for. They sought out vendors and manufacturers who insisted on producing the highest quality goods. Hamza's next trip was to go all the way to Constantinople, with stops along the way.

Before he left, Hamza and I talked. He suggested I give him a letter to the ambassador asking him to hand over the funds Judah and I had left with him. I did so, certain the ambassador would comply.

While we were gone my associate, not having the training and dedication necessary, had allowed my medicinal plant garden to degenerate. Hasdai provided me with the necessary replacements and sent me his gardener's most qualified apprentice. My garden was on its way to full recovery.

I try to continue to exercise with some regularity, but Judah became an enterprising businessman and merchant. It is increasingly difficult for either him or me to find the time to exercise and spar together. I am feeling more and more like a middle-aged man.

CHAPTER EIGHTEEN

I have learned, by virtue of living long enough, that friendships only survive if the individuals involved work at it. Effort must be made to accommodate personality traits, errors in judgement, and arguments. It is essential that arguments be resolved, but this can be difficult. It seems to me that there are two distinct personality types. One type needs confrontation immediately. Issues need to be resolved now rather than later. The other type avoids confrontation. This personality tends to rely on time to reach a solution, often by compromise.

In 964, a year after our return from the great adventure, I was forty-four years old and developed new interest, poetry. Cordoba is where Hispano/Hebrew poetry was first born and nurtured. The Arabs have a long history of maintaining a love affair, infatuation is perhaps more descriptive, of poetry. Poetry has played an important role in Islam from its beginning. The meters, forms and constructs of Arabic poetry are, almost, beyond any system of classification. Hebrew students living in the Empire of Cordoba, me included, learned to love and respect Arabic poetry as an integral part of their general education. The Hebrew scholars of Cordoba, inevitably, began to adapt and develop Hebrew poetry using Arabic forms and I became infatuated with it.

Of course, Hebrew poetry was not previously unknown. The first biblical examples are found in writings now over two thousand years old. The adoption and adaptation of Arabic forms beyond the rather simplistic rhyming found in Hebrew prayer books of the time was a new development. The Arab poets used the language of the Quran to sing songs of lament, praise, love, and beauty for hundreds of years. As the Hebrew scholars of Cordoba developed a deep appreciation for the beauty of Arab poetry, it was natural for them to adapt the various forms and meters into Hebrew. Dunash and Menahem were amongst those scholars who began to experiment in their own writings. Within a short time, while they were still close friends and collaborators, they started to adopt and include popular tunes sung by minstrels and the general population. These rhythms and constructs further developed the poetic art form and the works of Dunash and Menahem reflected this progress.

I am happy to say that my mentor, Hasdai ibn Shaprut, not only mentored and supported the regular work of both men, but he also encouraged and supported their poetic efforts by publishing their works. Not surprisingly their poems were frequently laced with praise for their benefactor. Dunash's *Te Shubot*, published by Hasdai, is prefaced by elaborate praise. It is the first example of a poem written in Hebrew but using the requirements of quantitative meter that characterizes Arabic poetry. One Arab tradition is to write alternating long and short syllables using accents in specific places. The result is a special kind of rhythm best appreciated when heard. This convention had never been attempted in Hebrew poetry, but Dunash accomplished it. In the Hebrew language there is no distinction between long and short syllables, but by using clever adaptations Dunash managed to overcome this fundamental difference between the two languages. Dunash's breakthrough techniques provided a mechanism to use the patterns of poetical composition, the subject matter, and the style of classical Arabic poetry found a place in the emerging Hebrew poetry.

One of Dunash's most celebrated poems starts with a familiar invitation to drink wine and goes on to describe the pleasures that derive from that activity. He manages to mimic the sensuality of Arabic poetry dealing with this subject. But then, perhaps because of the influence of his wife, Rebecca, he describes the life of a pious Hebrew living in the diaspora during this time of history. He makes it clear that there can be no meaningful joy in the life of a Hebrew while he is exiled from his homeland. His peoples' destiny is to follow the often-repeated tragic consequence of being faithful to their religion. While he is appreciative of his tranquil and tolerated existence in Cordoba, Dunash is nevertheless aware that historically the destiny of his people has been to be overwhelmed by calamity. We all understood that life for us Hebrews could change dramatically when Abd-Ar-Rahman III died, and another caliph took control. This understanding of the realities of life for the Hebrews was the motivation for my journey to the Khazar empire. While Judah and I were gone the poetry of Dunash and Menaham drove a wedge between them.

Without doubt the work of Dunash as a poet was influenced by Rebecca who was also a poet. He showed me a poem written by her. It was, perhaps, the first Hebrew poem in Arabic form authored by a woman. It was a short poem describing a woman, holding her son in her arms, and saying farewell to her husband who is leaving Cordoba. Emotionally, the reader or listener hopes the separation would be for only a short time, but we are left to ponder.

The poetry of Dunash recognized no boundaries. Although he did not name Menaham specifically, he allowed grievances with Menaham to find their way into his writings. Isaac ben Capron, Menaham's disciple, had an independent reputation as a poet of some repute. He defended his teacher while criticizing Dunash's technical innovations particularly for stretching Hebrew words beyond their biblical meaning. This manner of public argument, in written form, was a favorite form of dueling between Arabic and now Hebrew scholars. Isaac ben Capron then developed his own technical convention that other Hebrew poets quickly adopted. He devised a syllabic system that did away with the distinction between long and short syllables and was thus better adapted to Hebrew poetry.

As the rift between Dunash and Menahem grew Hasdai was eventually forced to choose a side. Dunash remained while Menahem drifted away, partially by choice, mostly because of Hasdai's neglect to keep the friendship alive. With time Menahem became bitter and vented his displeasure with Hasdai to some of his yeshiva students. When Hasdai heard of this, he stopped sending Menahem's regular allowance and when the criticism continued, he threatened to take back the building housing Menahem's yeshiva.

CHAPTER NINETEEN

In 966 Hasdai received news from one of the Rhadhonites trading in Cordoba, that during the previous year the Rus had formed an alliance with the Turkish Ghuzz, and Prince Sveyatoslav Igorevich led an army that soundly defeated that of the Khazars. The Khazar empire was in turmoil and its ability to survive in doubt. The news was devastating, we no longer had a safe haven.

Four years after my return to Cordoba, Dunash came to my house. His face was contorted with worry.

"Hasdai is ill, Yusuf. Please come and attend to him."

"Of course. I will go with you immediately. Is his medicine chest still fully stocked or do I need to bring medications?"

"He still keeps his chest up-to-date."

"Tell me his symptoms as we go," I said.

"Four days ago, he started coughing. The next morning, he was coughing more and appeared feverish. Then he developed diarrhea."

"I should have been sent for right away."

"I asked him, and he said not to bother you. He told me he was taking medicine on his own and would be better in a few days."

"Did he at least stay in bed?" I asked.

"Of course not."

I shook my head. "Why does the parent become more of a child the older he gets?"

"I suppose it is inevitable," said Dunash. "There is a poem somewhere in that observation. I have to work on it."

We arrived at Hasdai's house where we found him at his desk, writing.

"I am told you have not been feeling well for several days," I said.

"Shalom, Yusuf. I see Dunash is worried about me but doesn't obey my wishes."

"Yes, and you should be thankful that he came to get me."

He started coughing and couldn't stop. He got to his feet, bent over, still coughing, and began to sway. I caught him before he fell to the floor.

"Dunash, help me please. We need to get him to his bed."

He continued to cough but was weakening. His face was flushed. I could feel his fever as I held him up, holding his forearm in one hand and my other hand in his armpit. Dunash took his other arm. We half-carried, half-dragged him up the stairs to his bedroom and laid him on the bed.

"Help me get his robe and shirt off. I want to put him under the covers."

He was shivering with chills even though he had a raging fever. "Wait," he whispered.

We managed to get him over a chamber pot and he all but filled it with a malodorous watery stool. When he was done, we got him back into the bed and covered him with three wool blankets.

"Are you having abdominal cramps?" I asked.

He nodded.

"Fever, cough, diarrhea, what else? Muscle tremors, weakness, loss of balance, vomiting?"

He nodded, and began coughing again, more violently than previously. I gave him a dose of honey laced with the poppy extract. The cough gradually subsided.

"Let me listen to your lungs please, Hasdai."

He nodded his ascent and sat up. The blankets fell from his chest. He was shivering but his skin was hot to the touch. I listened with my ear to his back in several locations. He had another coughing fit.

"I can hear both moist and dry rales," I told him. "The infection has got a foothold in your lungs. You have pneumonia."

I gently pushed him back down and covered him again with the blankets. "You know the seriousness of this as well as I do," I said. "I will stay with you and do everything I can to make you comfortable, but this is very serious. You must trust me and do everything I ask of you."

He gave me a weak smile, then in a raspy voice said. "My student is now the teacher. My own words are being used against me."

"I will give you more of the honey and poppy extract for the cough. Hopefully it will also make you sleep. Do you think you can hold down some broth?"

"Not yet," he murmured.

I asked Dunash to send a servant to fetch Judah. "One of the three of us will need to stay with him at all times. I will give him medication to stop the diarrhea, but we must try to keep him hydrated with small sips of water or broth as frequently as possible. If he messes the bed, we must clean him and change the bedding right away. We cannot allow him to lay in his own waste."

I am, by design, always optimistic with my patients. It is important for them to believe their physician thinks he is going to make them well. I had trouble doing this with the man who had been my father, mentor, teacher, friend.

I can't believe he didn't call me sooner. Hasdai, Hasdai, what can I do to help you through this. You are too important to too many people to leave us now.

I did everything I could think of to improve in his comfort. His coughing subsided but his breathing became more and more labored. His lips began to turn blue. After three days he was weakening to the point of giving up. The effort it took for him to just inhale and exhale made him exhausted.

That afternoon the caliph and his grand vizier arrived to check on him.

I spoke with them outside his room. "His illness may be contagious, Excellencies. Please do not come too close to him, or to the three of us, and put these clean silk scarves over your nose and mouth to protect yourselves."

They complied and followed me into his bedroom. "Shaprut, can you hear me?" shouted the caliph.

Hasdai opened his eyes and tried to rise. I put my hand on his chest and he laid back against the pillows that propped him up to ease his breathing.

The caliph inhaled sharply. "Do what your student tells you, ibn Shaprut. I need you to get better. I order you to follow your physician's orders and get well. Do you understand me?"

Hasdai closed his eyes and nodded.

The caliph motioned for me to follow him out into the hallway. "Can he survive?"

I wiped away the tears streaming down my face. "Not unless he improves greatly in the next few hours, Your Excellency."

The caliph and the grand vizier both sighed deeply.

"He seems so old," said the grand vizier. "Do you know how old he is?"

"Yes, we celebrated his sixtieth birthday recently."

"That's a long life," observed the caliph. "Listen, physician, I need you to assume the position in my household that ibn Shaprut filled. Do you have confidence you can do that?"

That was unexpected. What will happen if I say no?. . . Do it Yusuf.

"I am confident as a physician and, I believe I do have some diplomatic skills, but I am not the man to act as your collector of customs, nor do I have Hasdai's skill level with languages."

"It is good that you are honest about your shortcomings compared to your mentor. I understand and appreciate that. We will find others to fill those roles."

After the caliph and grand vizier left, Hasdai motioned for me to come stand by his bed. His voice was raspy, barely audible. "I have left instructions for you, Yusuf. The document is in my patient files with your name." He stopped, took a deep breath, and continued. "I want all my belongings, investments and wealth to be divided equally among you, Dunash and Menahem."

"I thought you and Menahem were estranged," I said.

"Yes, that's my fault. I allowed the feud between him and Dunash to influence my relationship with him. I don't want him to struggle. Convince him and Dunash to become friendly to one another."

I put my hand on his arm and gave it a gentle squeeze. "If that is your wish, I will do my best to bring them together."

"One more thing, Yusuf. I want you to go through my correspondence with rabbis. Send them all a synopsis of what you believe is happening in King Joseph's empire. I no longer believe that place is safe for our people.." He took another deep breath and closed his eyes.

I found the document he had filed and took it with me that same day after leaving Judah with him. I went to both Dunash and Menahem and did my best to convince them that Hasdai wanted them to reconcile.

Dunash vowed he will do all he could to reconcile with Menahem, but Menahem resisted the idea. "Why now? What does he expect from me?

"Look at this document he left. He instructed me to give you a third of his wealth. He hopes you will accept this gift and use it to continue your good work. He hopes it will help you forget any past insults or slights and remember him with kindness."

"So, on his deathbed he wants to bribe me?"

I frowned. "Can you allow your problems with Dunash and him to wipe out the years of friendship and common goals you shared? Just put all that bad feeling aside and come to see him tomorrow."

I was doubtful Menahem would relent but two days later Dunash, Menahem, Judah, and I were with him when I heard the death rattle. I had heard it many times over the years and the sound of it always distresses me. I raised out of the chair I was in. When I got up Menahem, Judah, and Dunash all got to their feet. I walked slowly to the bed and took Hasdai's right hand in mine. He opened his eyes, looked at each of the three of us, smiled, and nodded then slowly exhaled. He was gone.

THE END

BIBLIOGRAPHY

1. BARTHOLOMEW, *10th Century Europe, 1876 antique map stock photo*, Image ID: FY31D4, Alamy.com

2. Brook, Kevin Alan, Sept. 2006, *The Jews of Khazaria, The Khazar Capital City of Atil,* 3rd edition, Rowman, and Littlefield.

3. Pelaez del Rosal, Jesus (editor), 1991, *The Jews in Cordoba (X-XII centuries)*, Artes Graficas Benzal, Madrid, translated by Patricia A. Sneesby.

4. Schwarz, Leo W. (editor), 1965, *The Jewish Caravan, Great Stories of Twenty-five Centuries*, Holt, Rinehart and Winston, New York, Chicago, San-Francisco.

5. Karasulas, Antony, 2004, *Mounted Archers of the Steppe 600 BC-AD 1300*, Osprey Publishing Ltd, Oxford.

6. Zhirohov, Mikhail, Nicolle, David, The Khazars, 2019 *A Judeo-Turkish Empire on the Steppes, 7th – 11th Centuries AD,* Osprey Publishing Ltd, Oxford.

7. Shpakovsky, Viacheslav, Nicolle, David, 2013, *Armies of the Volga Bulgars & Khanate of Kazan, 9th – 16th Centuries*, Osprey Publishing Ltd, Oxford.

8. Al-Hakan II, https://wikipedia.org

9. Alcazar of the (Caliphs) Cordoba, https://wikipedia.org

10. Ancient Ships, https://wikipedia.org

11. Atil, https://wikipedia.org

12. Cagliari, Sardinia, https://wikipedia.org

13. Caliphate of Cordoba 92501031, https://wikipedia.org

14. Cartagena, Spain, https://wikipedia.org

15. Conversion of the Khazars to Judaism, https://wikipedia.org

16. Crete under Muslim rule, https://wikipedia.org

17. Dunash-ben-Labrat, https://britannica.com/biography

18. Felucca, https://wikipedia.org

19. Guadalquivir River, https://britannica.com/place

20. Mindel, Nissan, *Hasdai ibn Shaprut [circa 4675-4735 (915-975)]*, Kehot Publication Society, Chabad.org

21. Hasdai ibn Shaprut, https://wikipedia.org

22. , Gottheil Richard, Kayserling, Meyer, 1906, *Hasdai Abu Yusuf ben Isaac ben Ezra ibn Shaprut*, Jewish Encyclopedia.com

23. Hebrew Calendar, https://wikipedia.com

24. History of Sardinia, https://wikipedia.com

25. History of the Jews in Sicily, https://wikipedia.com

26. Fumagalli, Marcello, *The formula of Theriac- the Teriaca (formula and ingredients of Venice Treacle (Theriac). The secret knowledge of how to make a Venice Theriac or Teriaca Andramaclus*, Google

27. *Sicily, Italy, History*, Jewish Virtual Library, Google

28. *Khazar Correspondence*, https://wikipedia.org

29. *Khazar Khaganate, 650-969 (with map),* Google

30. *Khazars,* https://wikipedia.org

31. *Khazars, early history,* https://wikipedia.org

32. *Kingdom of Leon,* https://wikipedia.org

33. *Local food delicacies of Sardinia,* Google

34. *Manufacture of opium,* Google

35. *Andalusia, The Kingdom of Spain 910,* map code Ax01026, Google

36. *Map of the Near East in 15th Century,* Google

37. *Medical Knowledge, Cordoba,* 10th Century, Google

38. *Menahem ben Saruq,* https: www.britannica.com/biography

39. Claudia, *The most delicious Sardinian food: Everything you must try,* Google

40. *Hasdai ibn Shaprut,* Temple Beth Am Library, Sephardic Tid-Bits, Google

41. Whitewright, Dr. Julian, *Ships; building and sailing in the ancient Mediterranean,* Google

42. *Tarragona,* https://wikipedia.org

43. *The Alcazar of Cordoba,* https://wikipedia.org

44. *Theriac,* https://wikipedia.org

CPSIA information can be obtained
at www.ICGtesting.com
Printed in the USA
BVHW041555111022
649158BV00009B/1314

9 781977 255990